my

TOWNIE HEART

Diana Sperrazza

A POST HILL PRESS BOOK
ISBN: 978-1-61868-891-0
ISBN (eBook): 978-1-61868-892-7

MY TOWNIE HEART
©2015 by Diana Sperrazza
All Rights Reserved

Cover design by Ryan Truso

Post Hill Press
275 Madison Avenue, 14th Floor
New York, NY 10016

http://posthillpress.com

Dedication

For my mother
Wilhelmina Hall
whose struggles and dreams
will never leave my heart
and for John C. Morris from
the old neighborhood

A Note from the Author

My Townie Heart draws heavily from my own experiences coming of age in a blue-collar neighborhood during the 1970s. Springfield, Massachusetts is a real place, but I've liberally expanded it to include parts of my hometown, West Springfield. That said, this book is a work of fiction. Any resemblance to actual events or locales or persons, living or dead, is entirely coincidental.

Acknowledgements

This book would not have come into existence without Janice Gary, my writing partner and author of the critically acclaimed book *Short Leash: A Memoir of Dog Walking and Deliverance*. It was Janice who helped me find the courage to acknowledge my own difficult past from which the writing was birthed. She also made this speedy television producer think more carefully about the words on each page.

A tremendous amount of gratitude goes out to novelist Alice Mattison, who understood what I was trying to do when I brought the beginnings of a manuscript to her workshop in Provincetown, Massachusetts, and provided generous and critical support throughout the entire process.

I'd also like to thank Sven Birkerts and Bob Shacochis, two writers I had the great fortune to have as teachers when I was a student in the Bennington MFA program, who offered early and essential support for my writing, and to Philip Lopate whose encouragement of my work and, very specifically, my voice, goes back even further.

I was the grateful recipient of residencies at both Casa Libre de la Solana in Tucson, Arizona and the Virginia Center for the Creative Arts, that provided valuable time and space for the writing and editing of this work.

Thanks go out to LeeAnn Dance and Cliff Hackel, two friends from my years at CNN, and to Kerry Hannon, who led me to Debra Englander and to publisher Michael L. Wilson at Post Hill Press. Thanks to all of you for believing enough in this book to get it to print.

I am also grateful to: Carolyn Lieberg, who thoughtfully edited a draft of this book, and to Meredith Davenport, who would not let me give up.

Last but not least: I want to thank my friend Jane Latman, who has never stopped believing in me or in this book. There are no words, Jane, only tears of gratitude.

I

Back Home

Tall and imposing in her beige pantsuit, my mother looked over at the empty red Samsonite suitcase lying on the floor, a present she and my dad had given to me when I graduated from high school.

I didn't know what to say and neither did she. Out in the dorm's hallway, someone turned up the music and yelled, "Everybody boogie!" It was that part in "Sugar Magnolia" where the Dead really start to jam and some asshole dancing outside in the hallway slammed into the door.

Startled, my mother gave me her best *j'accuse* look.

"What the *hell* is going on here? I thought you'd be packed already. You said you wanted to leave right away."

The suitcase sat before me with its metal jaws wide open, exposing a ladylike, powder-blue interior. In her dress pumps, my mother stepped over the suitcase, beer bottles full of cigarette butts, Chinese takeout cartons, and the random bits and pieces of clothing that littered the floor. She made a beeline for the only chair in the room, which stood next to my roommate Gail's bare mattress.

"You look terrible and this room looks like a flophouse."

"I know. I'm sorry, Mom."

There was, indeed, a lot for me to be sorry about. I was flunking out of the University of Massachusetts and, as a scholarship girl from a hick town in western Massachusetts, I had let everyone down, including myself. I ran my finger over the carpeting, trying to remember the mysterious Aztec mandalas that would appear in its salt and pepper weave whenever I took acid. Finally, I swallowed hard, got up, and started flinging random things into the suitcase.

My mother had been hearing the stories about UMass back in Springfield. How the drug pushers had been selling LSD to kids who would take it and jump off the nearest roof. How the school had let the dorms go coed, allowing rampant sex to go on even in broad daylight, and how those Jewish professors (yes, my mother was a lukewarm anti-Semite) were poisoning the minds of kids with Marxism and encouraging them to run off and live on communes. Now, it seemed that her own daughter had somehow become a captive to these forces, with disastrous results.

Throwing the last of what I could find of my clothes into the suitcase, I flipped the Samsonite's lid down fast.

"Where's your roommate?" she asked me then, as if this information would somehow make a difference.

"Gail? I don't know." I'd actually wanted to say goodbye to Gail, the only person in the dorm who cared about what happened to me, but under the circumstances, I wasn't about to go looking for her. We carried my stuff out of the dorm and drove back to Springfield in silence.

When I woke up the next morning in the upstairs bedroom on Chestnut Street that had been mine in childhood, I lit a cigarette and sat down on the floor, crossing my legs just as I had the day before on the floor of my dorm room. The red Samsonite sat next to me, still unopened. I'd slept naked and not bothered to unpack. If anything, I felt even crappier than the day before. I smoked that cigarette right down to its filter and left it standing straight up on the floor.

I got up and looked around the room, noticing that the odd collection of knickknacks I'd had since I was a kid still sat on each of the room's two windowsills. My favorites had been the tiny Limogenes tea set my Aunt Doreen had given me, and a ceramic statue of a cat playing a saxophone that had a little plaque under him that said "Play it Cool," which I had rescued from a trash can. The objects looked untouched by time. I picked up the tiny Limogenes tea tray and rubbed it between my thumb and forefinger. It was dusty, but underneath it became as cool and smooth to my touch as it had always been.

Strange, the survival of objects from one's childhood. They shouldn't be allowed to remain the same since you don't. I put the thing back on the shelf, feeling totally weird.

I had to move, to do something, so I squatted back down and swiftly undid the latches of the Samsonite. The suitcase had been presented to me, with much jubilation, at my graduation party in our backyard last summer. *Our daughter was off to college. The first one in our family ever to go!* All the relatives and neighbors had come over and there'd been a rum cake from the Venetian Bakery to mark the event. My father had even strung up a set of paper lanterns.

Now I spewed out its cargo of dirty clothes. There was a purple Indian print top that Gail had given me, an extra less-favored pair of jeans, a silky orange shirt from my mother I'd never worn, a raggedy bra with intractable brown stains under the arms, and a brand new pair of platform shoes with tooled flower designs on the fronts. My things smelled like patchouli and pot, Marlboros and tamari sauce. Burying my nose into them, I tried to find some patch of realness, some way to recognize myself at home with my family in the house on Chestnut Street. It was the clothes that smelled real to me now.

More than anything, I missed Gail and wondered what she was doing at that exact moment. After staring at the pile for another long minute, I fished out the spare pair of jeans, which was cleaner than the ones I'd taken off the night before, and a small brass hash pipe, before stuffing the rest of the things back in the suitcase.

When I closed the Samsonite and snapped up its latches, the smells disappeared. I pushed the suitcase under the bed.

Those first few days back at my parents' house, I spent my days in the dim interior light of the living room watching bad TV shows and awaiting my mother's predictable rotation of suppers – Monday's hot dogs and beans, Tuesday's stuffed peppers, and Wednesday's boiled dinner. My sister Jane was still living at home, which was one of the few good things about being back there. But mostly, I felt numb inside, which was better than the way I'd felt at school, but only slightly.

After supper on Wednesday, I decided that my sister and I needed to take a very necessary escape upstairs. After opening the windows, we sprawled across the double bed in the extra bedroom so we could talk and smoke dope in peace. Jane was better at rolling than I was. She passed me the joint when she was done.

"I think you need this more than I do. You look like a fucking zombie," she said.

"I AM a fucking zombie. You know how weird this is for me, to be back here."

"Yeah, that's why I still don't get why you're here."

"Because, Jane, I blew it." I slowly exhaled the lungful of pot smoke I'd kept in there for as long as possible. "Why do you want me to talk about it?"

"Cause I keep thinking it's good for you, that it's fuckin' bugging you and you need to get it out of your system or something."

I handed the joint back to her. "Jane, do me a favor, okay? Don't play my fucking therapist. Remember how you always hated that woman Mom made you go see? All those social worker types are so-o straight. I don't need to talk, okay? Maybe I'd talk to a real healer, like a shaman from Tibet or somebody like that, but not some middle-aged rich lady from Longmeadow."

Jane exhaled and leaned heavily back, making the old mahogany bed frame creak.

"Yeah, I know. The shrinks are full of fucking shit."

She was a big girl, and she was getting bigger. She had a dirty red flannel shirt on, and a pair of blue jeans a couple of sizes too big for her, which she had cinched with what looked like the sash from a man's bathrobe. My sister was five months pregnant. I knew this but my parents didn't. Since Jane had always dressed strangely and had a tendency to be heavy, they hadn't really noticed.

She had called me one night at UMass and told me about her pregnancy. I'd been up for a couple of days, jacked up on cocaine.

"Laura, how do you feel about being an auntie?" she'd asked me, right off the bat.

"You're kidding, right?"

"Nope. I'm knocked up and I'm going to keep it."

"What are you talking about? You're still in your first trimester, right? Get rid of it. I'll go with you. You could come up to Northampton and it's over in like, twenty minutes."

"No. I want the baby."

"Are you fucking out of your mind?" I had screamed into the phone. "What are you going to do with a kid?"

Actually, I was pretty much out of my own mind. The downward spiral that would make me leave school was already in full swing by then.

Now, here I was, my family's great success story of a daughter, back home and stinking up the house with my failure. My parents weren't talking about it, but there it was, the truth. We all knew I'd probably blown my one opportunity to get out of Springfield and get an education. And there was no stopping the shame of living with this knowledge, which I pretty much felt all the time, just under the surface. But tonight, the pot was helping a little bit, sawing off its worst edges. I looked over at my sister. In my stoned gaze, Jane looked like a fat, beautiful angel. Pregnancy was softening her face, giving her more color, and slightly curling the ends of her hair. Reclining on the bed, her belly exposed, she certainly looked pregnant. If my mother walked in now, she would know it too. Jane took a hit off the joint, unperturbed by anything it seemed.

"You should lay off this stuff," I said.

"Naw. A little grass isn't going to hurt the baby. Might help her be more mellow, you know?"

"You better check with a midwife about that. I don't think it's such a good idea."

"You always get too paranoid."

"Maybe. And what's the deal with the father? Does he know?"

"He'll know when it's the right time."

"Are you ever going to tell me who he is?"

"Yeah, everybody thinks they should know. Like it matters or something."

"What do you mean? Of course it matters," I said, sounding a little too straight, even to myself.

"Look, you're my sister. You know what people think of me in this town. Me telling who the father is won't change anything. Shit, Laura, it's just the way things are. Believe me, it's fuckin' easier when you just accept it."

I didn't say anything but I reached for the roach clip Jane was holding and sucked in the smoke, greedily filling my lungs with it. But no drug, not even heroin, would have been able to annihilate what I knew. It came bubbling back to the surface then, returning like a long lost relative, or an amputated limb. Once again, I took my sister in, that body, which had absorbed what had been done to it, now with the bloat of pregnancy upon it. Sure, she looked like an angel to me, but I knew more, saw more than that. I loved her but others would not. In reality, the flannel shirt and the bathrobe sash made her look like somebody you'd see at the Salvation Army or panhandling down by the bus station. Like somebody who was broken for life.

What I felt then was really very simple. I wanted to kill Timmy Morton more than anything else.

2

Merinski's

It was almost four o'clock on my second Tuesday back home, so it was stuffed peppers night again. My mother called me into the kitchen.

"Would you do me a favor, honey? Could you pick up a couple of pounds of hamburger at Merinski's for me?"

Since she was going out to show a house after supper, she had a ruffled pink nylon apron on over a blue polyester pants suit. I thought the apron-over-the-pantsuit thing made her look like a transvestite playing June Cleaver but I kept this fashion insight to myself.

I said I'd go to the market. At least it wasn't another job interview. I really needed a job, but hadn't found anything yet. I was flat broke but the last thing I wanted to do was ask my parents for money.

In the orangey evening light, I walked past the same row of houses on Chestnut Street I'd been passing my entire life. Since the next day was trash day, people had already hauled their cans out to the tree belt. In front of the Dolan's, who had more kids than anybody else, the trash overflowed – something my father frequently and bitterly complained about. I saw torn open red and white Hood milk cartons and Hawaiian Punch cans, their deep blue tins still exotic and bright, as they faced ultimate extinction. A rusted tricycle with no seat was wedged between the two trashcans. The late day sun glinted off the still shiny handlebars of the tricycle and it made me suddenly sad for the time when that tricycle had been brand new and beautiful, the apple of some Dolan kid's eye. Now it was just another piece of trash. Did anyone in the Dolan household care? Did that kid even think about the tricycle anymore? Did he remember it at all?

Everything changed, no matter what. The year before, I'd gone off to college where all everybody talked about was change (*change the system, change the rules, change your head*). I had trusted in all of it, believing it would set me free from this neighborhood.

I kept walking until I got to the end of Chestnut Street, where it met King's Highway. Here the cars were moving fast, trying to beat the light and get through the intersection.

King's Highway was the busy street we were never supposed to cross when we were kids. When Jane got hurt, before I knew what really happened, I'd thought there had been an accident at this corner, the boundary between our known world and the scarier one beyond it. A movie had instantly been made in the back of my brain that day. Of Jane getting hit by a car as she'd tried to cross King's Highway. Of an ambulance, its lights flashing ruby red, its sirens howling, coming to take her to the hospital. *She's gonna be all right*, the lips of one of the men in white would say over the din as they lifted her onto the stretcher.

All these years and that old movie played. If only Jane had been hit by a car. Scraped up, with a broken leg. A concussion, maybe. If nothing else, a more normal misfortune.

It was relief to join the stream of people going into Merinski's Market, probably all buying a few things for supper. Mr. Merinski already had his air conditioning on, even though the temperature had barely cracked eighty degrees. Through the frigid air, I made my way to the deli counter in the back where Mr. Merinski was busy with another customer. He was a large jowly man with a crew cut so short and so blond you could see his whole scalp. Even with the air conditioning on, he was sweating and I noticed the usual morbid blood stain in front of his butcher's apron. Over the hum of the big deli case, he spoke to me.

"What'll it be, Laura?"

"Just two pounds of hamburger, Mr. Merinski." There had never been a time I hadn't known him; the family lived around the corner from us on Hillside Avenue. In fact, Mrs. Merinski had been the one who'd waited for me at our house the day Jane had gotten hurt.

"How's your dad? Haven't seen him lately…"

"He's fine," I said, which was a total lie. I knew from my mother that Sal was a wreck these days, worried about his job.

"Well, tell him I say hello." He turned his back to me to wrap up the pink and white meat that has just emerged out of the grinder.

"You know, Patty's getting married two weeks from now at St. Thomas." Patty was his oldest daughter, who had graduated from high school with me.

"Really? Wow. That's great. Tell her congratulations for me." I didn't have to ask who Patty was marrying. She'd had the same boyfriend, Robert Demaris, all through high school. Patty was a nice girl with a wide Polish face. A little chubby, with thin blond hair like her dad's but thank God, not his jowls.

In the wavy glass of the deli case, I saw my own face reflected back. I had olive skin, dark brown frizzy hair, and brown eyes that had circles under them no matter how much sleep I got. I looked like my father's Sicilian side, rather than my mom's auburn-haired, blue-eyed Irish side. All the humidity had made my hair frizz out even more than usual, so it hung like a half-open umbrella around my face. When I stepped back, letting the glass reflect back all of me, I looked like a giant mushroom, or maybe a gnome with an oversized head. It was definitely a very trippy-looking image.

In high school, where you had to declare what you were (jock, straight, greaser, or freak); I had been a hippie freak. And in Springfield, freaks quickly blew town for the wider world or burned out and became junkies who scored and hung out all day at Forest Park.

Patty Merinski had stayed straight. I could picture her now as a bride, emerging from St. Thomas in her long-sleeved Catholic wedding dress. There would be a flurry of confetti, the ride in a rented white limo to the inevitable reception at the Knights of Columbus Hall over on Second Street.

I'd watched that particular scene play out about a million times before. At least I knew one thing with total certainty. I would never have a wedding like that and marry some local guy. Whatever I was going to do, whatever I was going to become, it wouldn't be that.

"Laura? Laura. Here's your meat." I'd been daydreaming and Mr. Merinski was trying to hand me the taped white package of *dead animal flesh* (I could hear Gail's voice in my head). "Well, there you go," he said, when I finally took it. He eyed me for a moment, like I was still ten, then wiped his hand on the bloody apron. "Now you take care, Laura. You take care of yourself." There was something about the way he had repeated that phrase about taking care of myself. I'd lived in the neighborhood long enough to have a pretty good idea of what it was. My early return from college was being talked about, once again putting the DiStefanos in a bad light.

So what's new? I thought, as the door to the market closed behind me with a heavy slam. The warmer air surrounded me. My family had always given the neighborhood plenty of grist for the gossip mill. Why would any of that change? I walked back up my street, past the row of houses and the Dolans' overflowing trashcans. When I got home, I curled up on the couch like I was a kid again and watched a rerun of the Donna Reed show until supper was ready.

Much later, I tried to call Gail but the phone in our old dorm room just rang and rang until I finally hung up.

3

Irish

I'd spent another whole day out there looking for a job, trying to look straight, with my hair pulled back and a navy blue skirt on, but no luck. It was hard to love McNally's, the worst dive bar in town, but when Jane called and said, let's have a beer, me, you, and Kimmy, it had seemed like a better deal than facing another supper with my parents, so I'd said okay.

I walked into the bar, which was already starting to fill up with regulars. Even before I sat down, there was one guy who started checking me out, big time. He's Irish, I thought, of that specific type that can only be found in New England – where these pale-faced, blue-eyed men can drink, cause suffering, and be loved their whole lives through, no matter what. Springfield, indeed, the whole state, was full of them.

I took a seat about six stools away from him to wait for Jane and Kimmy who, like usual, were late. The Irish guy was with a group listening to a story told by a big, blond biker guy. All of the sudden the biker guy must have delivered the story's punch line, because everybody started laughing at the same time.

As Irish laughed and casually leaned into the bar, I felt compelled to look. He was wearing a blue denim shirt, which was unbuttoned enough to expose a hairless sleek chest. His torso seemed to be hipless and totally boyish, reminding me of a picture I'd seen of Michaelango's David, and he had legs as long and straight as a racehorse's. Freckles, visible even in the bad bar light, were scattered across the long somewhat horsey face. The hair was shiny and the color of new pennies. He's Irish all right, I thought. Irish as the day is long, and just as full of trouble.

He caught me watching him and gave me a wide, totally flirtatious smile. A few moments later, he left his buddies and came over to talk to me.

"You waiting for someone special tonight or what?"

"Why, are you special?" I said it sarcastically, but with just enough of a smile, so that he would know I wasn't blowing him off.

"Well my mother thinks so. That count? Actually, I was hoping I might've lucked out for once in my fucking life and ended up at the right place at the right time. That is, in case you were looking…"

"Looking for what?" I interrupted him. "A guy? So I can get laid tonight? Too much trouble."

He laughed a big rowdy laugh. "Ooh, listen to you. You are a nasty girl! You always this bad, or were you just saving it up for me? Either way, let me buy you a drink."

He leaned that torso into the bar again, this time quite close to me. I suddenly felt reckless. How long had it been, exactly, since I'd been with somebody? Probably March, and it was almost June. I hadn't finished my first beer but I felt buzzed sitting next to this man, and the feeling seemed to be gaining momentum, like I could just skid over whatever I'd felt that day, that week, like a flat pebble skims over deep and heavy water.

"I'm Kevin, by the way." He reached over and grabbed my hand. Years later, I would remember the strength of that hand and the way the cuticles of the fingertips were edged with grime.

"I'm Laura." I said. In the dark of his pupils, shiny with excitement, I could see a reflection of myself.

"You're not from here, are you?" he said.

"Actually, I am. I was away at school for a while."

"Where?"

"UMass, but I'm back here now."

Just then, Jane and Kimmy walked in. They spotted me, but in observance of the universal code of conduct for chicks at a bar, they didn't come over, since I was clearly talking to a guy I was interested in. As I looked past Kevin the Irish guy's head, I saw Jane pointing to a booth in the back, letting me know where they were sitting in case I decided to ditch him.

The place was starting to fill up. Mick, the bartender, who had been waylaid by a group of drunken firemen, finally made his way back to our end of the bar.

"This girl," Kevin said, "needs a drink. But if she wants something top shelf, you better tell her she's got the wrong guy." As if to back up that statement, he put a five-dollar bill down on the bar. Mick brought us drafts and a shot each. When I tried to pay extra for the shots, Kevin laughed and Mick just left my money on the bar.

"Don't worry," Mick said, winking at me. "He's got some pull around here."

And so the night went. Kevin was a local and a year younger than me. We determined after a protracted discussion that we had attended the same junior high school, but had never actually met before. He'd gone to Cathedral, the Catholic high school, and I hadn't. He built fences now, for a company down on Union Street, which was close to where his family lived. I talked about how weird it was, living with my parents again. I talked about looking for a job. What I didn't talk about was UMass, or anything that had happened there.

Several rounds later, Jane and Kimmy came over and said hello. I introduced them to Kevin, but the band was playing by then and it was hard to hear. Besides, Kevin's hand had started to wander up and down my leg and I had to remind myself to keep breathing. We were in that first rush of what happens when things happen, so to speak.

Jane was in my left ear, almost yelling so I could hear her.

"So, Kimmy and I are going now okay? We have to go to Powers tonight. Sam's playing." Sam was Kimmy's drummer boyfriend. Powers was a hole in the wall that smelled like pee or old beer, depending on the evening, and it was in Chicopee, one of the few places in the world that was actually more dismal than Springfield.

"Well I guess I'll see you guys later," I said, yelling back. As I turned my head to do this, Kevin began kissing the side of my face.

Jane laughed. "Yeah, looks like I'll be seeing you later, all right. Much later. Like tomorrow," she said. "You sure you're okay?"

"Yeah, it's cool. I just want to have some fun and I know him from school, sort of. Nothing serious, just, you know…"

"Okay, I get it," she said. But as she moved away from us, she punched Kevin's arm with just enough force so that he turned around.

"What the hell…"

"You be good to her," she said to him, before disappearing into the crowd. I doubted that he'd heard her.

Kevin had an apartment of his own a few blocks away, which was where we went when the bar closed. But he was letting some guy he worked with stay there with him, and that guy was already asleep in the bedroom, so we ended up in the living room, on the couch.

He never turned on the lights and he broke the zipper on my jeans trying too hard to get them off me. That didn't exactly turn me on. In fact, it made me wonder why sex with this guy had seemed so desirable an hour before. But, I knew it was too late to change my mind. I'd had five beers and a couple of shots, and he'd had more than that and it was almost three in the morning. I prepared myself for a quick pounding. I figured at least it would be over fast, then I could go to sleep.

But it didn't go like I thought it would. His eyes, wide and vulnerable, watched my face when he entered me.

"I want you to feel this," he said, cupping my breasts in his hands and putting his lips around each nipple in turn, as if it was the rim of a delicate wine glass. Involuntarily, my body shuddered; I was not expecting this. When I came a few moments later, I decided to keep it to myself.

Afterwards, he got up and rolled out the couch so we could sleep.

"Who was that big fat girl, the one in the overalls, with the blond chick," he asked me as he smoked a cigarette. "I think I've seen her around."

It wasn't anything I hadn't heard before. He was talking about Jane the way all Springfield guys talked about her. I made him wait a moment before I said anything.

"She's my sister."

"Sorry."

"Let's just go to sleep, okay?" I turned over on my stomach to end the discussion. I didn't want to think about Jane right now, let alone talk about her.

"No really. I'm sorry."

"I believe you. But I'm really tired."

"I'm an asshole sometimes. So now you know. Just don't freak out on me about what I said, all right?" He had propped himself up on his side and was staring at me. He wanted an answer.

"Okay, I won't." I said it just to shut him up. He was still smoking, still watching me, when I fell asleep.

4

Coffee Shop

"Hey, Sleeping Beauty, it's eleven o'clock. Don't you have some job interview thing? You better get up." It was Jane's voice, not Kevin's. I jumped out of bed and threw my clothes on. I had left Kevin's place at dawn but I'd fallen back to sleep when I got home that morning.

"Shit. Jane, you have to help me. I'm going to be late." I was supposed to be downtown in a half an hour to apply for a waitressing job. The bus would take too long, so I bribed Jane into dropping me off on her way to work at Big O's Laundry, her latest part time job.

"So how was it?" For payment, Jane was getting details of my previous night with Kevin as we drove.

"Sexually, it went better than I expected. And he's a pretty decent guy, too."

"How big was it?" she asked, squinting a bit into the bright sunshine that was pushing through the windshield. We weren't talking about watermelons or snakes or even trucks. Even more than I was, Jane was obsessed with penis size.

"Big *enough*. You're awful, Jane." I tried to look peeved but I started laughing.

"I just like to know these things. You said he was Irish looking and Irish guys usually have small ones. You know, like little pickles."

"Well, this one didn't."

"Lucky for you, Sis." Jane shot me a big leer of a smile as we pulled up in front of the coffee shop. "So are you gonna see him again?"

"Who knows?" I said, still giggling, as I got out of the car.

An older Greek man named Ari ran the coffee shop, called the Athena. We sat in a tiny windowless office, its walls covered with pictures of people standing in front of the white buildings and blue waters of Greece. He pointed to one of them, a dark-haired woman squinting in the sun, standing in front of a church in what was probably her wedding gown. "Tasia, my wife. She dead now."

"I'm sorry," I said automatically.

He continued to look at the picture. "Beautiful woman. She die in childbirth." He sighed and looked back over at me. "Nobody understand the mind of God."

Hearing all that personal stuff made me feel a little weird. Still, I gave him my best smile because I needed this job.

He asked me if I knew who Athena was.

"She was the goddess of wisdom in Greek mythology." At least I remembered some things from my education.

He nodded, satisfied, then looked me up and down over the tops of his thick glasses. "You ever waitress before?"

"Yes, all through high school. I worked at the Pancake House on Riverdale Road."

"You do a good job there?

"Yes, I'm a hard worker."

"Why you not at school? You look like a smart girl…"

"I went for a while, but it didn't work out." Ari took this information in, pursing his lips.

"These days, everybody need school. That what the United States of America all about." I knew enough not to say anything. My grandparents had been the same way. It had been a crime not to fully exploit every opportunity for self-advancement in this country. Ari looked me over once again.

"You start tomorrow here, okay?"

It wasn't a bad gig. The coffee shop was in the same building as the YMCA on Worthington Street. There were a lot of regulars who ate there all the time and the tips were pretty good.

I'd been working at the Athena a few days when Kevin walked in and sat down at the counter. He was sweating into his blue tee shirt and wisps of his shaggy copper hair stuck to his neck. Seeing his bare arms made me think about being in bed with him.

"You look hot," I said. Then I flushed, realizing how what I'd said sounded.

Okay, I said to myself, this guy really does turn you on. It wasn't just the drinks the other night.

"I walked over here."

"You did what?"

"I walked here. My car's fucked up."

"You walked over the bridge?" I said, meaning the bridge over the Connecticut River, which cut the town in half.

"No, I walked on the water like Jesus Christ." He smiled. Clearly, he felt secure in his ability to amuse me. "I wanted to see you. I called the house and your sister said you were working 'til nine so I decided to walk.

A gaggle of old Polish ladies who were regulars sat down. I went over and got their orders. His eyes followed me as I moved around. Never had anybody paid so much attention to the way I wrestled a pie plate out of the stupid glassed-in dessert cooler.

"You could have just left a message you know," I said when I returned. I knew I sounded snotty but I liked teasing him. Plus, it covered up how turned on I felt.

"I wanted to see you *tonight*," he said. I was still getting hung up about the way he'd said *tonight* when he added, "We could have a beer or something when you get done."

"Sure" I said, as my heart began to beat way too fast.

The ladies took forever to finish their pie and coffee, talking loudly in Polish. Kevin kept drinking the coffee I poured for him and waited. Finally, they left and things slowed down. When it was five of nine, I took out the broom and started to sweep.

"Who that guy? He a customer or what?" Ari said, loud enough so Kevin would hear.

"It's all right. He's my friend and he's waiting for me." I was slightly worried. Maybe Ari didn't like the idea of somebody hanging around while we closed. But, when I went to put the broom away, he just smiled at me and said, "You tell him he a lucky guy."

5

Working Life

One night became two nights then two nights became three. Kevin and I were seeing each other, just falling into it, like you do in the beginning, magnetized by sex. I was sneaking around, leaving the house late and coming home early before anybody else was up so we could do it every night, no matter what. It had occurred to me more than once that I wasn't fooling anybody, that when the back door creaked at dawn, my parents probably heard me come in. But these days, it didn't seem like Sal and Margaret wanted to know too much about what I was doing. I'd already given them more than enough to think about.

At least I had the job at the Athena, which probably made them worry less about me. Working was very important to my parents. After all, and I had learned this at school, my parents could be classified socioeconomically as "working people." Even then, I'd thought it was a weird term. It made me think of horses with fucking blinders on, trudging through the muck.

In the way my father thought about things, work wasn't just something you did to put food on the table or pay the bills. It was about holding up your end of the bargain and making yourself useful in this world. Which was why Sal was freaking out these days. He was on the verge of losing his job at the Springfield Armory, where he'd worked for almost twenty-five years. He was also on the verge of fifty-two; not very good verges to be on, I thought, as I started getting ready for work myself.

It was almost two o'clock and I had to be at the Athena in an hour. I looked out the window to check if it was still raining and saw Jane trudging up Chestnut Street, coming home from her shift at Big O's. She was walking next to somebody. When I realized it was Gordon Valeaux, I got a little freaked out myself.

It seemed like it was part of my sister's nature to befriend some of the strangest, most marginal people around. She attracted them like some people attract stray dogs. Gordon, in fact, was a known weirdo who lived in the neighborhood. At twenty-five, he'd already been in and out of Northampton State Hospital a couple of times. He was a tall, hulking guy who always dressed in the same impeccably pressed pin stripe suit, black silk vest, and tan fedora, no matter what the season. Gordon's main weirdness, however, was his way of talking in two different voices. If you ran into him, you never knew which one you'd get. There was a soft, goodie-two-shoes voice in which he'd go on and on about the weather and other banalities, then this other voice in which he'd snicker and say rather vile, gross things to you.

One time I told some premed major I knew at school about the way Gordon acted and he said it might be something called Tourette's syndrome or else just plain old schizophrenia. At least I'd never heard of Gordon doing any of the horrible things he muttered about (one time he said he wanted to lick my cream hole), but still he was a scary guy and everybody avoided him. Everybody but Jane. From the window, I watched as she waved goodbye to him in front of the house.

"Why were you walking up the hill with Gordon Valeaux?" I said, as soon as she came in.

"Why not? Hey, he's a person too."

"But he's a creep, Jane. In fact, he's nuts."

"Well, he didn't act nuts today. People should just give him a chance. I think he does that weird voice thing just to get attention."

"Jane, he's schizo, that's why he's been in Northampton. You don't know *what* he might do."

"He won't do anything."

"You don't know that."

"Hey, he was nice to me. He asked about the baby and everything. That's more than a lot of people around here do." Jane had sat down at the kitchen table and was now impatiently tearing open the cellophane window of a box of Hostess donuts. The awful thing was, I understood her strange Jane-logic, even when I didn't want to. The broken people in this town were her community. Among them, she was a rose, a queen in their midst, someone who wouldn't criticize or judge, who might even inspire them. The first time I heard that Leonard Cohen song "Suzanne," I had decided that Leonard must have known my sister.

There was coffee on the stove my mother had left before she took off with Peg Brenner, her real estate partner. I poured myself a cup and sat down. I had absolutely no interest in those horrible Hostess donuts but Jane was happily eating her second.

"Jane, I'm not saying don't talk to people. I just worry when you hang out with people like Gordon. They're a little too close to the edge, you know?"

"Yeah, like you never do stuff that could get you into trouble. How 'bout that first night with Kevin? You went home with him and you knew him for like what, two hours?"

"But I knew him from school…"

"You did not. What, you passed him once in the hall, four years ago?" she said, definitely pissed off. "That's a load of crap."

I was amazed at how much like my father she could sound when she got mad. "Okay. I'm not trying to get all preachy on you, but honest to god, Jane. Gordon Valeaux? I don't trust that guy. Just because he hasn't done anything weird yet, doesn't mean he won't."

Jane put her latest donut down on the table. It created a puddle of powdered sugar where it lay perfectly intact except for one large bite taken out of it.

"Look, I was just talking to him. He was getting off the bus and I was walking up the hill from work and he saw me, so we just started walking together and talking. It was no big deal. Now I don't want to talk about this bullshit anymore." Jane had a way of totally turning off, of becoming as inanimate as a piece of linoleum when she wanted to. I watched her eyes glaze over as she mechanically drank her cup of coffee.

It was time for me get to work anyway. I got up from the table and dumped the rest of my coffee in the sink. I should have known it would be a mistake to try and tell Jane not to talk to Gordon. My sister would do what she wanted to do, like she always did. And Jane had always had this thing with danger. The fact that I had said something about Gordon would just make her want to hang out with him more the next time she got the chance.

"Whatsomematterwityou? You not yourself today, my girl," Ari said. I had overturned one of those stupid little metal creamers, trying to fill it with Half-and-Half.

"Sorry, Ari. Just not paying attention to what I'm doing." I started cleaning up the mess.

"You wanna get ahead, you gotta pay attention in this life." Ari waved his hands in the air for emphasis before retreating to his favorite perch behind the cash register at the Athena. It was a good thing Ari liked me – which he showed by lecturing me every chance he got. His main thing was how I had "tree-mend-dous opportunities" waiting for me out there, opportunities he never had growing up in Greece. Even though he was older than my parents, sometimes he seemed like a little kid to me, all wide-eyed about life in general. Other times, I thought he was wiser than I was ever going to be, especially if I kept hanging out in Springfield.

It had started to rain again so business was really slow. To keep from going totally nuts, I went into the kitchen so I could restock all the napkins and to-go cups that we kept under the counter. As I came out from behind the counter with an armload of these things, I saw Timmy Morton and another guy walk into the coffee shop and sit down in one of the booths. I stood totally still for half a second then turned around and went back into the kitchen. My mother had told me he was living in the neighborhood again while I was at UMass, but I'd forgotten this piece of information.

Almost six years had passed since I'd laid eyes on Timmy, but he looked pretty much the same. His hair was still dark, with the slight wave I remembered, but longer in the back, styled in the modified Prince Valiant hair cut that half the young male population in Springfield had. The buddy was smaller and darker – probably Puerto Rican, I thought — and he was wearing a red bandana.

I didn't want them to see me so I moved from the kitchen through the other less-used door, grabbed a rag and slipped into one of the big booths we reserved for large groups. Even though it was at the other end of the dining room, it was quiet and I could hear Timmy's creepy voice when Malvina, the older black waitress, took their order.

"I don't know what I want. Is this all you got?" he was saying to Malvina.

"We got what's on the menu, boys. That's it." A few seconds went by. I knew, without being able to see, that Malvina was furiously drumming her pencil on top of her order pad. "So what you fellas want? I don't got all day." Malvina was a former lady wrestler. She didn't take crap from anybody and she especially detested customers who took up too much of her time.

"All right, all right. Gimme the corned beef on rye." Timmy said irritably.

The other guy ordered a hamburger. Then I heard the squeak of Malvina's heavy white shoes as she walked away and Timmy saying something under his breath that ended with the words "black bitch," just to prove how much of a racist asshole he was. He went on, louder, so it was easier for me to hear. "You know whose fault it is that we got to eat here tonight? My mother's. I told her we were going to the game tonight. She could of stayed home and made supper instead of going off to warm her ass on some lousy bar stool, but did she do that? No. Women are always fuckin' with you," Timmy said.

He was a monster. I knew that. But as long as I stayed hidden away in the red-cushioned interior of the big booth, I felt safe enough. And it seemed important to hear what the monster had to say. I wiped down the booth's tabletop for the fourth time, my ears as rapt as a rabbit's, but Timmy and the other guy had started talking about cars – the most boring topic in the world as far as I was concerned. Almost hypnotically, I stopped moving the rag over the table's flecked-grey Formica surface. I looked at it more closely. It was exactly the same surface as our kitchen table, the one we had back then and still had now.

I had been ten years old. When I'd found our neighbor, Mrs. Merinski, on the day that changed everything, standing in our kitchen. I knew right away that something was really wrong. It was suppertime. What was this woman, who was not my mother, doing in our kitchen? And what was she doing wearing my mother's apron? Mrs. Merinski didn't really look at me. She kept pushing a yellow sponge over the same spot on our flecked-gray kitchen table.

"Laura, your sister's been hurt," she said in a monotone.

"Jane?" I said, which was stupid because I had no other sister. "What do you mean? Where is she? And where's my mother?"

She began to answer me, but I was having trouble hearing all the words.

"…to the hospital. They told me maybe she got hit by a car. It's pretty serious, honey. Your dad went right over there from the work and…"

It seemed then, as if I was listening to Mrs. Merinski from the end of a long tunnel because the words were beginning to have a funny echo to them. This wasn't real, not Mrs. Merinski wearing my mother's apron and not these words. It was a dream and I wanted to wake up. But the other part of my brain, the part that couldn't turn off, no matter how much I wanted it to, knew better. All the spittle inside of my mouth became solid, like the white paste they gave you at school.

My little sister got hit by a car. What if she dies like my grandma Kate did? If Jane dies, I would never see her again.

The thoughts churned through me, like clothes in the water of my mother's violently agitating washing machine. Once I'd tried to put my hand in that water, when my mother had opened the lid to throw a loose sock in.

"Don't ever put your hand in the machine." She had yelled at me, exasperated as usual, with my stupidity. She was always warning me about the world and what could happen.

"Don't take candy from people you don't know."

"Don't let boys look up your dress."

"Don't cross the street without looking both ways"

We weren't supposed to cross King's Highway, not ever. But Jane liked to do things that we weren't supposed to do. I needed for it to have happened there. It was someplace I knew. And because of that, I could make the pictures in my brain end happy. I allowed myself one short breath of hope and unglued my tongue for the top of my mouth. *Maybe it wouldn't be so bad.*

"Mrs. Merinski, did my sister get hit on King's Highway?"

"They didn't say, honey." Mrs. Merinski was trying to open a can of Franco American spaghetti for my supper, using the new can opener my father had just bought. Now the pictures I had of Jane being put in an ambulance on King's Highway were disappearing. Panicking, I ran to her side and started pulling at her arm with all my might.

"I have to go see Jane now. I don't want her to die. You have to take me!"

"Honey, you need to settle down." She pulled my fingers off her arm. "The doctors are taking care of your sister. I'm making you some supper…."

Then everything swung away from me, like I had been high up on a swing at Mittineague Park and its chain had broken, making me fall back to earth too fast. I saw the metal legs of the kitchen chair coming closer, then the green blur of the linoleum.

Jane is gonna die, I thought as I hit the floor. Then there was no kitchen, no Mrs. Merinski, just this black around me.

When I woke up, not all of me felt like it was there. Mrs. Merinski had to help me get my arms into the tops of my blue flowered pajamas and hold out the bottoms in front of me to step into, like I was a two year old. She made me sit down on the bed and gave me a glass of water I didn't want.

"You just got dehydrated, that's all. It was the shock…" she said, her voice trailing off.

I held the glass of water she had given me with both hands. It had pictures of the Roadrunner and the Coyote on it, one of the cartoons Jane and I liked to watch on Saturday mornings.

"Is my sister dead?" I was asking this from the faraway place that most of me had gone to.

"No, honey." I didn't believe her. She sounded like adults did when they lied to you about Santa Claus or the Easter Bunny. Then Mrs. Merinski put her face close to mine, like some relatives did when they were getting ready to kiss you, even if you didn't want them to. Her jaw trembled a little and she kept opening and closing her mouth, like she couldn't make up her mind up about what to say to me. She still had my mother's apron on, which was all wet in the front, probably from the water she had splashed in my face, trying to get me off the kitchen floor.

What I knew, suddenly, in every fiber of my ten-year-old being, was that she was very scared — actually terrified. In fact, I'd never seen an adult so scared in my entire life. All the million different things that had been flickering through my mind came to an abrupt stop, like music from a record player when somebody pulled the cord out. Finally, Mrs. Merinski took the glass out of my hands and put it on the nightstand between the two beds in the room.

"You should say your prayers and ask God to take care of your sister."

I knelt down by the side of my bed. Jane's empty bed was in front of me, the spread on it still smooth from my mother's hands that morning. Her bedspread had cowboys and Indians on it. Jane had begged to get it, even though my mother had said it wasn't meant for a girl. But Jane wasn't just any girl. She was my crazy wild little sister. I began to say the Now I Lay Me Down to Sleep Prayer, the one I'd said every night of my life, but it occurred to me that God might not be listening to prayers coming from 130 Chestnut Street.

I couldn't stay in the booth all night, I knew that. Ari was starting to look over at me, probably wondering what the hell I was doing still wiping down that table in the big booth.

I saw one of the regulars, Mr. Lane, come into the coffee shop and make his way over towards the counter. I would have to leave the booth and let Timmy see me; there was no way around it.

Like when I was a kid and really freaking out, I looked around for something that I could latch onto, that would make me feel better. My eyes focused on Malvina, who was bussing plates from the booth next to the one where Timmy was sitting. I told myself nothing bad could happen as long as Malvina was there. The ballsy way she'd acted with Timmy and his pal made me feel, if not exactly safe, at least protected. I stood up and left the big booth. As I walked across the open floor, I kept my eyes on her and away from the booth where Timmy sat. When I was behind the counter, I took Mr. Carrera's order, which was coffee and a piece of apple pie, like usual.

At first, it seemed like Timmy was ignoring me. I could see his profile, out of the corner of my eye and it wasn't moving. But as I delivered the pie, I ventured a direct look over at his booth. Timmy, the guy who'd raped and almost killed my sister, looked up at me. He smiled. Then his lips puckered and slowly released a silent kiss.

6

Supper Time

My mother put some pork chops, a small bowl of applesauce and a bowl of canned green beans on the table. It was Sunday so we were having supper early, like we usually did. Even though the box fan's blades turned in the kitchen window, it wasn't doing much good. The kitchen was still incredibly hot. I watched my parents and Jane eat, their mouths chewing in some sort of strange unison. Maybe that was inevitable, given all the eating they'd done together.

I wasn't hungry. At school, I'd stopped eating meat and I wasn't so crazy about eating it again. With my finger, I traced the pattern of one of the gray swirls on top of the kitchen table, thinking about seeing Timmy Morton at the Athena. I hadn't said a word about it to anyone and I wasn't sure I ever would.

"I forgot the bread," my mother said, finally breaking the silence. She had one of her polyester pantsuits on, this one in a yellowish green color she called celadon. My father watched her closely as she got up and plucked four slices of bread out of the open Wonder Bread loaf on the counter then put them on a plate and sat down again.

"You going out later?"

"Yeah. I'm showing that ranch on Rogers Avenue with Peg. I'll be back around six." Peg was Peg Brenner, my mother's business partner. She was a retired schoolteacher with dyed blond hair cut so short it almost looked butch. I actually got a kick out of her. She smoked more cigarettes than anybody I'd ever met in my life and talked non-stop, usually about how much money she was making. She always ended these monologues with the same brassy punch line: "How's them apples?" she'd say, eyebrows arched high, as she took a deep drag off her Newport. My father couldn't stand her. When he thought nobody was listening, he called her a ball buster under his breath.

My mother and Peg Brenner were hardly bra burners, but lady real estate brokers were still a novelty in the Springfield area. Sometimes when people called the house, they assumed Peg and my mother were interior decorators, not realtors, which always made me laugh. But my mother's new life was no laughing matter to my father.

"It's Sunday, you know. It's supposed to be the day of rest." He gave my mother a look. "Or is Peg an atheist?"

"Methodist, actually. Sal, nowadays the world doesn't stop because it's Sunday. Today's the only day the clients can make it." My mother was trying for that middle ground, not getting into it with my father, but not giving in to him either. She looked very modern in her pantsuit, with her coral lipstick on and her auburn hair done up in a French twist. Like a surgeon, she carefully cut the meat from the bone of the chop. "You know, you won't be complaining when we sell it and get that commission."

Money, and the fact that my mother was capable of making some, were sore points with my father. A year ago, Secretary of Defense Robert McNamara had announced that the Springfield Armory was going to be sold to General Electric. My father couldn't understand "what the hell McNamara was thinking." The war in Vietnam was going strong, in fact, he was shipping more and more M16s over there every day, and why would you want people who didn't even work for the government making your guns anyways? His conversations these days were filled with new words, "phase-out" and "private industry," which he would spit out like swear words, when he talked about it. Now he squinted, looking at the chop on his plate more closely.

"Did you buy these chops at Merinski's?"

"I stopped there with Peg on my way home yesterday."

"You think we got money to burn, like that Brenner woman? Everybody knows that Polack's scale is fixed." My mother said nothing. She knew the volcano inside my father was rumbling, waiting to spew. But in her face, there was still a hope it might pass, that another meal together wouldn't be ruined.

Then my father's hand came down, loud and flat against the table.

"So now you go anywhere Peg Brenner tells you to, like the two of you are married? Who the hell is wearing the pants around here – me or her?"

Jane had been engrossed, devouring the second pork chop on her plate, but now she stopped eating and leaned back in her chair. She squared her shoulders against the flying vinyl wings of the kitchen chair like some gladiator, prepared to do battle in the hot humid air of our kitchen.

"What the fuck gives you the right to talk to her like that?" Jane said, looking directly at my father. Even for Jane, using the f word with my father was incredibly ballsy. I elbowed her and gave her a look that said, "Are you crazy?" But Jane wouldn't look back at me; instead, she leaned harder into my father's angle of sight.

"You're just pissed off about everything. But it's not our fault they're closing the Armory down," she said. "Why don't you just lighten up?" My father's face went white with rage. I was afraid he was going to hit her.

"In my own house, you talk to me like this? It figures. You never had a lick of sense, not for one day in your entire goddamn life. No wonder you always get into trouble." He would never say it, even when he was this angry, but we knew what he meant. The attack had been Jane's fault somehow in his mind.

"You don't think I know what the hell is going on, but I do. This one over here…" He was jabbing his finger at me now, "is out every night and comes home at dawn. And *you*, now you're going to have some bastard's baby and we're all going to have to go on, like nothing happened. Well I'm not going to stand for it." His left hand, fisted already, began to pound the table, accentuating key words.

"You all wanna live like that, you can go to *California* and find some *commune* to live on. See who pays the goddamn bills then. You can bet your ass it won't be me. I won't take it!"

In the dead silence that followed, my mother picked her plate up from the table and walked it to the sink. Jane, still in her gladiator pose, was ready to fire back but she stopped, stultified by my mother's calm trip to the sink. My father sniffed the air, sensing some change in the wind.

The kitchen became so quiet I could actually hear the clock on the wall above the stove tick as its minute hand, thick and black like the line on Merinski's scale, moved. The balance of power was shifting and my father knew it. Robert McNamara's stupidity, my mother's career in real estate, and the fact that both his daughters were going to hell were just the latest signs. He stared down at his empty plate and said nothing.

My mother opened the cabinet above the sink, removing the bottle of Seagram's that my father always kept there. I noticed her wedding set, two gold bands with an almost pathetically small diamond on one of them, as she put the bottle on the table in front of my father. Then she reached into the cabinet again, retrieving a shot glass with a picture of a blue trout jumping over the word "Florida." She put it next to the bottle on the table.

"Sal, have a shot. You need to calm down. Nobody's going anywhere. When Jane has that baby, she stays here. And Laura stays here as long as she needs to so she can figure out things. It's their home. That's the way it's going to be. I'm going out now."

I watched the luminescence of my mother's celadon pantsuit fading as she disappeared into the darkness of the living room lit only by the TV set that was left on all the time now, like a night light for a child. Increasingly, that child was my father. Years ago, he'd been the one in charge, but all that was changing.

Eventually my father took the bottle of Seagram's and the shot glass, and retreated like some sad-eyed Robert E. Lee to his lounger chair in the living room. Jane and I cleared away the dishes and went upstairs. We lit up a joint without saying anything. Then finally, Jane said, "I guess they knew about the baby all along. Just as well it came out now, I suppose."

7

McNally's

At least the secrets were out in the open. I didn't have to sneak around when I got home from Kevin's in the morning and everybody had finally acknowledged Jane's pregnancy. About a week after the fight, Jane quit her job at Big O's saying it was too hard to haul laundry anymore. Meanwhile, Peg and my mother sold the house on Rogers Avenue and collected a nice juicy commission. And my father just shut up about everything for a while, which was a very good thing as far as I was concerned.

I had a Saturday off from the Athena, so Kevin and I drove over to hear a band play in Forest Park. Afterwards we stopped at McNally's for something to eat. Kevin was being strange. He didn't want to sit at the bar like we usually did, so we waited for a table. The place was noisy and crowded, full of police and firemen's softball teams having burgers and getting drunk. When we finally sat down, he reached across the table and took my hand.

"I think I'm in love with you," he said. I was totally shocked. It was true we were having great sex together, but I hadn't thought about things beyond that. As far as I was concerned, Kevin was a townie guy and townie guys were not what I saw in my future. I took an elaborate time-consuming slug from my beer bottle.

"Laura, did you hear what I said?"

"Yeah, I just didn't think we were – serious like that." It was suddenly hard to talk, to physically make my mouth move.

"So you're not?"

"Not what?"

"In love with me?"

"I don't think I've ever been in love with anybody in my life."

It was a lie, actually. I'd been in love with John Shea who lived in my dorm at school. We'd had a thing for a few months until the roof party, when he had wandered off with some blond girl from the dorm next to ours. Everybody could hear them screwing in the stairwell as the party wound down. The next day I'd gone to his room and tearfully told him that even though I didn't believe in monogamy (a tool for sexual repression) it was not okay for him to go off and do it with somebody else if I was literally on the other side of the wall. The "L" word, despite my best intentions, slipped out as I talked. I knew I'd crossed some kind of line.

"Look babe," John had been blunt. "Don't get all heavy about me. I never said I was your boyfriend or anything."

The din in McNally's was getting louder. Kevin was watching me, still waiting for an answer, trying with all his might not to lose it.

"So, why do you think you're in love me?" It was all I could think of asking, under the circumstances.

"Fuck if I know Laura," he said, exasperated. "It just happens, that's all. One minute you're alone and then the next minute boom – you're with somebody. That night I was in here, hanging around with the guys, then *I saw you…*" These last three words were said very deliberately and he paused, like that should have made the whole thing crystal clear to me. I was trying to figure out what to say next when he sprang up from the table, making sure the chair scraped the floor as brutally as possible.

"I gotta go to the men's room. You're taking the piss right out of me here." Kevin was used to women being more interested in him than he was in them. Now he was caught on a line I hadn't really meant to throw and he didn't like it one bit.

With John, I'd been the one who wanted more. But I was just a Springfield townie chick to him. When the novelty wore off, it was easy enough for him to move on. I stared across the room at the IRA poster the bar's owner Dan Coughlin had put up. One thing was for sure. I had a thing for Irish guys, although John Shea and Kevin Mahoney were hardly cut from the same cloth. My mother would have described John's family as lace curtain Irish, since they could have passed for WASPs with their house in Belmont and their summer place on the Vineyard. I had fallen for John because of his sarcasm and his reckless entitled audacity. That, along with the killer mane of black hair and eyes the color of blue lake water.

Kevin was shanty-Irish, more like my mother's family. He had grown up in a ramshackle house down on Kelso Avenue, the oldest of seven siblings. There was a long-suffering mother named Eileen and his father Andrew, who had an impeccable alcoholic pedigree, religiously drinking up his paycheck from the railroad every week. Not that this was so unusual in town. The bars were full of men like his father who drank as a lifestyle. They drank every night; they drank in the morning to get over the night before and they drank in the afternoon to get ready to drink more that night. Most of these guys weren't so old, but by the time they were thirty, they looked forty-five. One of the reasons I knew for sure I'd never be walking down the aisle in a white dress at St. Thomas' was the terror I felt, just thinking about waking up one morning and finding myself married to a guy like that.

Kevin came back. Apparently taking a piss hadn't made him feel any better because he sat down and glared at me. "I can't believe this," he said, his voice tight and hard. "Here I tell you how I feel, like women always say they want you to do, and you're acting like you don't give a damn." The hand that had held mine a few minutes ago was balling itself up into a fist.

I thought of John again. I still hated the fucker, but being on the other side now, I could feel the claustrophobia of somebody getting too close, ready to suffocate you with their needs. I liked sleeping with Kevin but it was probably better to end the whole thing. Maybe he'd hate me for it, but I couldn't be with someone like him and I knew it. I put both of my hands down in front of me on the table and started giving him the break up talk. "Look, I got some things going on right now and…"

There was a sudden rush of noise. I stopped talking and looked up. It was him again, appearing out of nowhere like he had in the coffee shop. Timmy Morton and two other guys were at the door, trying to get in. Pat the bouncer, an enormous guy in overalls with a long braid down his back, was blocking their way like some hippie linebacker.

Dan Coughlin, the bad drunk who owned McNally's, intervened. "Let'em in," he yelled to Pat. "They're okay."

"That one's a creep. You pay me to keep people like him out," Pat said.

"Just let them in. So they'll have a few beers and go home. No big deal…"

The Morton family must have done something major for Dan Coughlin, I thought. Timmy and his buddies sauntered in and headed towards the table across from us. The dispute had gotten the room's attention, so people were looking up from their drinks.

"All right everybody. No worries. Me and my pals are so glad we are able to join you tonight." Timmy said. He smiled manically, looking like Johnny Carson on speed.

Kevin watched him, with lowered eyes. "What a total asshole," he said, but I doubted he knew who Timmy was to my family or me.

"Kevin, that guy creeps me out. Let's just leave," I said.

"You shouldn't let a jerk off like him bother you," he said. "We were talking about things…"

"I can't, not in here. Let's go. We can talk later."

"Okay." Since he was, after all, a man trying to win me over, Kevin started to put some money down on the table and I stood up, ready to go.

"Well, if it's not Laura DiStefano from the neighborhood," Timmy said, turning to us.

I decided not to say anything. I turned around and started looking for my purse which was somewhere under the table. Later on, I would wonder if my ignoring him had egged him on.

"Hey buddy, looks like you lucked out." Timmy raised his voice, making sure he had Kevin's attention. "Got yourself one of those good looking DiStefano women. They're all good looking, aren't they? Especially this one here, but so's the mother, even the little sister, before she got fat. Glad I got her when the getting' was still good. Know what I mean, buddy?"

There was a silent second, maybe two, before Kevin crossed the narrow space between the two tables and slammed his fist into Timmy's face, which made that sickening dead meat kind of sound when he did. Pat the bouncer appeared out of nowhere and forced his way between them to stop the fight but not before hitting Timmy in the mouth again, taking the opportunity to settle whatever the old score between them had been.

A crowd quickly formed hoping for more action. Many of the faces were vaguely familiar from school but I couldn't have remembered any of their names, even if I'd wanted to. Some were making catcalls, others laughed.

Indeed, I thought, I was back in Springfield, and I cursed the twisted turn of events, which had led me back to this town's barrooms and townies, and most of all, to my own past.

"You fuckin' assholes are through here. I see either of you in here again, I'm calling the cops." As Pat yelled more stupid male blather, Timmy cursed loudly and rubbed his jaw. Kevin just stood there, ramrod straight, ready to take another shot.

"Kevin." I got behind him and said his name only once. He turned and looked at me, his eyes changing. Dan Coughlin was arguing loudly with Pat and the guys Timmy had come in with. Someone threw a bottle and the crowd began to sway and emit a kind of rumbling noise that made me think of the cattle in that opening scene from the TV show *Rawhide*. Before the situation could totally fall apart, I took Kevin's hand and we disappeared, stepping out into the hot humid evening.

We never did have the talk I thought we would have, where I would have told him that I didn't want to get involved, leaving out the part about not wanting to get involved specifically with him because he was a townie and how it conflicted with my plan (ok, almost a plan) to go back to school. We went back to his place and turned on the TV and smoked a joint. Both of us were edgy and somewhat freaked out.

"Why did you hit him? You're lucky the bouncer had it in for him or he would have come after you."

"After he said the thing about your sister, I finally realized who he was. He was the one who hurt your sister, that they sent away."

"Yes but you didn't have to hit him and start a fight" I said, realizing even as I said it that it was a stupid chick sort of thing to say.

"Of course I had to hit him. What did you expect me to do? Stand there like some pussy and let him say that crap about you and your sister?" he snapped.

I pulled the quilt over me. In fact, I was secretly glad Kevin had hit him. "You know, he showed up at the coffee shop a few weeks ago and now he showed up tonight at McNally's. It's freaking me out. I knew he was back in the neighborhood, but I didn't expect he'd be turning up every time I turn around. He's crazy and he's scaring me."

"That's why you have to stand up to the motherfucker."

"You don't know what he's like. You don't know what he did to Jane." I didn't usually cry (another chick thing I thought was manipulative and stupid) but now I couldn't stop. Kevin got up and brought me some toilet paper so I could blow my nose.

"Look. Why don't you tell me about it?" he asked. "I got time. I can't go to sleep now anyway, after all that shit at the bar."

Even though it was still hot in the room, I burrowed in close to Kevin. That part of me that wanted to end things with him in McNally's had vanished. Right now, the fact that this man loved me made me feel safe. So why not tell him the story? Why not let the memories, which flowed underneath everything, finally speak? What had happened to Jane lay in the back of my brain like it was a living thing, a snake shiny and fat with memory. I lit another cigarette and sat up in bed, letting the thing uncoil and make big loops in my head.

8

Memory

"She thinks she's really something," Marie DeLuca said to Gloria Serrano as they drank coffee in the kitchen. I was standing in the little hallway outside of the Serrano kitchen and the women hadn't seen me yet. It was a hot July afternoon and I'd been playing Candy Land with Donna and her cousin Tina outside on the picnic table and had gone inside to get a drink.

Mrs. Serrano didn't like us kids tracking dirt through her kitchen when we were thirsty, so she'd set up a little table with a plastic pitcher of KoolAid and a stack of Dixie cups in the hallway. I was a quiet child by nature, a trait that let me sneak up on adults sometimes and hear things they normally wouldn't say around kids. That sentence made me curious: "She thinks she's really something." Who were they talking about, I wondered. Maybe it was some actress, like Connie Stevens.

"You know Margaret actually knocked on Thelma and Dan's door to collect the rent when they were two days late. Just stood there, until they wrote her out the check."

Upon hearing my mother's name, I stood absolutely still with the Dixie cup of cherry KoolAid still in my hand, afraid any movement on my part would give me away. I both did and did not want to hear what they might say next.

"That Margaret shows off sometimes. Just because she and Sal own that two-family, she thinks she's the Queen of Sheba."

At ten, I already knew I should keep my mouth shut. I had figured certain things out about relationships between adults. I knew telling my mother what a neighbor said about her might change something. And I liked the way things were, the way all of us kids were welcome in any of the neighbors' backyards, how our mothers would get together in somebody's kitchen and talk and talk, never running out of things to say. The way things were made me glow inside with a happiness I couldn't explain.

So, I had to keep it to myself, this thing that they had said about my mother. But it made me afraid that somehow it would come out of me when I least expected, like in that fairytale about the little girl who had frogs leap out of her mouth at the end. I couldn't remember why that had happened to her in the story, but I was afraid that my secret would suddenly spring out of me and terrible things would happen.

A few days later, Jane and I were alone, sitting in the kitchen eating cereal. My father had left for work and I heard the squeaky pulley sounds of the clothesline, so I knew my mother was out on the porch, hanging clothes. I had been taking ballet lessons that summer and at last, my mother had bought the pink tutu with rhinestones on it that I would wear for the recital. I woke up early that morning to try it on again. Even though Jane wasn't a girlie girl like I was, she liked glittery things and wanted to try it on too. I was afraid she would rip it, so I said no.

She got mad. "Laura, you're a show-off, wearing that stupid thing." She must have said it ten times, in a particularly irritating monotone.

I wanted her to shut up. "I don't care if you call me a show-off," I said. "Mrs. Serrano said Mom was a show-off. So what?" I thought my mother was still out on the porch, but the creaking sounds from the clothesline had stopped. She was standing in the kitchen.

"Mrs. Serrano said WHAT about me?"

"I don't remember what she said, Mom. I just thought I did." She grabbed me with one arm and pulled me away from the table. A wisp of the little pink tutu caught in the chair and remained there.

"I never want to hear things like that out of *your* mouth again." With her other hand, she slapped my face, hard enough so I knew she meant business.

"And you…" She grabbed Jane by the arm. "I don't want *you* going over to the Serranos' today. You stay away from that house."

Kevin took the cigarette out of my hand. I'd stopped talking, lost in the memories. More for myself than for Kevin, I summed up the story so far. "Because of something I said that day, my mother got mad and wouldn't let Jane play at the Serranos' like she usually did. Instead, she rode her bike to the cemetery where Timmy Morton saw her. That's why it's partly my fault."

Kevin opened up a new pack of cigarettes. "It's not any of your fault." I didn't want to argue with him. It was so late and part of me wanted to stop telling the story. Kevin lit another cigarette and handed it to me, his way of encouraging me to keep talking.

"So how did he get her to go with him?"

"Well, basically because he told her he'd let her have a cigarette." I glanced at my own cigarette now as its smoke curled and disappeared into the air. "She was seven years old. I don't think she had words for what he did to her. She didn't talk about it, except to some policewoman who asked her questions while she was still in the hospital. But one day, two years later, she told me everything."

I sat up straighter in bed and put the mostly unsmoked cigarette out. I pulled the battered quilt over my shoulders. It didn't feel right to be naked to tell the next part.

It was a summer day – the sun shining perfect yellow light, the sky the exact color of a sky-blue crayon. After asking our mother, Jane and I rolled our bathing suits into towels and raced to the pool, only stopping to buy Hostess chocolate cupcakes, Jane's favorite, at a little store on the way. I made Jane hurry up. The way I saw it, summer came around the corner like the ice cream truck did. If you didn't run out in time, you missed it.

We swam for hours, until we couldn't lift our arms up anymore. Then we sat down on the cement near the edge of the pool to eat our Hostess cupcakes, shivering a little in our wet bathing suits. It was getting close to suppertime and we both dreaded going home. In the two years since the attack, our parents had changed. Our mother rarely got out of her bathrobe now and was incapable of cooking anything other than frozen dinners. Our father sat in his chair every night and got drunk in front of the TV, whose volume he insisted on keeping up too loud. Sometimes I wanted to scream at them "You're supposed to be our mother and father. Why are you acting this way?" but I knew I never would.

I watched Jane as she finished her cupcake, licking the wrapping clean like she always did when she ate something chocolate. Someone walked behind me, blocking the sun for a moment. Jane's face changed.

"What's the matter?"

"I thought it was him," she said. There weren't many people left at the pool since it was getting late but I saw one of the lifeguards picking up a towel someone had left on a bench. He did look a lot like Timmy.

"It's not him. He's in Bridgewater. You know that."

"I know," she said. Then she got absolutely still, this sister of mine, who was always wiggling around. I could feel something change, as if the seconds that normally made time move forward stopped and waited for something.

"Do you want me to tell you what he did?" Jane said.

"Only if you want to," I said. "I never wanted to make you, like that time Mom tried to send you to that stupid counselor."

"You're not making me."

"Ok, then tell me."

"I was riding my bike past the gate of the cemetery on King's Highway and Timmy was just standing there, like he was waiting for something. So he yells at me and said 'You better come talk to me or I'll tell your Ma.' He knew I wasn't supposed to be riding my bike up there. I go up to him and he's smoking a cigarette and I say that I'll tell his Mom on him if he tells on me. He kind of laughs. So then, he says, 'I bet you wanna try having a smoke, right? Bet you never done that. If you go into the cemetery with me, I promise I'll let you.' So I go with him and we put my bike near some bushes so no one will take it and we keep walking and go all the way back, near where the woods start. Then he lights up a cigarette and he gives me this weird little smile, then he kind of starts laughing. I didn't know what he was laughing about, so I laughed too, because he was a teenager and I figured he would tell me what was so funny. Then he stops laughing, just like that.

'Say, kid. You sure you still wanna cigarette?' he says. I say, yeah. So he lights one up for me with his and then he gives it to me. But I start coughing when I try to smoke it. And then it starts. The really bad part. He gets all mad at me after that.

'You think you're a big girl now, with your cigarette? Is that what you think you are? Well, you can't smoke like a big girl,' he says. Then he takes the cigarette away from me, like he just grabs it from my mouth and he puts it under his foot and he crushes it real hard. Then he takes something out of his pocket. It's all folded up and the paper looks kind of smeary.

'I'll show you what big girls do. You're gonna learn,' he says.

There are black and white pictures on the paper. One of them shows a man putting his thing into a lady's mouth; another one shows a man sitting down on a chair and a lady sitting on top of him, facing away from him and he was putting his thing into her too. I stare at the pictures for a second but I don't know what to do. Then I decide to run, because he's being so creepy with his stupid pictures and crazy talk. I try to run away but he just reaches out and grabs at the waistband of my blue shorts and he won't let me go. I start screaming so he hits me in the mouth real hard and shoves me down on the ground. I get blood in my mouth and there are these old leaves on the ground and I get them in my mouth too so I can't cry or scream or anything. I go to lift my head up but he punches it. So I lie still. Then he tries to rip my blue shorts from the back where he's holding on to them, but he can't get the waistband part to rip, so he takes both hands and gets them off me. He puts his whole arm on my back, to keep me on my stomach on the ground. And he starts swearing under his breath and grunting.

I thought at first he had put a stick up me, it hurt so bad. I wasn't sure what he was do- ing but I knew he's hurting me in some way that's different and dirty. Boys in school talked about putting their weenies up girls' twats, and that were what caused babies and stuff, but I didn't know much about all that.

So he just kept grunting and the thing inside me keeps going up me further and further and I thought maybe he would just split me open into two halves, like a cantaloupe when you cut it. When he was done, he stands up and puts his foot on my back. 'I'm not through with you bitch,' he says to me. I try to get up, just raise my head up a little bit, because I am so scared and I hurt so much but he just steps down on my back harder.

'You stay there bitch. You're my bitch now and you do what I tell you to do and you stay on the ground.' I still try to push myself up off the ground again to get away. I try real hard, even though Timmy's got his foot on my back. I push up and kind of crawl and I get a couple of inches away from him. But it doesn't work. He gets even madder at me. He grabs me by my hair and yanks me down on the ground again. The dirt's coming into my mouth. Then he puts his cigarette out, into my back. I cry out, real loud, even with the dirt in my mouth. I feel like that dog you and me saw once, that got hit by a car. That dog knew he was going to die – remember, we could tell by the noises it made? Well, that was me. He starts to punch me in the head over and over again and then I stop remembering. Everything goes into black."

When Jane had finished talking, we just sat there on our towels and didn't say anything to each other. Then the lifeguard who looked a little like Timmy Morton climbed down from his chair and told us we had to leave, so we did.

We walked in silence, and I felt like we had become one person, my sister and I. As we approached the house, we could see the familiar bluish light of the TV through our living room window.

"Don't ever tell them this stuff," she said.

"I won't," I said.

Kevin was looking intently at me as I finished the story.

"She never talked about it again. Not ever. Just at the pool that day."

"I wish I had crushed that motherfucker's skull tonight, when I had the chance," he said.

"Just as well you didn't know the whole story. I'd be bailing you out of jail right now."

"Yeah, right. Well, it would have been worth it."

"Why? Nothing can change what happened." I was suddenly exhausted, not just by the night, but by every single thing that had ever happened in my life. I picked out a strand of the filling from the polyester quilt that was stuck in my hair. Instead of making me feel better, telling the story had made me feel sick. Sick of talking, sick of remembering, but most of all sick of possessing this story that had no happy ending, no big redemptive moment, no lesson learned. Just pain. It made me feel like all the spiritual shit at school I'd read about was just that: Shit.

"You're right, nothing can change what that bastard did, but having his ass kicked might remind him that no matter what the lawyers and his family can do for him, other people are not going to forget. The cops should have fucking thrown away the key when they locked him up." Kevin was riled up all over again, almost like he'd been hours ago at McNally's. I was afraid he'd keep talking and smoking for hours now, tripping out on a new testosterone surge.

I wondered if telling him had been a mistake. I really didn't know. All I wanted to do was go to sleep and I knew what I would have to do to shut him up. I began to kiss his chest, salty with sweat, but still smooth and warm. He stopped talking. I kept on, working my way slowly and deliberately down his body. Maybe it was a weird thing to do after telling what happened to my sister, but I was outside of my body, watching myself from some other place, almost like what Gail used to call astral projecting.

He was already hard; now he stiffened more. I knew it would be faster if I took him in my mouth, so I did.

9

After This

Kimmy said the police broke up the brawl at McNally's after we left, but it was no big deal, just another run of the mill bar fight. Timmy wouldn't get into any trouble. The owner, Dan Coughlin, knew that one of Timmy's uncles was a Selectman and held sway over whose liquor licenses got renewed and whose didn't.

The Mortons were a force in town. Even though they liked to claim a Mayflower ancestor way back, they'd been nobodies until Timmy's grandfather made a fortune by buying up blocks of tenements in the South End and jacking up the rents of the Italian immigrants who lived there. In the last thirty years, the Mortons had morphed their way out of being slumlords and become very successful developers in town.

Timmy's father Jerome was one of four brothers who had all been expected to enter the family business. But Jerome hadn't been cut from the same piece of cloth. At sixteen, he left home and enlisted in the Navy. After the war, he married Mary McCarthy, the drop-dead gorgeous but dirt-poor farm girl he fell in love with. Estranged from his father, he took the job he still had now, at a machine shop in Holyoke. When they bought the house on Chestnut Street, Mary was pregnant with Timmy. By the time he was a baby, she was already drinking too much.

According to my mother, Mary had married Jerome believing his father would eventually forgive him and bring him into the family business. But as time went on, she realized that it wasn't going to happen. Jerome hated his old man and liked being a working guy who didn't have to wear a suit or have business lunches with the local pols. Mary realized she would see none of the Morton money and that the good looks, which had gotten her off the family's farm, weren't going to get her further than Chestnut Street. Maybe it wasn't the worst fate, but Mary didn't take it so well.

One summer afternoon when I was still a kid, I went down an open hatchway into the Mortons' cellar, chasing a wayward soccer ball. I saw the woman I still called Mrs. Morton in action. The washing machine was on, the water already filling the tub, so she hadn't heard me. I watched as she poured Clorox into the machine then put the jug back on the shelf. Her hand reached for the tall glass bottle next to it. She unscrewed its cap and raised it to her lips. With her head serenely thrown back, her eyes shut, she looked like people did when they knelt at the altar to receive Communion. I was horrified, like I'd seen her naked.

There was no doubt Mary Morton had screwed Timmy up, but no one would know exactly how until much later. He'd been just another kid in the neighborhood when we were growing up, big for his age and with his mother's good looks. Jane and I would see him around sometimes, but mostly he'd ignore us like older boys generally tended to do.

Then there'd been the afternoon when a white Cadillac convertible with New Jersey plates drove up our street, hitting the brakes too fast before it stopped in front of the Mortons' house. I was playing hopscotch with Donna Serrano and Jane on the sidewalk. We watched as one of the back doors flew open and the large hairy arm of a man appeared, pushing Mrs. Morton, who looked as limp as a Raggedy Ann doll, out of the car and onto the curb. The door slammed shut and the car sped away.

The white blouse and gray straight skirt she had on still made her look dressed up, but her nylons were all torn up and there were scrapes on her knees. One hand gripped her purse, but it had opened and her stuff had fallen out. I saw a compact, its smooth pat of powder cracked into flesh-colored splinters, a pack of Pall Malls, her turquoise Lady Buxton wallet and a mostly empty bottle of vodka.

Timmy had been playing ball with his pals until the Caddy had screeched to a halt in front of his house and unloaded Mary Morton. "Mom!" he kept yelling as he ran over to her, one of his hands still in a catcher's mitt.

Public displays of drunkenness were not that unusual in my neighborhood but this was much worse than somebody's dad weaving unsteadily up the street. *It was his mother. Drunk and dumped like garbage out of some stranger's car.*

Timmy crouched next to her. "Get up," he pleaded. "Mom, you have to get up."

Mrs. Morton opened one eye. "Timmy?" she said weakly. When she moved her legs, you could see strips of white thigh and her garters, gripping what was left of the nylons.

Timmy's hand eased her gray skirt down to cover them up.

Timmy the boy disappeared then, at least from my memories. When I started seeing him around again, he was a teenager who liked to smoke cigarettes and hang out in front of Joe's, the variety store up on King's Highway. There was this smell that came off him, if you got too close. And getting too close was what he wanted you to do, basically.

"Want to meet me in the woods later?" he asked me once, when I ran into him on Chestnut Street. He meant the woods behind the cemetery, where he would attack my sister a few years later. But it wasn't a big deal at the time; he'd asked other girls there too and nothing seemed to happen to them.

"No, I can't go. I'll get in trouble," I said. The truth was, even if my mother hadn't made the rule about crossing King's Highway, I would never have gone with him. I was the cautious, scaredy cat one. It was my sister who would do things, not me. And Timmy would figure this out too, in time.

After the night of the fight, when I told Kevin what had happened to Jane, things were different between us. I started talking about the stuff that had happened at school, mostly the drugs and a little about John Shea. He was sympathetic but only to a certain point.

"What did you think was going to happen, sleeping with some guy from fuckin' Belmont who's always going to think he's better than you? And there's plenty of drugs around here to get screwed up on. You didn't need to go to Amherst for that. Should have just skipped the whole school thing, if you ask me."

Like my father (which was definitely freakish), Kevin didn't believe in college. He thought people should just read on their own if they really wanted to know about something. He actually checked out books from the library by famous people like Machiavelli, Socrates, Shakespeare – anybody he'd heard of who "had something going on upstairs." He'd read a slew of them until he was ready to go on to somebody else. This made him kind of lopsidedly smart – he knew a lot about some things, next to nothing about others.

It was Friday night and Kevin called me, as I was finishing up at the Athena. "Hey, college girl."

"What do you want, townie?" I asked. We were at that point where it was okay to jive each other about these things.

"A little affection, a lot of sex."

"What about a discussion on Marx?" I knew he was reading something by him that week.

"No way."

"C'mon. We could talk about how the working man will eventually triumph over his capitalistic oppressors"

"Marx was full of shit. Nothing's ever going to change. If you don't work, you don't eat. Rather watch the game on TV and drown my troubles. You coming over?"

"Sure," I said.

It wasn't that my doubts about being with Kevin had disappeared, but they'd gone in some kind of suspended animation like the Robinson family at the beginning of *Lost in Space*. Since I wasn't planning on marrying the guy, I left them alone.

We had a perfectly good night together. But later on, I dreamt of Timmy and his mother like they were that afternoon. Timmy's hand keeps smoothing Mary Morton's skirt down over her garters. I hear my mother's voice then, from that time when she finally told me everything. *She was sleeping with him. You know, doing things to him.* The knowledge floods over the dam of my childhood innocence. In the dream, I panic and try to grab Timmy's hand away from his mother's skirt. If I can save him from the darkness that lies underneath there, I can save my sister and change the story completely. But, as I struggle, Timmy's hand becomes an amputee's stump and Mary turns to a block of salt like that woman in the Old Testament.

When I woke up in a cold sweat in the dark of Kevin's bedroom, it took me a long time to remember where I was and that everything was okay. In fact, I had to say it to myself over and over again, *it's okay it's okay it's okay*, like a mantra to make myself finally settle down and go back to sleep.

10

Equinox

"You need a change." Gail was on the phone and I'd just told her about the fight, the dream, and everything else going on in my life. She had an immediate solution. "Just come up. We're throwing a party at our new house for the fall equinox next week."

"But I have this job at a coffee shop and I can't just take off…"

"Tell your boss it's a family emergency. It kind of is, you know. A gathering of your clan counts as family and you need to *connect*." At the end of the semester, Gail had moved into a group house in Leverett, a country town just outside of Amherst, with ten other people from UMass.

"Say yes. It's the right thing."

"Ok. Unless my boss freaks out, I'll come"

It was hard asking Ari for a Sunday off since it was our busiest day and he usually counted on Malvina and me to handle the crowd that came in after church. I finally asked him as he was cleaning the grill. Through the greasy steam, he gave me his sad hound dog look.

"If it is something you must absolutely do, then you do it, my girl. In life, the old must endure the young."

I told Kevin that I was going up to Amherst to see my old roommate Gail. I left it at that; I didn't think it was time for my two worlds to meet. A few days later, I was driving north up Route 91 in my mother's old green Pontiac, noticing that there were fewer smokestacks and less smog in this part of the state – probably the only good things to come out of so much industry and so many jobs leaving the area. As I rode by a closed up brick factory, its wide dark windows seemed to stare back at me, asking questions that were the same as my own. What will happen next? What am I supposed to be doing?

Still, I was glad for the grey ribbon of highway unwinding in front of me, taking me out of Springfield and back to what I thought of as a new and better world – Amherst and its surrounding towns full of hippies, natural food coops, radical lesbians, and former anti-war activists. If there was an issue, there was an activist for it somewhere in this part of the Connecticut River valley.

I took the Northampton exit and headed west, watching the strip malls give way to farms and watching my own thoughts turn into regrets. *Why couldn't I have kept it together enough so that I wasn't waitressing my life away in Springfield? Why had I left Amherst and limped home like some wounded animal?* I thought about turning around then, that maybe I was still too freaked out to show up at some party, but I didn't want to disappoint Gail.

I saw the yellow house that she'd told me to look for. With its big screened porch, the place looked like somebody's Grandma's house. I gunned the old car to get up the steep driveway. Then there was Gail, splendidly frumpy in an ancient calico dress, running out to greet me, her mane of wildly curly blond hair flying behind her.

"Oh my god, you're here, finally. Look at you! You are so beautiful!" Gail's greetings were legendary for their exuberance. "You must be getting laid a lot or else you're doing Kundalini yoga or something. You practically glow!" I didn't think I looked good; I'd probably put on ten pounds from all the shit I was eating at the coffee shop and at my parents' house. But it was true that I was getting laid, thanks to Kevin, so maybe that showed. I relaxed into Gail's generous bear hug, smelling the same mix of patchouli and slightly raunchy body odor I remembered from living with her.

"You have to see the house. It's totally amazing." She took me on a grand tour of the new place. In the living room, there were two dented-up sofas and a coffee table made from four red milk crates and a long shaky board. A poster of the Grateful Dead's big-footed trucker stepping over a rainbow clashed gloriously with the room's faded Colonial wallpaper. Indian print bedspreads, which Gail dubbed "hippie drapes," hung rather crazily around the windows.

There was a labyrinth of rooms up on the second and third floors used as bedrooms. Most of them were empty but the door to Jason and Linda's room was shut. "They're probably in there, screwing as usual. It's the house's official conjugal suite." Gail said. Indeed, I noticed someone had tacked up a sign on the door that said as much.

We sat down at the table in the kitchen, a large square room painted an egg yolk yellow with an absolutely huge water heater in one corner and a smell, sort of like rotten apples, new bread, and old ashtray mixed together. Gail lit the old stove's burner with a match and put the teakettle on. Two other burners were going full blast, cooking up large vats of things for the party.

It was like we'd seen each other the day before. We talked about my thing with Kevin and her thing with this guy from Seattle she'd met at a bluegrass festival. (He'd insisted they were soul mates from a previous life but Gail wasn't so sure.)

Gail filled my cup with yerba mate tea. "You know, John is coming."

I crossed my legs and very consciously locked them together. "That really sucks. Is that chick coming with him?

She made a face at me. "Laura, you've got to lighten up about him. And you shouldn't call Vanessa a chick. She's a woman, just like we are." Gail liked to reprimand me about that sort of thing.

"What if I'm not over it and I still hate her guts?"

"Well you should get over it, fast. That was almost a year ago. So you guys had a thing for a while and now he's with somebody else. Besides, you're sleeping with that sexy townie dude, right? So let it be, already."

Gail's Earthmotherness had spoken. I drank my tea and tried to mellow out. Even though I loved her to death, this trait of hers bugged me. If people were Tarot cards, Gail would have been the Empress. She had this way of making pronouncements from her throne that people actually listened to. The best I could be, Tarot-wise, was probably the dark haired Queen of Pentacles who always looked overworked and underpaid. I'd always suspected she'd been ordered to sit there and hold up that heavy looking pentacle against her will.

"So how's it going with Jane?" Gail opened a box of Pepperidge Farm Milano cookies and passed them to me. Even though they were full of sugar, we loved them.

"She's due in another month. Everything's totally fucked in Springfield. You know that."

"That's why I didn't want you to go back there when you were freaking out at the dorm last year. Just because they're your biological family doesn't mean you belong there. You should move up here. Another woman in the house would keep things balanced. You know, too many guys in one space isn't such a good thing."

Gail got up from the table to retrieve an aluminum canister that could have come from my mother's kitchen and removed a large baggie of pot. With her trademark lilac rolling papers, she began rolling us a joint. As she did, I felt it again, the pull of the Hippie Dream, although we never called it that.

In the dark of our dorm room, Gail and I used to lie in our beds, trying on different futures like little girls trying on dresses. First of all, we were soldiers in the sexual revolution, so sleeping with lots of guys (or women, if we decided to go that way) was a given. Later, maybe we could become radical lawyers and take on the patriarchy. Or grow organic vegetables and home birth a bunch of kids. Or become artisans and live in Spain and throw pots all day.

I had believed in the Dream, more than the Catholic Church, more than anything my parents ever taught me. Moving home, it had slipped out of my reach. But now, getting stoned and watching my friend in the thrall of full-blown hippie domesticity as she sliced carrots into big homely-looking ovals for a vegetarian stew, the dream shook loose and landed, a ripe apple at my feet. I picked it up and believed again. Maybe I could still have this other life. I could get back to it. Somehow, it could still happen.

There was a lot of noise through the kitchen's open windows. Two vans with Vermont plates were driving up the rocky driveway. A VW bug and a truck followed right behind them. The party was arriving, like an invading army. An hour later, sixty people filled the house. Gail took big vats of beans, rice, and veggies off the stove and people began to line up cafeteria-style to fill their plates. Several pans of brownies were put out, understood by everyone to contain hash. A few guys wrestled the speakers out onto the porch and the dancing started.

By eleven I had been dancing for hours in the scruffy backyard like some stoned amnesiac, feeling fine, feeling like I'd never left this scene at all. Then I saw John and the chick (she would never be Vanessa to me) making their way through the crowd. His hair was slightly shorter than it usually was and he looked great. So did the chick, who was dressed in a blue sari with silver threading, identical to the one John had given me last year after his trip to India. They brushed by me and gave me the most casual of greetings (Hey, howyadoing?) before moving along. I stopped dancing and just stood there, a grim fake smile plastered on my face. Maybe he'd brought back a carton of blue saris, I thought, for all the girls he planned on fucking over the next few years. I watched their backs disappear into the kitchen. No, I wasn't over it. Like I usually did when faced with feelings, I headed for the bathroom, choosing the one on the third floor because it was farthest away.

I opened the door and caught Tommy Boy just as he was zipping up. Tommy Boy was one of the low-level drug dealers I knew from the dorm who kept us awash in pot and other substances. He was a smallish compact guy with dark hair cut into a shag who wore granny glasses with blue lenses in them. Like most drug dealers, he was ultra-friendly but nobody knew that much about him, except that he wasn't a student, was older than any of us, and was never called anything but Tommy Boy.

Highly amused by the bathroom intrusion, Tommy Boy laughed and asked if he could watch while I peed, just to make it even. I said no, that I was too uptight for that sort of thing. Very politely, he stationed himself on the better side of the bathroom door and waited until I was done. We went back downstairs together and I was actually relieved he was with me, in case I ran into John and the chick again. The party was reaching its climax. The first floor was jammed; people were hanging out on the steps, even infiltrating the bedrooms on the second floor. Tommy Boy's eyes flicked back and forth, like he was counting bills or pounds of product.

"Shit. Look at all these fucking people. Did somebody tell the entire state about this party? Let's go back upstairs and get high." Without knowing why, I went with him. We came to the room I'd seen earlier with the sign next to it that actually read The Jason Parker – Linda LaPierre Conjugal Chamber. We entered the dark empty room, its space dominated by a big king-sized bed. We sat, matrimonial style, against its massive Art Deco headboard. I found a candle next to the bed and lit it. Tommy Boy extracted a small brass pipe, exactly like the one I had, from the front pocket of his jeans jacket.

"Where'd you get that?" I asked.

"Phases," he said, naming a popular Amherst head shop. All the brass pipes in the Northeast corridor probably came from there, but this shared bit of trivia was comforting. Weirdly, I thought about the way my mother and her friends in the neighborhood would have the same kind of conversations about what grocery stores they went to, or what cake mixes they used, their way of saying, "Yeah, we're the same kind of people." We smoked his hash, which, no surprise, was very strong and very good, and started idly gossiping about some of the people at the party.

I suppose I knew when we went into the room. I might have even known when I ran into him in the bathroom. I certainly knew when we got high together. We were already in bed, after all. We kissed and groped a bit. Then he took off my jeans and sort of slid into me, like it was no big deal, just a little something extra for the evening. At one point, I looked up and realized he still had his blue glasses on. They still stood perfectly in place, as he moved, back and forth, inside me. I couldn't see his eyes and the way the glasses had gone opaque in the semi-dark made his face seem unreal, like a Halloween mask. This struck me as weird, even more than the fact that I was having sex with him. I wanted him to stop and at least take off his glasses but I was too stoned to say anything. He finished then lay heavily on top of me. After a while, I realized he was asleep. Slowly, I rolled him off me so he wouldn't wake up. I got out of the bed. When I stood up and felt his wetness between my legs, I knew the sex had been a big mistake.

I put my clothes on and crept down the hall to the bathroom. Using a facecloth I found in the sink, I tried to wash (as if I could wash away what I had just done, which of course was ridiculous). I thought of Kevin but I wouldn't let myself go there. I knew why I'd fucked Tommy Boy. The reason was walking around downstairs with a woman in a blue sari.

More than anything, I wanted to find Gail so she could tell me it was okay that I had fucked up like this. I felt totally sober as I waded through the rowdy party crowd. Couples, mostly hetero but some not, sprouted up here and there on the couches and on the floor, entwined like romantic crabgrass. Ritchie and Sidney, two guys who lived in the house, were starting a bonfire in the backyard but Gail was nowhere to be found. Just as I was beginning to wonder if she too had gone off with somebody, I saw her, totally focused in on a red haired woman wearing an embroidered white caftan who looked really pregnant. They had cordoned themselves off in a corner of the living room. The woman was sobbing and I saw Gail's lips moving, as she talked non-stop, in full-blown counselor mode. When she put her arm around the woman's waist, I was amazed at how pissed off this gesture made me. Did she have to help every stray woman in her path? What was I supposed to do, stand in line?

Pissed off with everything, I turned around and walked through the kitchen, going through the screened porch to get outside. There were three people sitting on the steps doing hits of amyl nitrate poppers. They laughed uproariously, virtual hyenas, as I passed.

The bonfire out back seemed to be the only place to go. At least I could just stand there and watch the fire and not have to talk to anybody. As the flames grew, someone put on a David Bowie album. The words to "Changes" rang out of the huge speakers. People began to sway, all loosey goosey, and form a circle around the fire. I scanned the faces in the crowd; some I knew, but many I didn't. Who were all these people? Bowie's voice told us to turn and face the strange, and now the lyric seemed to have been written for me. Tommy Boy's Halloween mask of a face flashed before me, but it already seemed like a memory from a different night, a different life. Then, across the circle, I saw John and the chick with a blanket wrapped around them, Woodstock-style. The two of them looked like countercultural poster children, so fucking smug in their hip-ness they made me sick.

I remembered again, how the hippie dream had failed me. I knew it should never have risen or fallen on what some guy did to me; it should have been about the tribe and Higher Consciousness and making the world a better place. *John.* Who the fuck was he anyway? Just some spoiled brat from Belmont. Still, whatever remained of the dream seemed to leave me then. What was I doing here? All of it – the party, the people, the house itself – seemed so flimsy, it could have been made out of cardboard. And it was easy to imagine the flames from the bonfire just leaping up and devouring it all. Right now, I wouldn't care if they did.

I found the Pontiac and drove back to Springfield.

II

Sunday

I sat on the edge of the bed. My stomach rocked uncertainly and my head felt too big for its skull. I reached for my jeans, which sat in a pile next to the bed, the crotch stained and turned inside out. Remembering what I'd done, I felt like a slut. I pulled them on. The gauze shirt I'd worn failed the sniff test, so I stole a tee shirt from Jane's room and walked downstairs.

It was Sunday morning. My mother, the sole member of our family who still went to church, was at eleven fifteen Mass up the street at St. Thomas. Lost to the church for decades now, my father sat alone in the living room behind his Sunday paper. The TV was on, but he wasn't watching it.

"Morning, Dad," I said.

What might have been a low hello came from behind the newspaper. Since I was hung over this morning myself, I felt a vague sympathy for my father who was probably in the same condition. I walked on, into the kitchen.

"Hey. You're up. And you got my tee shirt on. You want coffee?" Jane, enormous in a candy-pink bathrobe that no longer hid her big belly, was standing in the kitchen holding the glass coffeepot under the faucet. She had another TV on, this one on the kitchen counter. Lately, small televisions had begun appearing in every room of the house, giving my parents and Jane plenty of opportunities to turn them on and not watch them.

"Yeah. A whole pot."

"Better pace yourself, Queen Caffeine. And I want that tee shirt back, by the way." Jane turned away from me and scooped coffee into the top of the coffee maker.

"So how'd it go last night?"

"Shitty. Real shitty. I shouldn't have gone."

"You saw that guy."

"Yeah, with the chick he dumped me for."

"Well, fuck'em both. That's what I say. Except for that Gail-girl, those people up there all seem like major assholes. I don't know why you give a shit about them."

Jane sounded just like Kevin – not the person I wanted to think about this morning. I sat down and didn't say anything, but Jane wasn't ready to let it go.

"I just don't get you sometimes," she said. "I mean, why go up there when you got a hot guy down here who's crazy about you?"

Leave it to my sister to put a knife in the wound.

A rerun of a game show was on TV. A skinny woman dressed like a Christmas package was trying to guess the price of a washer dryer combination. When she dramatically over-bid, the crowd moaned with a Roman Coliseum's contempt for her naïveté.

"Look. I didn't go to that party to get laid," I said. "You might not think so, but I need to see those people. They're part of my life."

Then, like a bad dream, the night before came back to me. The scenes were worthy of a Hieronymus Bosch painting. There was me screwing Tommy Boy, blue granny glasses and all; those guys doing poppers laughing like hyenas; hordes of people, their faces mask-like and strange, as David Bowie sang about cc-changes and the strange.

I reached over and shut the TV off with a sharp click, satisfied with the way it stopped the announcer dead in his tracks, with his mouth open. The coffee pot gurgled loudly as if applauding my decision.

"Why'd you do that?"

"Because it's a stupid show. Why do we have to have the TV on all the time anyway?"

Jane scrutinized me from across the table, fluffy pink arms folded over her amble chest. "OK. What happened last night that's got you so bitched out?

"If you really want to know, I screwed some drug dealer I sort of knew at the party and now I feel like crap about it."

She shrugged her shoulders the same way she used to in grade school, looking at her own bad report cards. "Course you went for it with the drug dealer guy. There was that asshole with his new babe hanging around." With some effort, she got out of her chair to pour us coffee. "Look Laura, I know how you are. Don't get all Catholic about this. Getting some nookie at a party like that – just forget about it. That's all there is to do. If you tell Kevin, he'll freak out."

"Well, I shouldn't have done it."

"Yeah, probably. But you'll make it worse by telling him."

I drank my coffee and started to feel better. Sometimes my sister, as crazy as she was, knew what the hell she was talking about.

So I didn't tell him. Summer was ending and I took more shifts at the Athena, feeling like I should try and save some money for whatever it was that I would do next. Because of the Watergate hearings that summer, Ari had installed a TV at the coffee shop. (Wherever I went now, there was another TV. It drove me crazy.) One evening when it was slow, we were hanging around watching the news when something about Nixon firing the special prosecutor, Archibald Cox, came on.

Ari scrutinized the President who appeared in the report, angrily defending what he was doing. He shook his head sadly. "When a man is afraid, he is like a little child. That is what is wrong with this man, this American president Nixon."

"Oh come on, Ari. Nixon's just a piece of shit." I was squatting down under the counter, restocking all our paper products. I didn't know as much about Watergate as Ari, but I knew everything there was to know about Nixon.

"You with your mouth. You do not understand. Nixon, he go to China, he a big man. Everybody love him. Now he go all crazy when they don't. These politics. I feel sorry for him. He need a big daddy, somebody to tell him what to do now." Ari turned the volume down when a commercial started but I got the feeling Ari would volunteer for the job if he could.

Even though I didn't give a flying fuck about Nixon, there was something about Ari's desire to be a big daddy that really got to me. What would it be like, to have a father or anybody who was older, who could really watch out for me? Ever since I was sixteen, I'd made all my own decisions about college, about sex, about anything that mattered, but lately I'd begun to wonder. How much did I really know, anyway?

12

November

"Laura, you have to wake up. I'm having the baby." It was after midnight, two whole weeks before Jane's due date. I turned on the lamp. Jane was crouching next to my bed, with a giant wet spot down the front of her nightgown. Her water had broken. At least I remembered that much from the birthing class.

"Did you call Dr. Anderson yet?"

"No"

"Did you wake Mom up?"

"No. Can you get me something to put on? I'm all wet."

It seemed like the last thing in the world to worry about but I wasn't going to argue with her. "All right. Wait a minute." I went to her room and found one of her favorite mumus. As Jane pulled the wet nightgown off, the swell of a contraction crested across her naked belly, making me think of the waves at Misquamicut beach when we were kids.

"How far apart are your contractions?"

"I don't know. I just woke up with them. What's the difference? It's happening!"

"You're supposed to time them, like Dr. Anderson said." Refusing to follow rules was one of my sister's best or worst traits, depending on how you looked at it. But rules about births were suddenly very good in my book. Certain things were supposed to happen at certain times. If the rules were followed, then everything would be okay. And that's what I wanted, more than anything, for things to be okay.

"Let me know when the next one starts. I'm going to time it." The Mickey Mouse watch I liked to wear was lying on the nightstand where I'd taken it off hours before. Now Mickey would need to move those skinny black arms of his and take us to where we needed to go – that moment when this baby was safely born. It would happen. If we were lucky. If we followed the rules.

It was 2:08 when the next contraction started. "Oh my god." Jane gasped for air. Her eyes opened so wide I thought they might pop out of their sockets. "It's going to kill me, Laura. Make it stop." I had never seen my sister terrified before. Afraid, yes, but not like this. It struck me then. *This is how she must have looked when Timmy attacked her*. He had seen this fear on my sister's face, and it hadn't stopped him. A wave of murderous intent swelled in me.

"You're not going to die. Just breathe." I was saying it to her and to myself, actually. "It's what's supposed to happen." I looked at my watch. According to Mickey's arms, it was 2:14 so this contraction came only six minutes after the last one. It occurred to me then that things were happening fast, maybe too fast for somebody just starting labor. "Remember what they said at that birthing class? You have to breathe through them."

We had gone to exactly one Lamaze natural childbirth class together, then Jane had decided to blow them off. It was dawning on me, how potentially fucked we were for not going to all of them so we actually knew what to do. I should have made Jane go, I thought. Shoulda woulda coulda. Panic, like a red rubber ball, began to bounce uncontrollably inside of me.

"It's coming again!" she said.

I grabbed Jane's arm hard. "Jane, keep breathing. Don't freak out."

"I AM freaking out. This baby is going to kill me."

"No it won't. I won't let it," I said to my sister.

As soon as the contraction ended, I called Dr. Anderson, the Swedish doctor who delivered all the hippie girls' babies in the area, because she wouldn't let the hospital drug you up, like they had in our mother's generation.

"Yes?" Dr. Anderson answered the phone on the first ring and sounded totally composed and alert, like it was the middle of the day. Shaky as a schoolgirl, I answered all her questions. "Please bring your sister to the hospital immediately. Her labor is proceeding very swiftly. I will be there, forthwith," she said, in her strange slightly British-accented English. I turned back to my sister.

"Jane, we've got to get to the hospital. I need to tell Mom. I'll be right back."

She was sitting on the edge of my bed, hunched over like a wounded bear. "Okay. But hurry."

I raced down the steps. When I was a kid, I used to just burst into my parents' room when I was sick or afraid, a small bullet of human need. But I wasn't a child anymore. I made myself knock, my knuckles white against the paneled mahogany of their door. I could picture my parents sleeping in their four-poster Colonial bed. I suddenly wondered, totally out of whack with the present moment, if they still had sex, these people who happened to be my parents. Being middle-aged seemed as distant and as impenetrable as death to me. In your late forties, did you still want to? Who knew?

I heard my mother's voice and opened the door. She raised a head full of pink curlers off the pillow and turned on the lamp on the nightstand. "What's wrong? Is it Jane?"

"Yeah. She's in labor."

"Okay, I'm getting up. I don't want to wake your father up." Her voice had the same slightly exasperated edge to it I remembered from waking her up as a child and it calmed me down a little. My mother appeared a few moments later in her old striped bathrobe and white scuffs. She closed the bedroom door. "How's she doing?"

"Her contractions are six minutes apart and her water broke. She's real scared, Mom."

"Well, she's never had a baby before. What do you expect? Are you going to the hospital?

"Yeah. Right now.

"Okay. Let me help you get her downstairs."

We got stuck on the steps while she had another contraction, and she threw up once, but we got Jane into the car. It was a November night with only a little sliver of a moon out. The wind blew cold, churning up the fallen leaves in the driveway. The curlers still in her hair, my mother leaned into the window of the Pontiac. "Are you sure you don't want me to come?"

The plan had always been for me to go with Jane to the hospital. Jane hadn't wanted my mother there. "It's my thing, not hers," was the way she put it. I had fantasized about being a kind of midwife at the birth, helping to usher in this new being, but I was more scared than I thought I'd be. *Yes, I wanted my mother to come.* But it was Jane's call. I repeated my mother's question to her, as if I was some translator at the UN. "Jane, do you what Mom to come?"

Wrapped up in a green quilt, her face bleached from pain, Jane shook her head no. The firmness of that answer surprised me.

"I'll call you from the hospital as soon as I can," I said.

Dr. Anderson examined Jane with rubber-gloved Swedish efficiency and made her pronouncement. It was already too late for an epidural, too late for anything but to get the baby delivered. Since she was fully dilated, they wheeled my sister straight into the delivery room next door. In a flash, they had Jane's legs up in stirrups. The nurses positioned a mirror down there, so Jane could see herself deliver, but she hardly seemed interested.

"Laura…" Jane started to say, until a contraction ripped through her body. My sister tightened her iron grip on my arm and let out a long sharp scream. We were at Misquamicut again and it was high tide. A wave was cresting way over our heads and we couldn't get away. We should never have gone so far from shore, I knew this now. The wave was going to take us under completely. "You're the oldest." I heard my mother's voice in my head. "You're supposed to know better."

Dr. Anderson was saying something to me. "The baby is in distress. We must do a C section immediately."

"Jane doesn't want a C. She can't have a C!"

"There is no choice." Dr Anderson's face was granite. "She will lose the baby. You understand? I need you to help us and tell your sister what we must do." She pointed to the double doors at the end of the room. "You will go behind those doors when we give her the general anesthesia."

"What do you mean? I have to stay here!"

"You tell your sister now. Then you must go. It is the law."

The room was cold and the lights made everybody look horrible. "Jane, listen to me." I bent down and put my cold hands on her face. Jane's eyes were slits. She didn't really look human, more like an animal in extreme distress, but I knew she could hear me. "They have to take the baby now. It can't wait to be born. They going to do a C and I have to stand out in the hall while they do it, but I swear to you, it will be okay." I kissed the middle of her forehead. "They're going to give you something now."

With both of my hands pressed against the heavy glass pane of the door, I watched Dr. Anderson's back and the backs of a number of nurses as the huddled around the crack they must have made in my sister. Just when I thought that it was taking too long and that something must be wrong, Dr. Anderson turned and stepped away from the table, allowing me to see. A nurse held a baby, all wrapped in white, with a triangle of a pink face. It seemed to be crying, although I couldn't hear through the doors. A moment later Dr. Anderson came out of the room and removed her mask. Her face broke like the sun after clouds.

"It's a girl," she said, merrily. "Another girl for the two of you."

I called my mother and told her. As my sister slept, I went back to the nursery. After putting on a gown and mask, they let me stand by the bassinette. I couldn't seem to get enough of looking at this new person, who occasionally stirred and mewed like a kitten. The tiny arms and legs were just bumps under the blanket, but the itty-bitty face looked familiar, like pictures of Jane and me when we were born.

How Jane had made this person was really impossible to understand. The prayer I'd said every night of my childhood put itself on my lips. Hail Mary, full of grace. The Lord is with thee. Blessed is the fruit of *thy* womb, my sister. For all she had endured, this baby would have to be blessed in this life. It couldn't be any other way.

13

Damage

Jane came home from the hospital with a baby who still needed a name, along with an ugly incision from the Caesarian. Because they did it fast, it was no bikini cut. The thing ran straight up and down her belly and was at least nine inches long. Dr. Anderson's tight black stitches had sewn the skin together, but you could still see the dried blood deep inside. I cleaned the wound every night, after Jane put the baby down. An expert I was not, but Dr. Anderson had told me exactly what to do.

"Well if it ain't Nancy Nurse," Jane said. I neatly laid out all the necessary stuff on a dinky red play table that had survived our childhood, ready to do my chore. Back then, I'd liked playing nurse; now I wasn't so sure.

"Hey, I'm the one with the stuff that stings, so you better be nice to me. Lie down." Jane obeyed, lying down on the bed with just her nursing bra and nylon panties on. With a neatly folded pad of gauze wet with hydrogen peroxide, I gently dabbed at my sister's incision and the two tracks of skin that bordered the deep and sudden cut. The skin there was inflamed, a shade of pink that reminded me of rose buds and something else.

After the attack, there had been a piece of skin on the left side of Jane's forehead that was the same shade of pink. Even though her bangs covered most of it, this strange patch of skin was the first thing I noticed after she'd come home from the hospital. It made her look like she'd been patched together with Play Dough. Later, I would find out that a plastic surgeon had taken skin from her thigh and grafted it up there. The wound, that place where Timmy had attempted to bash her head in, had been too big to close any other way.

On that first Sunday after Jane came home, my mother invited company over. It was a month after the attack. We were still in that time period when gratitude that Jane had survived blotted out everything else. But it would be the last time my mother had people over to the house like that and the beginning of the time when the company stopped coming, when we would all realize that nothing was ever going to be quite the same.

That afternoon, Jane and I sat in the clothes we'd worn to church as family members and neighbors trooped in to welcome Jane home. My mother had made several Bundt cakes for the occasion and she had pulled out the good silverware we rarely used, a wedding gift from some wealthy Irish relatives. Our company sat stiffly on the edges of the kitchen and dining room chairs, coffee cups and cake plates dangerously balanced in their laps, sneaking glances over at Jane. They talked about anything, except what had happened to my sister. Of course they wanted to get a good look at her (how could they not?) but they wouldn't have been caught dead staring at her.

My little sister looked different. She'd lost a lot of weight. At some point, the nurses had cut her long shiny brown hair. Even though they left her bangs alone, to cover up the new weird skin on her forehead, they'd shaved a strip of scalp to stitch up a wound in the back of her head. My mother had seemed oblivious to Jane's appearance earlier, but that changed when the company came.

"Look at this hair." As she talked to my Aunt Doreen, she reached over and nervously fingered Jane's head like she was looking for nits. "It looks like hell. I've got to take her over to Frank and Tito's tomorrow and have them fix it." She must have said this eight or nine times to various people, like someone who keeps repeating the details of an accident hoping that it will finally make some sense.

Jane kept pushing my mother's hand away from her head. She wouldn't talk to anybody, not even to me. Instead, she sat there and ate her way through most of one of the Bundt cakes and some of the other pastries people had brought. Years later, Jane would tell me, "That day when the company came over. When Mom kept yakking about my hair. I knew what was going on. Those people couldn't help it, but I knew they were all thinking the same thing: *I wonder what he did to her?*

What he did to her. According to the court records, Timmy was convicted of forcible rape on a minor under the age of twelve, oral and anal sodomy, and aggravated assault and battery. For these crimes, he would be incarcerated for two years in a juvenile detention facility in Bridgewater. It would have been much more if the DA hadn't been a family friend of the Mortons' and agreed to drop the attempted manslaughter charges.

During the court proceeding, Timmy insisted that Jane had followed him into the cemetery that day because she wanted him to be her boyfriend. That she'd gotten mad at him after they'd had consensual sex. That she'd started hitting him and that all he had really done was defend himself. It must have been freakish for my parents to sit there and hear this story but they did.

In the interests of protecting me, I was told very little about what had happened. But listening by my bedroom door late at night, I heard my parents talking about it. In fact, they couldn't shut up about it. I had just turned eleven. I don't know what scared me more – what Timmy had actually done to my sister or how powerless and crazed my parents sounded.

All I wanted was for everything to be okay again. By then I'd learned to stop counting on God for that. If He was so great, why had this happened to Jane at all? At least the shows on TV, where all wrongs got resolved by the end of the hour, gave me some hope. What my family needed was someone like one of those guys on Dragnet. Or maybe Raymond Burr, the guy who played Perry Mason, which was my mother's favorite show. It seemed like he knew how to take care of things. I actually tried to write a letter to Raymond Burr once, explaining what had happened to Jane. I knew he was an actor, but I still thought he might be able to help us. When my mother found me writing the letter at the kitchen table one Saturday morning, she snatched it away from me and threw it in the trash.

"Don't be telling people our personal business," she said.

But the thing was, everyone knew our personal business. It had been in the papers and on the news. They didn't go into all the details or use Jane or Timmy's names, but everybody in town knew who and what they were talking about.

The day after people came over to the house, I went with Jane and my mother to Frank and Tito's, a beauty parlor near our house that was run by a guy named Giovanni, who, as they say used to say, was as queer as a three dollar bill. The place was done up in a poorman's Liberace décor, with black wrought iron furniture, purple velvet drapes, and a statue of a little boy leaking water out of his tiny penis, right in the front where you came in.

Donna, the brunette receptionist, who had one of those big bouffant hairdos Italian women wore back then, told us to sit down on one of the wrought iron love seats to wait. Then I saw *her*. Mrs. Morton was on the other side of the large plate glass window, staring at us.

"Mom!" I yelled, freaked to see her standing there.

My mother looked out the window, saw Mary Morton and violently turned her head away. It must have been that movement, my mother's head jerking away from her, which got Mrs. Morton's attention. She lurched through the door and stood in front of us, smelling like Tabu perfume, hard liquor, and Dentyne gum. I thought of that time I'd seen her in the basement, the way she had lifted the bottle to her lips, and the time she got dumped from the car on Chestnut Street as her son crouched next to her.

"I want to see your daughter and make sure she's all right," she was saying. Before any of us could move, she bent down and put her face close to Jane and me. At this range, her breath stank of whiskey, overpowering the Dentyne gum she was chewing. Her red lipstick had smeared, running outside the lines of her lips, which I watched in horrible fascination as she continued to talk. "You know he didn't mean to do it. He's a good boy…"

Like an iron bar in an amusement park ride, my mother's arm suddenly came down in front of us, pushing us back into the wrought iron loveseat and away from Mary Morton. My mother started yelling, like a rubber band had snapped inside her. "If you try and touch my daughters, I swear I'll kill you."

Donna the receptionist and the ladies having their hair done all froze. The only sound in the shop was the white noise of the hair dryers. Then from somewhere in the back, Giovanni appeared and strode up to the front, with his Guinea charm in high gear and a smile as wide as a diva's.

"Mrs. Morton, why don't you go home now? Your family, they need to see you." Mrs. Morton had started to whimper and was trying to blow her nose on an old tissue she'd taken from her purse that already had lipstick and snot on it. "You people don't understand. He's a good boy," she repeated again for Giovanni's sake.

"Yes, it's time to go. *Ciao* for now. You come back some other time and I cut your hair for you." In a move worthy of Fred Astaire, Giovanni took her by the elbow and steered her out the door. Jane hadn't moved a muscle since Mrs. Morton entered the shop and she didn't when Giovanni came back in and addressed my mother.

"Now Mrs. DiStefano, you need to relax. I make you a nice espresso, okay?" Giovanni went back to make the coffee and the beauty parlor's regular sounds resumed.

But my mother was quietly sobbing, reaching over to Jane who sat between us. Her fingers moved frantically, trying to fix the bangs so the funny pink skin wouldn't show. *My baby,* she kept saying. Jane let her do this, but the look on my sister's face silently pleaded for my help. She was being drawn into some black hole fueled by my mother's pity and she wanted out.

Giovanni came back with a small white cup of espresso and put it down on the glass table next to the loveseat. "You drink, Mrs. DiStefano. You have a little espresso. You so upset. You drink this."

I knew then that it was up to me to fix things, to try and undo that bad thing that had happened. Gently, I pushed my mother's hand away from Jane's face. "Mom, drink your coffee. Giovanni's going to cut Jane's hair now. Everything's going to be all right. She'll look real nice. Right, Giovanni?"

I finished cleaning Jane's incision, reaching again for the roll of gauze and the small scissors on the red play table. When I used to play nurse as a kid (girls didn't play doctor back then), it had been my operating table. My dolls would have to submit to operations done with my mother's tweezers and a butter knife stolen from the kitchen. Afterwards, I enthusiastically bandaged them up with gauze and adhesive tape, or ordinary Band-Aids if that's all we had. But Jane used to get bored with this game so she'd drag the neighborhood cats in for operations to liven things up. Of course, it ruined the whole thing. They wouldn't stay still and the bandages would never stick to their fur. We got into some big fights about those cats. Playing hospital always brought out this side of me that loved order and efficiency and the side of Jane that loved to disrupt it.

But these days, Jane was a good patient and I was a good Nancy Nurse. She didn't flinch or complain; she let me do what had to be done. We heard the baby fuss in Jane's room but she miraculously fell back to sleep.

"Maybe she'll sleep a few more hours," I said.

"Maybe hell will freeze over. That kid likes to eat. My boobs are ready to explode."

"Stay still. I'm almost done." I moved my fingers lightly over the incision again as I put the new dressing on.

Like that other wound, the uneven pink skin reminded me. There was a borderland between what could not be changed and what remained. It was something I knew my sister understood better than I ever would.

14

Family Matters

Things were better for a while. My sister finally named her child Tabitha, after the baby in that TV show, *Bewitched*, and like magic, we all fell in love with her, even my father. Now there was no more talk about Jane or me leaving. Even my mother stayed home more, willing to let Peg Brenner fend for herself in the real estate jungle.

In the beginning, I was worried about how my sister would react to being a mother. But as I watched Jane nursing Tabitha, the baby's tiny hand curled around my sister's finger, it seemed that the baby was taking care of something in my sister that had needed taking care of for a very long time.

A kind of equilibrium began to settle in me, as if I was rooted to things again. Life was simple. I worked at the coffee shop with Ari. I saw Kevin. I hung out with Jane and the baby. I did these things and they made me happy. Whole days would go by and I'd forget how I'd fucked up school and how I was supposed to be figuring out what to do with my life. I had to admit it – the baby totally changed my sister's life but her arrival had steadied all of us in some weird way. We had someone new to think about and that was a change for the better.

About two months after Tabitha was born, I got home from the coffee shop and there was a letter for me from the UMass Scholarship office. It said that even though I was still on academic probation, I could return to school and regain my scholarship if I got counseling and kept my grades at an acceptable level. Somehow, the school was giving me this special one-time dispensation. I would be forgiven, it seemed, if I promised never to screw up again.

I read the letter, then put it right in the middle of the bed, not quite sure of what to think. I got ready to go to Kevin's. The plan, as much as I had one, was to stay in Springfield until I could figure out some way to get back to Amherst. But I wasn't so sure anymore. Two things were true, really. I wanted to go back there and I was afraid of going back there.

At Kevin's house, the get-out of jail free card from UMass was on my mind while we watched the football game. We were eating our way through an entire bag of potato chips as the Patriots played badly against the dreaded Dallas Cowboys.

"They seem to have this thing, where they feel like they have to lose," Kevin said to me at one point, exasperated when the kicker missed a field goal.

"You think?" What I was actually thinking about was the letter, playing out what would happen if I were to take UMass up on its offer. I looked over at Kevin. Amherst might be a short trip up Route 91, but it wasn't just about the miles. If I were to go back, it'd be over between us. Kevin would never leave Springfield.

As the first quarter ended, we heard someone coming up the steps in the hall. It turned out to be Andrew, Kevin's dad, who I'd met only once before, although Kevin had told me plenty about him. Andrew worked for the railroad and, like all railroad guys, he drank.

According to Kevin, Andrew had never adjusted to family life. He was almost forty when he married Kevin's mom Eileen. She'd been barely seventeen, pregnant with Kevin, and totally naïve about what she was getting herself into.

Andrew would drop out of sight for weeks at a time, often staying on in the various cities the railroad sent him to without letting her or anybody else know where he was. Sometimes he just stayed in town and became a bachelor again, sleeping in a cot at the yard and eating all his meals in the same dive tavern. True to his character, Andrew had been missing in action for about a week when he showed up at Kevin's door that evening.

"Dad, where you been? Have you gone home yet?" Kevin asked.

"Nope, not yet." Andrew sat down and lit a Lucky Strike, placing it between two fingers that looked like they'd been stained with varnish instead of tobacco. If someone put Kevin in a time machine, this is how he'd look, I thought. The copper hair was iron gray; the long face had wrinkles that ran like rivers around the sides of his mouth. "Been in New York City, in the Big Apple, baby. Had myself quite the time."

"Well, you look like hell. Didn't you sleep?"

"Sleepin's for dead people."

"You should let Ma know you're back"

"I will, by and by. Wanted to watch the game so I stopped by. No law against seeing the game at my son's place, right?"

"Yeah, but she worries. You know that."

"Well, I'll be getting home soon enough. Be makin' your mother a lucky woman tonight." He laughed a bawdy hee-haw kind of laugh, letting us know how hilarious he found this idea. Kevin shot him a look, then got up and made a call from the kitchen phone.

"Yeah, he's here. Just thought you should know." There was a long pause. "You wanna talk to him?" Another silence. "All right. I don't care. I love you too, Ma. Bye."

Andrew seemed to ignore the call. When Kevin came back and sat down, the three of us settled in to watch the game. But I couldn't help noticing how Andrew's hand shook a little as he scooped up the last of the potato chips. After a while, he got up and went into the kitchen.

We could hear him in there – the dull squeak of the cabinet door above the refrigerator, the clink of bottles making purposeful contact with each other. I knew Kevin kept liquor up there and apparently so did Andrew. He returned with a big plastic cup of something, smiling a little shyly at us, before settling back into the chair. He made several more trips to the kitchen, cup in hand, and by half time, as a line of blond women in cowboy hats and sequins kicked up their heels, Andrew was passed out in his chair, snoring loudly, his mouth hanging rather grotesquely open.

When I got a whiff of something I thought was a fart, I crinkled my nose. "Kevin, it smells like a sewer in here. Is he farting? It's totally gross."

"It's him, but it's not a fart. The way he's been hitting it, he's shit his pants. He does that when he's on a good bender." Kevin looked over at him. "That's my dad. A step away from the gutter in the good times, actually sitting in it, the rest of the time. Sorry. If I knew he was going to show up like this, I would have told you to stay away."

"It's okay." I took a hunk of his shiny copper hair, placed it behind his ear and kissed the side of his face. "What your dad does isn't your fault."

"I know," he said, unconvinced. He laid his head in my lap and I stroked his hair. For a few minutes, we stayed like that, then his face sort of crumbled and he made the kind of choked anguished sounds guys make, who never learned how to cry as little boys. "I never wanted you to see him like this."

"It's okay."

"I should be used to the way he is. Don't know why I'm letting it get to me now."

"You never get used to some things."

Andrew continued to snore and stink up the room. After a while, Kevin sat back up and lit a cigarette. We watched the game and didn't talk. It started snowing in Boston. After a while, we realized it was snowing in Springfield too, the first real snow of the season.

"It's really coming down. I better wake the bastard up so he can walk home," Kevin said. After a number of attempts, he succeeded in rousing Andrew and getting him out of the chair. Holding onto the railing for dear life, he made his way down the steps. Out on the porch, we set him in the right direction. The house Kevin's family was renting was only a few blocks away. Still we watched him, making sure that's where he was headed, until he became a dark spot moving up the whitening street.

Although it didn't look like he'd gotten the chair dirty, we got out some Lysol and wiped it down, just to be sure, actually cracking a few jokes while we did this. We hardly noticed when the Patriots lost the game.

It didn't seem like a big deal to me, that time with Andrew. But something was changing in me. I was beginning to realize that Kevin and I were alike in this very particular way. Both of us hated the people we loved and we suffered for it. And when you encounter people with pain similar to your own, you have a choice. You can jump back after touching that hot stove of sameness or you can jump into the fire, allowing it to forge a true bond.

When I got home the next morning, Jane was dressing Tabitha in her little pink snowsuit with rabbit ears on the hood. A foot of snow covered the roads, but Jane wanted to go out.

"Laura, come out with us. It's her first snow," she said. So I went with them and we walked up past St. Thomas, almost all the way to Frank 'n Titos, marveling at the winter wonderland around us gleaming in the bright winter sun.

When we finally returned, Sal and Margaret were both sitting in the living room and there was something about the way they smiled as they watched Tabitha, rosy from the outdoors and squealing with delight; that made me want to cry. I hadn't seen my parents happy like that for a long time.

The letter from UMass was still sitting on the bed where I'd left it. I put it back in its envelope and carefully tucked it behind a jewelry box I'd gotten on a family vacation to Lake George a long time ago. It stayed there for a few weeks. Then, right before Christmas, I threw the letter out.

15

Sufi Dancing

Gail was an indomitable force. Even though we hadn't been in touch for months, she wasn't going to let me settle into life in Springfield without a fight.

"My god, it's a new year and you're still there. When are you going to get out of that place? You need better energy around you." She had called just to give me a talking to. I quickly decided that I wouldn't tell her I'd turned down the offer from UMass to reinstate my scholarship. It was hard enough explaining it to myself, never mind Gail.

"Look, give me a break. I got a boyfriend here and my sister just had a baby, so there's a lot going on right now. Did I tell you she actually named her Tabitha? You would not believe how cute she is. And this kid's an old soul, believe me…"

"Yeah, well. Good for your sister. But it's you I'm worried about…"

"Don't worry about me. You're starting to be a pain in the ass about this. I'm okay."

"Tell you what. I'll stop bugging you but only if you come up for the Sufi dancing this weekend."

"Come up for the what?"

"The Sufi Dancing. You've heard of Sufis, right? They're sort of like hippie Muslims. They have these dances up in Brattleboro. It's a group meditation thing. The energy is really great. You have to come."

I thought about it. I really did want to connect with Gail even though the Sufi thing sounded pretty out there. But then so was Gail sometimes; she was like a kid at the hippie carnival, willing to try anything new that came along. I figured I'd go. What harm could it a little dancing do?

The Sufi dancing would be held on a Sunday night. It was the end of January, the depth of the New England winter and bitterly cold. Very reluctantly, I got into the Pontiac and made the drive to Brattleboro, Vermont, an hour north of Springfield. It took a while to find the old Grange Hall where it was being held. But it was worth the trouble just to see my friend standing there, like a blond Amazon, in the parking lot.

I always forgot how striking Gail could be. She was over six feet tall, with a chaotic mass of blond curls that snaked down her back. Underneath an ancient man's coat, she'd dressed for the dance, wearing a threadbare red velvet skirt with loads of beads and a string of bells wrapped around her waist, making her look a little like a belly dancer on acid. She had a few scraggly-looking guys in tow who didn't look particularly happy to be there. Knowing Gail, she'd corralled them into coming.

"Thank god you're here! It's late. They're already starting to line up. We'll talk later, okay?"

She gave me a quick but fierce hug, took me by the hand and pulled me into the hall, which had same floor wax smell I remembered from my old elementary school. There were candles all over the place and some banners with symbols on them tacked to the wall. A couple of guys in white dashiki shirts strummed guitars and a few more were playing weird percussion instruments I'd never seen before. This old guy with a longish gray ponytail and a gray beard stood in the middle of the room yelling what sounded like insults at everybody in an annoying Brooklyn accent.

"If you want world peace, people, we have to make the circle. Come on, it's a sacred dance we're doing here, not the hokey-pokey!"

I took an instant dislike to this guy. He was a type I knew well – old geezers who crashed hippie events trying to be cool, but who really had some demented power trip going on. If they had ponytails, they thought they could pass. But as far as I was concerned, these guys belonged in the tar pits with the rest of their royally fucked up generation.

Reluctantly, I joined hands with Gail and one of the scraggly guys. Everybody in the room finally formed the necessary giant circle and the old dude talked for a while. "This is a dance about developing a heart with wings, which is a major Sufi image that's come down to us…blah blah blah." I was beginning to think this thing was going to be totally weird. Gail read the look on my face. "Just wait," she said in a loud whisper and squeezed my hand. At least the instructions were pretty easy – step and turn three times, then bow in front of the next person – that sort of thing.

The music started and in the beginning we all danced like the stiff and self-conscious white people we all were. But the guys in the dashikis kept playing and somehow we all got into it. It was as corny as square dancing, and maybe because of that, it started to be fun. The old guy mostly stayed in the center of the circle, bleating out the moves so we all knew what to do next. Sometimes he would take people by the shoulders and move them around like chess pieces if they forgot where they were supposed to go.

There were all kinds of people there – organic farming people, guys in overalls and shit-kickers, women in long granny dresses and braids; a few boring academic types and Brattleboro townie guys with Lucky Strikes rolled up in the sleeves of their tee shirts, desperate for something to do that night. But after awhile, I forgot about all these things. Everybody's hand began to feel the same.

"A salaam aleikem, Peace be with you," we chanted as we danced into the night. Gail and the scraggly guys whirled by, smiling like lunatics, making me think of the times in high school my friends and I went on amusement park rides, stoned out of our minds.

Sufis were big on spinning. The old guy grabbed the smallish red-haired woman who was standing next to him to show us how to do this. You anchored your feet firmly on the ground, joined hands with your partner, then leaned back and spun around fast, keeping your eyes on the other person so you wouldn't get dizzy.

When the music started again, it was my turn to dance with him. When the moment came, I let myself fall back into the spin and stared straight into his eyes. His face was lined like an old person's, but his eyes shone like a little kid's. We spun around, going faster and faster, until nothing else mattered. When we finally stopped spinning, I forgot about his geezer repulsiveness and let him put his arms around me, giving in to something I couldn't name.

Then he talked to me like he knew everything about me. Who knew why? Maybe he did have magical Sufi powers. "You don't have to be afraid, young lady. You've got a good strong heart. You just need to trust it." He kissed me in the very center of my forehead then, like he was giving me a blessing. Then the old guy, whose name was Larry I later found out, jumped back in the middle of the circle to lead the last dance of the night.

Afterwards Gail and me were sitting in some ultra-smoky dive bar we'd found in the center of town. The scraggly guys had reverted back to their sullen selves the minute the dance ended and had gone off to play darts with some local bar flies. I told Gail what had happened to me, dancing with Larry, and she got all excited. "Sounds like your heart chakra opened or something. That guy is very heavy-duty. He's an official Sufi master. Maybe he laid some spiritual energy on you. You know, yogis and people like that, they can do that."

"Maybe he did. In the beginning I just thought he was some old dude who was there to hit on hippie chicks, but I totally blissed out, dancing with him." Whatever had happened, splinters of the feeling remained while I hung out with Gail at the bar. We drank a few beers and didn't talk much, just happy to be with each other.

When I got into the car an hour later, I was still feeling high. But as I drove away from Brattleboro, I started crying as this slideshow of people whirled, Sufi-style, through my brain. There was Jane, holding Tabitha. Sal and Margaret. Kevin. I loved them, but they felt like weights holding me down. Then I thought about Gail and the feelings I had for her and how I'd loved John the motherfucker even though it'd just been some stupid sex thing between us.

That scene in *The Wizard of Oz* came back to me. Dorothy had been knocked unconscious and was dreaming; the farmhouse had been taken up into the funnel of some vast tornado. Why, I wondered, was I thinking about that movie again?

I drove on in the dark, crossing the state line back into Massachusetts. Like somebody punched me in the stomach, I finally knew what it meant. In a way, the tornado in my life was about the people I loved. Because I'd never really gotten it straight, where I left off and they began and what I was supposed to do about them.

Larry the Sufi guy had said that I had a good heart, that I was strong, and not to worry. But as I turned into my parents' driveway, the last of the dancing high wore off. Now I was back to where I'd started and I desperately hoped he was right, that somehow he was seeing things from his Sufi-masterfulness that I couldn't know.

16

Gang of Three

Sitting at the counter, I watched Juan as he put my breakfast on the grill: two eggs, home fries, and three strips of bacon. It was way too early; we hadn't even opened yet. A big breakfast was one of the nice perks Ari gave all of the waitresses when we worked the morning shift. As the smell of bacon rose from the grill, I wondered how I'd ever thought I could be a vegetarian working as a waitress in Springfield.

Outside in the cold, a few cars moved quickly up Worthington Street. The sun still wasn't up yet and the grayness seemed stuck to the street. Whatever happened in my own life, this city would take no prisoners; I knew that much for sure. A line from Allen Ginsberg's poem, "Howl," drifted back to me. It seemed like a century ago when I'd read it in my Beat Literature class – something about cooking up rotten animal flesh, dreaming about the pure vegetable kingdom. (No, I didn't like the idea of eating animals. It was a horrible thing, even though I knew I would eat every bit of the bacon on my plate when my breakfast arrived.)

The idea of a back-to-the-land movement – Ginsberg's pure vegetable kingdom updated for the times – had fascinated me back at school. *Living on the Earth*, that book by Alicia Bay Laurel, with the drawing on the cover of an ecstatic woman with her pubic hair in full view, had been in heavy rotation at the dorm. Like everybody else, I'd fallen in love with it. These days, Amherst was becoming all about food co-ops and collectives and natural this and natural that. Plenty of people believed that some sort of apocalyptical reckoning with Mother Earth was imminent, akin to Jesus' second coming.

Sufi dancing aside, I didn't know what I really believed in anymore. Ever since I'd turned sixteen, my brain had been trying to absorb too much new material, with women's lib, the drugs, radical politics, and now the living natural stuff. I knew part of the reason I'd flipped out at school (besides John) was because all these different ways of thinking began to clash like swords in my brain. Was I supposed to buy into the system and change it? Or go off in the woods, build a hut, and smoke dope?

It didn't help, living in a place where no one had even heard of Allen Ginsberg, never mind Alicia Bay Laurel. In Springfield, peoples' knowledge of the counterculture stopped somewhere around the time of Timothy Leary. Their idea of heavy reading was Harold Robbins and any real interest they'd had in liberal politics had come to a dead stop when Lee Harvey Oswald's bullet entered John F. Kennedy's brain. It made me feel so lonely I got up and poured myself another cup of coffee from the pot on the Bunn warmer.

Then Juan put my breakfast in front of me. I ate all the bacon, just like I knew I would. As I was finishing my breakfast, Ari arrived carrying the blue bank bag with the day's cash, which he'd hidden inside an ordinary brown shopping bag. He headed straight for the cash register, putting bills and coins into various drawers. Ready for the day, he got himself a cup of coffee and sat down next to me at the counter. Sighing deeply, he looked me over like he was a doctor, looking for signs of trouble.

"So what are you doing with your life, my girl?" Ari didn't screw around. He liked to say whatever was on his mind. Greek men, as I would discover years later when I actually went to Greece, were often very direct like that, although often not as benevolent as Ari.

"Ari, why are you asking me that? You know I don't know what to do with my life!"

"You are young, but you will not always be so. You work for me now, and that is good, you make some money, you look after your sister and her baby. Family always important. Always. But this is America."

"So?"

"Girls back in Andros, they grow up, get married, have babies, never go anywhere, always do the same thing. But this a different country, you can make different life. True for men, true for women here too."

"My god, Ari. You sound like Gloria Steinem."

"Who is this Gloria Stein?"

"It doesn't matter. But a lot of people your age don't see things that way."

"When I was young, I tell my father the dream I have. I want to go to America, start my own café. My father disappointed, wants me to stay on Andros, work in his grocery store. But then he say to me, you a man, and a man must follow his dream. So I go. Then my father force my sister Maria to work in the store instead. She very smart girl but he won't let her go to school – just work work work all the time. He slap her when she talk about university!"

Ari's eyebrows rose high on his forehead, angered again by his father who sounded like a total Fascist.

"People in town, they say about my sister Maria, she a woman, she have to do what her father want. I say that is wrong! She is a free human being!" Once again, the high eyebrows. "So this is what I do. I send my sister money and she come here and never go back. She live her life!" I drained my cup of coffee, appreciating Ari's story. You never knew with people, even if they were old.

Lowering his voice, Ari swiveled on his stool and leaned in, close to my face, making sure I got his point. "I ask what you want to do because you young, you very lucky to have chance to decide. And this life here, not enough for you. You like my sister, very smart. You been here six months. Why you not go back to school, girl?"

I didn't say anything. I was getting really tired of people asking me that. I knew Ari meant well, but what was I supposed to do, abandon my family in Springfield and go back to Amherst? To do what, exactly? Wait for the arrival of the pure vegetable kingdom, which

I wasn't even sure I believed in? As I recalled, the rest of that poem, "Howl," was about going crazy and how some poor guy ended up in a mental hospital. But I couldn't explain all of this to Ari. Seeing that I was upset, he reached over and squeezed my hand.

"Okay, I talk enough for one day. Me with my big Greek mouth. I shut up now."

Malvina showed up for her shift just then, in a huff because she had to come in through the back door in the alley. It was 7:05, five minutes past our usual opening time, and Ari hadn't unlocked the front door yet.

"What kinda business you all running here? The damn door's still locked!" she said. Sighing, Ari got up, unlocked the door, and opened for the day.

It was a busy Wednesday, what I liked to call a hamster-on-a-wheel kind of day, where you had to keep moving, no matter what. Take the order, put the ticket up, deliver plates full of food, pick up the empty dirty ones. Then do it over and over again for what felt like a million times.

After the lunch rush ended, three guys came in and sat down in one of the booths. I remembered one of them; he'd come in months before with Timmy Morton. This guy was Latin handsome, but he was the type who knew it. He wore a red bandana around his neck, just like the time before.

Like some bad rerun, he and his friends sat down in Malvina's section and I stayed as far away as possible, removing myself to a distant booth in the back. But after those first few minutes, I realized I was freaking out about nothing, really. They were just three losers, one who happened to know Timmy, an even bigger loser. Wasn't it time I got over it?

I looked over at Malvina taking their order. I couldn't hear what she was saying, but her pencil began to drum faster and faster on top of her order pad. Besides the one with the red bandana, there was a short guy in a Red Sox cap, and a tall skinny one with dirty blond hair and an annoying laugh. Finally, she turned away from them, savagely pushing the order pad into the pocket of her apron. When she walked back behind the counter, I caught up with her as she was pouring their Cokes at the soda fountain.

"Those guys you just waited on. Do you remember that guy with the red bandana? That creep's been in here before."

"Red bandana man? Yeah, I thought I'd seen him before."

"Are they giving you a hard time?"

"Those boys just a tad slow if you ask me. They kept askin' me how much is this, how much is that, like they couldn't read the menu. Guess they counting their pennies, or maybe they just retards," Malvina laughed hard as she put the three glasses of Cokes together between her two hands to take back to the booth.

There was a surge of new customers, probably because it had started to rain, which magically seemed to increase people's need for food and drink. Twenty minutes or maybe more went by before I heard Malvina's voice above the usual dining din.

"Ari! Make 'em stop. They ain't paid!"

Ari was in his usual spot behind the cash register, carefully placing change into the wax-like hand of a very elderly man paying his check. I looked up, just in time to see bandana man and his pals' backs as they bounded out the door. Ari saw them too. But instead of going after them, Ari waited patiently for the old man to count his change and put his wallet away.

Malvina and I rushed over to the big window that faced out to Worthington Street.

We watched the three of them; they had already made it across the busy street. It would be impossible to catch them now.

"You shoulda stopped those little punks," Malvina said to Ari, who only now was joining us at the window. "You could still call the cops and have them picked up."

But Ari just raised his large hand in the air, like a referee at a football game. "They not worth it. They are bad people. Life will take care of such dirt."

I kept my eyes on them, as they walked on the far side of Worthington Street. They all had the same bouncy hoodlum walk, powered by a certain spring in their knees. They made me think of wolves or coyotes that had emerged in the daylight from some dark feral place. I decided to call them the Gang of Three – a term I remembered from some course I took on the Maoist Revolution in China. I remembered even less about that than the Ginsberg poem, but for whatever reason, I liked calling on what remained of my education to name the things that were happening around me now.

By late afternoon, the coffee shop cleared out and I ended up sitting at the counter with Ari again, back to the same place I'd been that morning. Malvina had rushed out as soon as possible, still pissed off that Ari hadn't done more to catch the three guys. We were both quiet. Ari looked particularly tired and didn't seem to want to talk about what had happened that day or about my life, thank god.

I had yet another cup of coffee and my thoughts returned to Allen Ginsberg. In the end, the pure vegetable kingdom seemed like a fantasy to me. The evil in this world was a whole lot more inevitable, like the Gang of Three. The rage stirred in me again, a return to the old darkness.

17

Spring

When the forsythia bushes on Chestnut Street bloomed and the last of the snow re-ceded, revealing what was left of last summer's old lawns, I knew spring had arrived. But I wasn't sure how I felt about this. I'd gotten used to winter and the change caught me by surprise. How did things know when to come up from the ground? Why was the warmth returning anyway? I knew the scientific answers to these questions, but they never satisfied the weird mystery of the season.

It was a Sunday morning and Kevin was still asleep. Kneeling in bed, I bent the Vene-tian blind a little harder, to get a better look at what was going on out there. It must have woken Kevin up. Suddenly his arms were around my waist. Like a wrestler, he pulled me down back into bed.

Lately Kevin had his own case of spring fever going. Basically, that meant he wanted to ball all the time. We'd had a particularly long session the night before but it didn't seem to be slowing him down this morning. That was certainly fine with me; I could never get enough of Kevin. And it wasn't just the sex. I loved him – no doubt. I loved the sad anger he had about his father. I loved the fact that he still tried to protect his mother. I loved the way his hands were dented up and dirty from working. I loved his sarcastic wit and relentless ranting when he decided something he was thinking about was really important. I loved how he wouldn't take any bullshit from me, or from anybody else. Most of all, I loved how when I was with him, he smelled like home to me, like the place I would always belong to, wherever I went and whatever I did.

Like some mutt, I buried my nose into his hair, bright as a copper penny on the white pillow, then into the space on his neck underneath his ear, where his smell was especially strong. Because my face was buried deep in his neck, my hand wandered blindly down the smooth flesh of his chest until it found his cock, already hard. As I stroked it, he made a big cat sound – something between a purr and a growl. I moved on top of him and used my hand to put him inside of me. He opened his eyes wide, like he always did when we made love.

"You want to come?" he asked.

"No. Stay like this." I didn't want to bother doing the things I generally did to come, like rubbing myself just right. I wanted him in me. This kind of desire was new for me – the simple urge to be like earth, open and waiting for rain to make it wet. After a few minutes, he came inside me, quick and hard.

We got out of bed, dressed without showering and walked up the street to St. Thomas cemetery, which was what we liked to do when I didn't have to work on a Sunday. Easter had just gone by so some graves had pots of mums or lilies on them, the sunshine glinting off their foil wrapping. As we walked, we saw drained bottles from the Saturday night before and some roaches left on some of the bigger stones. High school kids had been here, you could tell by the empties of what they'd left behind – Boone's Farm apple wine and cans of Bud. The real drunks that came through here left different mementos: flasks of Wild Irish Rose and bottles of that all-time alcoholics' favorite, Thunderbird.

"I wish I'd known you in high school." Kevin said, as we came across more of these party leftovers.

"I don't know if that would have been such a good thing. You would have thought I was a complete bitch and I would have thought you were some townie delinquent."

"No way. I would have won you over. I had my charms, even back then. Too bad you ran off to college."

"Well, I'm back now, aren't I? Let's sit here." I spotted my favorite grave, where a child named Lisa Higgins was buried. She'd died when she was five, in the same year I was born. The grave itself was made into the shape of a bench, so you actually could sit down on it. No one had left a potted plant. I hoped that meant the parents had finally stopped coming to this bench to sit and mourn her. That or maybe they themselves had died. The little girl had been dead the entire time I'd been alive, almost twenty years.

"Why do we have to sit on this one? It's too damn low." Kevin lit a cigarette, his knees awkwardly crunched up in front of him.

"Because it's so sweet. I think Lisa's my spiritual twin or something. She died exactly one month before I was born."

"Sometimes you are so fucking weird, do you know that?"

"Yeah, I know that. If I'm so weird, why do you like me so much?"

"Who says I like you? Maybe I'm just using you for the sex."

"Well then, go ahead and use me all you want." Laughing hard, he grabbed me in a big bear hug and rolled us off Lisa's bench and into the slightly damp but warm grass behind it.

"So, do you want to be used right now? How about right here, over poor little Lisa?

"You don't have the balls."

"Try me." He lifted my shirt up and undid the metal button on my jeans. "Damn. You've got your fucking leotard on. Those things shouldn't be allowed. They stop normal reproductive urges."

"Only for the weak." I had thrown down the ultimate gauntlet. Kevin reached down, unzipped my jeans and wrestled them to my hips.

"People will see us!"

"Not if we stay behind the bench." Pushing the crotch of my black leotard and my panties to one side, he licked two of his fingers and entered me with his hand. Closing my eyes, I grew deliriously uncaring about where we were and who might see us. He knew how I liked things to go. He took his time. After I was sufficiently wet, he pushed the two fingers deeper into me. I came suddenly, like warm Coke exploding from its bottle. While his hand was still buried inside of me, I opened my eyes. Kevin was hovering over me and smiling broadly. His jeans were still zipped up.

"Just wanted to even things out from this morning," he said.

We were walking back down Chestnut Street when we ran into my sister and her best friend Kimmy, out for a walk themselves with Tabitha in her carriage. The sun was shining, clearly about its business of dispensing only good things that morning. Maybe they weren't exactly Madonna and child, but my sister and Tabitha looked pretty good. Even Kimmy, forever pale and junkie-skinny, looked vaguely healthy.

"Hey, so this is Tabitha. Now she's a cutie." I realized Kevin hadn't met the baby yet. Bending down, he peered into her small face and lightly touched the tip of her nose. Tabitha gave him a little squeal and her most charming baby smile.

Turning to Jane, he said, "This Tabitha is a lot prettier than the one on TV. She's going to be putting a lot of men under her spell, just you wait."

My sister laughed. "We'll see. You two look pretty charmed-up, yourselves. Laura, did you know your fly is unzipped?" My sister gave me a stagy wink; I suspected she could smell the sex coming off us. We all started laughing. Kimmy, forever doomed to play the dumb blond in any scenario, just stood there and said, "What? What's so funny?" Then she started laughing too. Whether she got it or not, the hilarity was contagious.

As all of us stood in the sun on Chestnut Street, time seemed to skip, like the needle on Kevin's stereo did when it played his scratchy records. I could see a future me with Kevin, walking another baby down Chestnut Street, running into Kimmy, my sister and a little kid named Tabitha. Then the picture froze and something inside fluttered against my chest. *No, this is not for you.* But I wasn't in the mood to get too heavy. Like a small bird, the feeling flew away into that day's vast sunshine.

Usually, I went home on Sunday nights, since I had to work early on Mondays. But Kevin didn't want me to leave. He wanted to walk down to the center of town and blow some of his paycheck and eat at Lanazotti's. It was getting dark and cooling off, so I dashed home and put on the heavy black sweater I'd bought at the Goodwill near Smith College, during one of me and Gail's bargain shopping extravaganzas (the Smithies really threw out great stuff, we had discovered). I hadn't worn it since the equinox party. Putting it on made me think of Tommy boy, which turned my stomach a little. Sex with Kevin was so much better and – kinder. It was strange to describe it like that, but it was the truth.

We walked down the hill to the restaurant. The neon sign I remembered from childhood blinked in the window: Lanazotti's Steak and Chops. Frank Lanazotti, the proprietor, was my father's age. In fact, my father and he knew each other from the Elks Club bar and a few other local watering holes. As we waited for a table, I looked at the wall of photos he had covered the entryway with. There was Frank with Congressman Boland, with Bishop Weldon. Frank with his wife Evelyn and their five kids, with a Christmas tree behind them. Frank with his arm around the snug waist of Miss Massachusetts 1965. He was a large man with a big Fifties-style pompadour of a haircut, always sporting a two-highball smile on his face, at least when the camera flashed.

A slightly grayer, somewhat stooped version of Frank greeted us and led us to a table. Frank was a guy who could never contain how pleased he was with himself, and he didn't then, on our short walk to the table.

"Tell your old man, come down to the Elks Club this Friday. I'm getting installed as president of the lodge. We never see him down there no more. And didya know my Christine's going to be valedictorian of her class in June. Same as her brother Frankie Junior, last year. Smart as whips. They're chips off the old block, if I do say so for myself."

I knew I'd forget to tell my father all of Frank Lanazotti's wonderful news. He handed us menus and thankfully left us alone. We got salads, then NY strips, which came with a side of pasta, like everything did at Lanazotti's. Frank Lanazotti might be an asshole, but he served great food in generous portions. We practically inhaled our meals then ordered coffee and cannoli.

As we waited for dessert, the light of a red candle stuck into a Chianti bottle shone down on the red-checkered tablecloth and broke up the semi-darkness. The bottle of Chianti we were actually drinking was mostly gone and its contents buzzed merrily in my brain. It was quieter in the restaurant. The crowd had thinned out and most of the people with little kids had finally gone home. Kevin picked my hand up off the tablecloth, the same way he had the night we'd met.

"Marry me," he said.

18

Marry Me

What I'd actually said to Kevin, sitting at the table at Lanazotti's, was that I didn't believe in marriage. I had launched into the problems with the institution like I was at some women's lib meeting. A woman became a piece of property in marriage, I said, and nobody was going to own me. I'd never get married because both the fascist state and the damn archaic church dominated the institution. Deep down, there was plenty of Catholic in Kevin. I knew I was smashing some image he had of me as his bride in a white dress on the steps of St. Thomas, but it had to be done, like ripping a Band-Aid off an old cut.

By the time we left Lanazotti's, the warm wine glow was totally gone. Since it was a Sunday night, there were no greasers around, gunning their engines and racing cars up and down Elm Street, but there were plenty of rowdy kids still hanging out on the commons, trying to score nickel bags of dope. They made me feel impossibly old. We walked in silence until we got to the corner of Westfield Street. Kevin lit a cigarette, making a small point of light in the dark.

"Okay, so I get it, Laura. Getting married freaks you out so much you had to get on some damn soapbox about women's lib. If that's the way it is, what the hell. We won't get married."

That morning, seeing a future me with Kevin and a baby on Chestnut Street had, if not totally captivated me, at least made me stop and wonder. Now I shivered thinking about it. It was still early spring and the temperature was dropping. I pulled the sleeves of my black sweater down to cover my hands.

"Why can't we just stay the way we are, anyway? Why do we even have to think about this shit *now*?" I finally said.

"If that's what you want, okay." He might have been ending the argument but the corners of his mouth flattened out like he'd just given away his last dime. "You know I fucking love you and I can't help it."

"You've got to be kidding," Gail said the next day on the phone, when I told her Kevin had proposed to me. "You said no, right? I mean, don't you think you're carrying this thing too far? Fucking him is one thing, marrying him is another. What does this guy do? Work in a factory? It'd be like throwing your whole life away."

I didn't say anything for a moment. I was watching my mother in the kitchen, trying to open a big can of baked beans, one of the jumbo size cans my father liked to buy at the Stop 'n Shop. After a struggle, she finally got the steel teeth of the electric can opener into the thing.

"Laura? You there? C'mon woman, tell me what you said."

I held the green receiver tight, as if the phone might suddenly stop working and sever the connection we had. "Of course I said no, I wasn't going to marry him. Do you really think I'm going to sell out for some schmaltzy happily-ever-after thing with a guy from my home town?" Talking to Gail, everything seemed so certain, so crystal clear.

"Okay, so that's settled? I don't have to come over there and save you from holy wedlock, right?"

"Right." I said it and I meant it.

"And you're coming up to Northampton next week, right?"

"Right."

I got off the phone. Supper was almost ready. In the kitchen, hot dogs, slippery with sizzling fat, tumbled out of the frying pan and into a plate my mother had set down on the counter. In her supper rotations, Monday nights had always meant hot dogs and beans. Even in the frozen food years, when my mother had ditched us for Peg Brenner and real estate, even in the years after what happened to Jane when our family life had threatened to go entirely off its sprockets, this meal had endured. *If Timmy had killed my sister*. If even the hot dog and beans suppers had disappeared, what would have happened then? It was both troubling and strangely reassuring, returning to this my first life.

"Laura, where's Jane? Supper's ready," my mother said.

"I think she's putting Tabitha down."

"Will you yell upstairs and tell her it's on the table? Sal, you going to sit down with us or what?"

My father sat in his chair, poring over the evening paper, even though we got the same news on TV.

"Give me a sec. They're releasing those tapes. I hope they're going to fry Nixon's ass!" He chuckled loudly behind the newspaper. Reading about Watergate and the Nixon White House's descent into hell was deeply satisfying to him, since he held Richard Nixon personally responsible for closing down the Springfield Armory and taking his job away. It was a far cry from Ari, who wanted to help the guy out.

"I'm going to fry *your* ass if we have to wait and my supper gets cold!" I heard it then – the same exasperation in my mother's voice, like a long-lost melody from another suppertime years ago.

Same old suppertime, same old. I was a kid, maybe seven years old, and the kitchen was painted a different color. A pressure cooker my mother no longer used was sputtering on the stove, cooking corned beef and cabbage, my least favorite meal. My parents were sputtering too, arguing on and on about money.

My mother took the pressure cooker off the stove and put it in the sink. As she opened it and peeled the slimy rubber thing off inside the pot, the steam and the smell of the dreaded dinner began to escape and fill the kitchen.

"What do you think I am, made of money?" My father was shouting as he took his seat at the head of the table.

"Goddamn it, Sal. How are we going to pay the electric this month?"

I hated them arguing and I hated corned beef and cabbage and suddenly I was yelling too, in my high-pitched irritating child's voice. "I don't want to eat supper tonight! I hate this food!"

My father was already warmed up from arguing with my mother. Because I was sitting at the other end of the table, which was out of smacking range, he brought his hand down and struck the table instead of me. "You don't talk that way in this house. You eat what we put in front of you. Now I don't want to hear another peep out of you!" This was followed by his favorite mantra, delivered at top volume, that great leveler of better expectations I would hear over and over throughout my childhood: *"Who the hell do you think you ARE, anyway?"*

I couldn't explain it to people like Gail. Where I was from, parents believed they needed to bring you down a peg in preparation for a life that promised to do more of the same. The idea was to lower your expectations, make sure you learned how to get along and not ask for too much. Because if you did ask for more, you could end up even worse off.

Who the hell did I think I was?

I had answered the question silently in my head then, so I wouldn't get hit, and I would answer it again and again the same way during the rest of my childhood.

I can be whoever I want to be and it won't be anything like you.

Later that night, after everybody had gone to bed, I sat in the living room looking at the dents in the furniture my family had made from sitting in the same spots night after night. It was quiet for once, since I'd turned the TV off. Now the sofa and my father's recliner seemed to ask me the same old question: *Who the hell did I think I was, these days?* The truth was there in the dark of the room: No matter what, I was their daughter and that was never going to change. The reason I would never marry anybody wasn't because of some women's lib thing. It was fear, really. I didn't want to give anybody else a crack at having that much power over me, ever again.

19

Sonya

It was a week later and I was on my way to Northampton to see Gail but I'd left the house early. There was time, I realized, to make a detour and go to Amherst. The University of Massachusetts, Amherst College and Hampshire College – three of the illustrious Five Colleges that gave the Western Massachusetts something to brag about, were located here, about thirty miles north of Springfield. Mt. Holyoke in South Hadley, and Smith College in Northampton, where I would meet Gail later, were actually a little closer.

I was nervous as I parked the Pontiac in the big lot across from my old dorm at UMass. Like magnetic north on a compass, I'd been drawn back to my old dorm this morning, but for what?

In the gray light, the brick building looked modern and anonymous; it was just one of a bunch of nearly identical dorms that stood crowded up against each other in this corner of the campus. Now it was hard to believe I'd actually lived here. Counting three floors up and seven windows in to be sure, I spotted the window of the room Gail and I used to have which belonged to somebody else these days. I took a sip of the coffee I'd bought on the way, burning my tongue slightly on it, remembering how my exile from higher education had begun.

So there had been the badly lopsided relationship with John and then the break up, when he said I was getting too possessive. After that, John started telling people in the dorm that I was weird and not that smart. And what John thought went, at least with most of the crowd we hung out with. I'd assumed these people were my friends too. But after a while, whenever I walked into one of their rooms to hang out, there would be this weird silence underneath whatever music was playing on the stereo. I had gotten the message. It wasn't just John who didn't want me; none of them did.

Why had I cared so much about John and his snotty friends accepting me? Because they'd made me feel like I was getting closer to some fantasy I had about the kind of person I *should* be: A more confident, more sophisticatedly hip edition of the person who left Springfield. So, when they dropped me, I was like some junkie who'd lost her fix. I stopped going to classes, holing up in the dorm room for days at a time. I started doing a little coke to medicate; to make up for the drug-like effect that acceptance by John and his friends had given me. When the coke wore off, of course I did a little more. I kept this up until Gail finally took all my coke away. Then I got the notice that my scholarship was being suspended. (What had I thought would happen, when I stopped going to classes and my grades slipped?) The next day, I'd called my mother and asked her to come and take me home, ending what was left of my college career.

I chugged the rest of the coffee and threw the Styrofoam cup out of the window, enjoying the feeling of littering on UMass property. At least I hadn't lost Gail. She hadn't given a fuck what John or his friends thought of me or anything else. Gail had never needed their validation. She believed she was great, as is.

I thought of the letter that I'd never followed up on, that would have let me come back to school. Maybe I'd done the right thing after all. Too much had happened here for me to ever come back.

I turned the key in the ignition and left the parking lot with more speed than was necessary, leaving Amherst and going west towards Northampton, letting Route 9 with its shopping centers and never-ending traffic take me away.

Twenty minutes later, I found a parking space on Pleasant Street and started walking the few blocks to the café where I was supposed to meet Gail and Sonya in downtown Northampton. The town was a strange place, for sure. Smith and Mt. Holyoke, two of the snootiest girls' colleges were here, but so was the state's largest state hospital. As usual, the Smithies and Mt. Holyoke girls who I saw on the street were all dressed the same; suede jackets and Frye boots this year. The discharged mental patients all wore the same clothes too – chinos that had seen the inside of too many washing machines and the same cheap black tie shoes that slid on the town's wet sidewalks like an old car's bald tires. The people that actually lived there, just like the working people in Springfield, had this way of walking by both of these types, the Smithies and the mental cases, with the same hard *you're not our kind* look.

A slow chilly drizzle had started and my hair was frizzing out, but that was okay. In fact, everything was okay for the moment. I'd been afraid to go back and see my old dorm and now I'd done it and it hadn't made me shrivel up and die.

When I got to Main Street, I turned left. I was supposed to meet Gail and her friend Sonya at Beardsley's, a café that was further down the street, smack in the middle of the small downtown. When I got there, the café's windows were all steamed up, making the place look comfy and warm. I went inside. Gail and Sonya weren't there yet but I got a table and sat down.

The first time I'd been to Beardsley's, the place had smelled delicious, like baked bread, cigarettes, and people with money, and it did now, too. I'd been with John and some other people and we'd all been really stoned. The fancy pastries, the prints on the wall, and the waitresses who pronounced the French items on the menus so perfectly, swishing around in black skirts that trailed so far behind them they collected crumbs had just blown me away. I'd blurted out, "This must be just like Paris." John had winced noticeably and then joined in the group's laughter.

I made myself stop remembering.

Aubrey Beardsley was the café's patron saint, so his black and white prints covered the café's walls. From a distance, the pictures looked innocent enough, but close up, you could spot plenty of genitalia. I was checking out the print nearest to my table just to pass the time, when Gail and another woman who I assumed was Sonya walked in.

"So you're Laura. Well. About time we met." Before I had a chance to say anything, Sonya had me in a big close hug. After she gave me a good squeeze, she passed me on to Gail like I was a large piece of fruit.

Sonya, I noted during the hug, was a strange-looking woman. She had these very round small eyes and a canine alertness about her that seemed a little dangerous. She also had a rather noticeable moustache growing on her upper lip. My Italian aunts, no strangers to the tragedy of facial hair, would have slipped her a tube of Nair, pronto.

"Hey, glad you could make it. I was afraid I wouldn't be able to pry you away from that fiancée of yours!" Gail said. As usual, she looked great, majestic in a blue silk cocktail dress from the Forties with only a few noticeable stains in the front, which she wore over her thermal underwear.

"Well, I told him we were shopping for my trousseau," I said. Pushed up against her armpit, I got a whiff of Gail's usual smell, b.o. mixed with jasmine oil.

"Oh my god. You're not really getting *married*? You're kidding, right?" When Sonya asked me this, her small eyes darted around like unpopped popcorn kernels.

"Of course I'm kidding." It was a total relief to be able to joke about Kevin's marriage proposal with these women.

Gail and Sonya had gone to boarding school at Northfield Mt. Hermon together so they spent a few minutes gossiping, catching up on who had most recently gotten busted for drugs. Like many New England prep schools, Northfield Mt. Hermon had been full of upper middle class kids who'd used their parents' generous allowances to launch themselves into the drug trade. Now they were getting busted and costing those parents another bundle.

I sat there, silent, playing with my red cloth napkin. Even though I'd said it would be okay on the phone, I felt a little resentful that Gail had invited Sonya. I hadn't seen Gail for a while and now I had to endure the two of them talking about their druggie school friends. But that was Gail. No matter what the event, she always thought it was fine to include other people. Besides, she'd told me Sonya was leaving the area the next week, moving to Santa Fe, New Mexico.

The waitress who'd been ignoring us finally came by. We ordered coffee and lots of different pastries. Very directly, Sonya shifted her attention to me. "So what's your deal right now? Gail says that you're living with your parents and your sister had this baby. And there's some townie guy you're shtupping, somebody named Kevin, right?"

Gail looked over at me, a little nervous how I'd react.

"Right," I said, wondering just how much Gail had told her. It was weird, but suddenly I felt like my mother. I wasn't sure I wanted Sonya to know so much about my family. The best thing to do was to change the subject. "Why are you moving to Santa Fe?"

"This woman I knew went out there to start a woman's center. I was just about to start my MSW and she called me up and wanted me to be their rape crisis counselor."

"That sounds interesting," I said, figuring I'd keep her talking about herself, so she couldn't ask me a lot of questions.

"It's more than interesting, honey," Sonya said, sounding a little snotty. She released me from her laser-gaze and turned it on Gail who squirmed a little in her seat. "She knows, right?"

Gail nodded her head no.

"Well, that's fucking weird. If I know about her sister, she should know about me."

"You told her about *Jane*?" I said.

"Okay, maybe I fucked up, but you know I can't keep my mouth shut," Gail said, giving me her best cow eyes, the ones that said, "you know you love me no matter what." This was true, of course, but I was still somewhat ticked off.

"Don't get mad at Gail," Sonya said, even though she was the one who'd gotten pissed off first. "She told me because I've been raped. That's why I'm taking the job in Santa Fe."

The words sounded loud in the café, but Sonya didn't seem to care and she didn't lower her voice as she told the story.

"It happened to me when I was fourteen, when I was still living in Newton. At least I was older than your sister. I went for a walk in the woods behind the school with this guy who played violin with me in the school orchestra. In the middle of a normal conversation, he pushed me up against a tree and started doing it to me, just like that. It hurt like hell. There was something totally psycho about him, because afterwards, he began talking to me like nothing had happened. He actually turned his back, so I could fix my clothes. I had this pink and white flowered skirt on. All I could think about was whether the blood I could feel on my underpants was showing through on the hem of my skirt. Then, like a zombie, I followed him out of the woods. I was afraid of what else he might do to me if I tried to run. Both of our mothers were in the school parking lot, waiting to pick each of us up. I got into the car and just acted normal, like I was playing myself on TV. After that, when I'd see him at orchestra practices, I'd pretend like it hadn't happened and so would he. It was so crazy, I never told anybody."

As Sonya spoke, I started clenching my fists underneath the little café table. The pink skin the plastic surgeon had to put on my sister's forehead came into my head, like some weird Frankenstein flashback. I was angry – not only at the rapist but at Sonya. It made no sense, but I was.

"You never even told your mother? How did you know he wasn't going to do it again, to somebody else?"

Looking at me carefully, Sonya placed her small but very muscular hands down on the table. No rings, no bracelets, just hands that had lots of lines in them, like these pieces of flesh were much older than all of us.

"My mother spent time in the camps during the war and was never really right after that. Even at fourteen, I knew that she was too fucked up to help me. And with my father, it was hopeless, because the guy was Jewish and from a good family. He wouldn't have believed me. I talked my parents into sending me to Northfield Mt. Hermon for my last two years of high school just to get away from Newton. When I got there, I slept with a few guys, just to see what would happen. But I realized it wasn't just because of the rape. Sex with men wasn't for me. I figured out I liked being with women. Gail was the first person I told who didn't freak out about it. Anyway, I knew about your sister, so I thought you should know about me."

The three of us were silent for a moment. Outside, on the other side of the wall, I could hear somebody walking by, probably an ex-mental patient, saying "goddam son of a bitch, goddam son of a bitch," over and over again in a kind of monotone.

I didn't quite know what to make of Sonya Bernstein. She was from Newton. And these Newton girls, with their smarts and entitled jap-ness had always made me feel inferi-

or and had, therefore, always pissed me off. John had even dumped me for one. But Sonya defied this stereotype. She had crossed over to the other side long ago, where nothing was for sure or safe anymore, and I knew it.

When she finished the story, Sonya's muscular hand lightly touched my arm – in solidarity, I guessed, over her rape and my sister's. I wouldn't have admitted it to my Amherst friends, but lesbians still creeped me out. Part of me wanted to move my arm away from her hand but I didn't move a muscle.

"I don't know how it is for your sister," she said. "But I believe in talking about this stuff. It's like you're taking back what happened to you. Now I never let anybody shut me up, about anything." The hand withdrew, but the heat of it lingered on my arm for a moment.

"Okay," she said then, meaning that she, Sonya, was done with talking about the whole rape thing and would now be moving on to something else. This was Sonya in action, I realized. She liked to dominate any scene, but instead of resenting it, she made you glad she was. With the calculated finesse of a standup comic, she started cracking outrageous jokes – mostly involving penises being put in unlikely place, telling them just loudly enough so that a few guys at the next table, who had that wimpy pinched look that could only mean they went to Amherst College, began to turn around and stare at her. Sonya paid absolutely no attention to them, so we didn't either. She'd created a zone around us no one else could enter.

We had more coffee, even though we were already flying on the caffeine.

"So what about this boyfriend? Is he good in the sack?" Sonya asked, looking for a good segue out of the penis jokes. I took the cue. It was easy to talk about Kevin, if I kept it about the sex. She really liked the cemetery story, especially the part about me and my leotard. I liked telling it, even though it was a little weird, since Sonya actually slept with women.

We stayed so long the waitress came over and asked us to pay up because her shift was ending. Sonya insisted on treating us, plucking bills from a large and very worn man's wallet that she kept together with a rubber band. Then she looked across the table at me again, like I'd passed some sort of test.

"Look, if you ever come out to Santa Fe, get in touch." She plucked a napkin off the table. "I start working at the Women's Center next month. This is the number, I think." With ink-stained fingers, she wrote her name and a number that started with a five-zero-five area code on the napkin. "Anyways, the coffee's getting to me. Got to pee." She wandered off to the Ladies Room, making the table strangely quiet and empty with her absence. I put the napkin in my pocket.

20

Orange Sunset

The door on the Pontiac wasn't closing right. I had to slam it with both hands, hard, a couple of times to finally make it catch. Still, the Pontiac monstrosity, as the car was affectionately known by my family, didn't fail me. It started right up and I pointed it south, driving out of the center of Northampton towards Route 91, back to Springfield.

The conversation with Sonya left me thinking about a lot of things, but more than anything it made me wonder about Santa Fe. Did it look like California during its Spanish mission phase? Or was it more bona fide desert, with cacti and – what were they called in the Westerns – sagebrush? – blowing across the horizon? The name intrigued me. Santa Fe. Solid and old but exotic at the same time.

I'd never been to Europe, or even west of the Mississippi, like my Amherst friends had and this lack of travel depressed me. In my puny universe, the West still meant those epic pictures of pioneers and covered wagons from school, with the Summer of Love stuff, of hippies frolicking in San Francisco, as a sort of weird add-on. I thought of my Uncle Jimmy, my mother's brother, who hadn't given a shit about what anyone said and had moved to California. He'd pulled a Jed Clampett – literally packed up a dilapidated Ford station wagon with his wife and three kids, and left Springfield for Hollywood, where he planned on breaking into pictures. My father had shaken his head in utter contempt as Jimmy and his family backed out of our driveway and waved goodbye. Even though my uncle never got the big break he'd fantasized about, he ended up with a union job running the property management unit at Universal. Pretty good for crazy Uncle Jimmy, I thought.

The sun was setting as I drove on and the light filling the sky behind Holyoke's decrepit paper mills was a strange and wonderful orange, a shade of the color I'd never seen before. What would it be like to go west, like Sonya was doing, and start a new life? Different possibilities, vastly different futures were out there somewhere and thinking about them gave me the queasy fluttery feeling in my stomach I always got when I was scared and excited at the same time. *I could leave all of this. I could just keep driving. Until I got to New Mexico, or until the Pontiac died, whichever came first.*

I took the next exit to Springfield, merging with the heavy traffic on Riverdale Road. Back to reality, at least all the reality that was mine for the time being. Since it was six o'clock, I knew Kevin would be home. When I got there, he was sitting on the couch like some inanimate object, watching the Channel 22 News.

"Hey," he said when I sat down.

"Hey yourself," I said. Kevin always smoked a lot when something was bugging him. Judging by the number of relatively fresh cigarette butts I saw smooshed up in the ashtray, he was in quite the mood. "So what's going on?"

"I don't know. You tell me," he said.

"I went to Northampton to see Gail. You knew I was going up there today."

"Yeah."

I hated when he got all monosyllabic on me. "So what's your problem?" I asked after a while.

"Nothing. Got no problem."

We watched as the newscaster flubbed a line, looked a tad uncertain then attacked the sentence again, like the mistake had never happened.

"Want to get something to eat?" he said, staring at the TV. He was still economizing his syllables but sounding at least half human.

"We could, but I'm not that hungry. I ate a lot of pastries at the café."

"Well, I need to eat something," he said, retreating back into his Arctic Circle.

"Well okay, Mr. Huffy."

"I'm not being huffy."

"Okay, you're not being huffy." I didn't want to argue with him. In fact, I never wanted to argue with anyone ever again in my whole life. Northampton had tired me out and left me with this feeling, as I stood in the middle of Kevin's living room, of being neither here nor there. "We could go to McNally's," I said.

"Okay." Kevin got up from the couch and clicked the news off.

McNally's was exactly like it always was, dank. There were the usual drunks hanging out and Mick was behind the bar, pouring. Like some gatekeeper, he was doling out the liquor tickets these drinkers needed tonight, so they could get to where they wanted to go. I liked Mick; it wasn't his fault the only place his patrons wanted to go was oblivion.

We sat at a table next to the bar and ordered. Neither of us talked. From the ancient jukebox, the Eagles sang that song about another tequila sunset, or was it sunrise? Whatever they were singing, it made me think of the sunset I'd seen driving down Route 91 earlier. The whole subject of sunrises and sunsets made me sad as I sucked down my first beer then ordered another one. I had really enjoyed being with Sonya and Gail and now I was back here, back in town, and all that meant suddenly seemed to enter my personal space and fog it up. Kevin's food came fast. After he practically inhaled a cheeseburger and finished his second beer, he said, "I just don't like it when you go up there. You know that."

"Why? Gail's my friend and I wanted to see her. What's wrong with that? For chrissake, we were roommates."

"If you two are so close, why doesn't she ever come here? It makes me wonder what you're doing up there." His eyes slanted with suspicion. "Are you really seeing your old roommate? Or are you going up there and fucking around on me?"

"Jesus, now you're getting paranoid. I met Gail in Northampton and she brought along her friend Sonya who is, by the way, a fucking lesbian and we had *coffee* and talked. Because that's what we like to do, *talk*. Believe me, you wouldn't have wanted to be there. How does that translate into me fucking around?"

"What about last month, when you went to that dance?"

"We went *Sufi* dancing, which might as well have been *square* dancing, for all the sex that was in it. And it was with a bunch of hicks in Vermont!"

"Then why didn't you want me to come with you? And what about that party, the one you went to, right after we met?" He meant the equinox party, the night I'd ended up with Tommy Boy. No way had I seen that one coming. There was a bad taste in my mouth that suddenly turned metallic. I took a large gulp of beer and drank the shot that had appeared next to it down neat to wash it away.

Kevin's question still hung out there, unanswered, in the air between us. I didn't say anything and neither did he. As a wave of warmth from the alcohol began to flood over me, I looked over at the drunks at the bar. Maybe I'd never really understood them before. Oblivion suddenly seemed like an attractive destination. Everyone had something they were running away from. Why had I ever thought I was so different?

From the speakers over the bar, the Eagles song played again. Someone here really liked it a lot. I realized I was getting drunk. Still, another shot of courage didn't seem like a bad idea. Getting lit was making me see things. I was tired of everything. Tired of sitting in the middle, not knowing which way to go with my life. Tired of my sister and her baby and working at the coffee shop. Tired of myself and all the guilt and the fear that seemed to cloud everything I did, no matter what.

When I looked at Kevin, his face looked like a sulky little girl's, which totally annoyed the shit out of me. More than anything else, I was tired of Kevin and his precious townie-ness. Why couldn't he grow up and figure a few things out, like how to get himself out of this goddamn town? I caught Mick's eye and he brought me another shot. Feeling reckless, I drank it down. Then I lit a cigarette. Maybe this was the moment I should just clear the decks and leave for New Mexico, for Paris, for somewhere. What was I waiting for? If I didn't, twenty years down the road, I might still be sitting here at McNally's, on this same bar stool.

The need for escape was in my blood now, riding on top of the alcohol like the Lone Ranger on Silver. It wasn't my goddamn screwed up sister that held me here, it was Kevin and his suffocating possessiveness and I knew how to fix that.

"Since you're so sure I'm such a fucking whore, I'll tell you exactly what I did." I knew I was drunk and being ugly but I didn't care. "I fucked somebody I used to know from school at that party. Are you fucking happy now?"

In a reflexive action, Kevin's arm came down, sweeping away everything on the table, the bottles, the glasses and the empty plate with splotches of ketchup still on it. In the crash that followed, the bar got very quiet. Then a guy playing pool in the back yelled, "Hey asshole! You fuckin' screwed up my shot!"

As if he'd been waiting for that remark, Kevin bolted from his chair. He stood up and looked down at me. His face seemed dead, the eyes gone to glass, the lips stretched into one long colorless slit. Then he left.

Mick came out from the back with a broom and dustpan. "Don't worry about it. It's just a few lousy glasses," he said, looking older than he did behind the bar. I knew I didn't have to explain anything to Mick. Everyone knew he'd been divorced twice, the last time from a stripper half his age. He swept up the stuff dispassionately, like he was the busboy.

I sat there feeling like I couldn't move. I made myself wiggle each foot, then each leg and arm, like I'd survived a car crash, and a doctor was telling me to do these things. Then Kimmy appeared out of nowhere, smelling soothingly like menthol cigarettes. I hadn't even known she was in the bar. Her tall blond body folded, crouching down next to my chair. "Laura, are you okay? What the hell happened? I was in the back, playing pool with Dougie and I heard the noise."

"Kevin and I. We had a fight." It was a tremendous effort to form words.

"You look really fucked up. Do you want me to take you home?"

"Yeah, maybe in a minute."

"Did he hurt you?"

"No. He got mad. He threw everything down…" I was a kindergartener again, straining to talk with a vastly limited vocabulary. Kimmy's pale moon face loomed closer to mine. Her presence registered as a dull throb, an ache of connection to my normal world, cutting through the shock and the alcohol floating through my system. What had I done? I started shaking like a child afraid of punishment.

"Let me take you home, Laura. I'll help you. Let's go."

"Okay" I said. Kimmy was stronger than I thought. As skinny as she was, she managed to pull me to my feet and I leaned most of my weight onto her. We made our way out of McNally's and into her old Chevy.

Kimmy dropped me off in front of my house, which was totally dark. I turned my house key into the worn lock on the back door and crept through the kitchen and up the steps to my room. I hadn't been sleeping at home very much so the bed felt strange. The springs seemed to have gotten used to life without me. They heaved and sighed when I lay down.

I didn't want anybody to hear me. I put a pillow over my head and started to cry, the way I used to cry when I was a kid, so hard that my stomach hurt. Why had I told Kevin about Tommy Boy? Had I really wanted to break us up in the middle of McNally's like that? And why the fuck had I gotten so drunk?

I burrowed deeper under the covers, pulling the pillow tighter over my head. Losing Kevin felt like losing a limb. Why had I done this? Because New Mexico, or at least the idea of it, had gotten a hold of me. If there was a different life out there, trying to find me, I knew I was losing my chance at it. It was slipping away, like the orange light behind Holyoke's paper mills.

Did I really want a loser life with Kevin living in this town, full of tequila sunrises or sunsets or whatever the fuck they were – the only kind I'd ever get to see from the bar at McNally's? It was what I was heading for. So I had put an axe to it. Just cut it off.

But it was Kevin, the reality of us together, our bodies, our touching, not some disembodied future that I had amputated. The memory of his arm then, coming down, sweeping all the stuff off the table, everything falling and breaking and smashing into bits.

Somehow, I fell asleep. But, thanks to the booze, I kept bobbing back to the surface and waking up, like I was wearing one of those inflatable swimming rings Jane and me used to have when we were little.

I'm in the Dorothy nightmare again, but this time I'm the mean witch on the broomstick, riding by the window of the house as it was flying into the cyclone. Dorothy's asleep

and doesn't wake up as I ride by. I get confused because I'm not good little Dorothy any-
more. How did I become the witch? Who am I and what side am I on anyway?

Dreaming then waking, then dreaming again. At seven, when the baby started crying, Jane got up and I woke up for real, The *Wizard of Oz* reruns finally ending in my head. For about ten seconds, I thought that the day had ended with me talking to Gail and Sonya at Beardsley's, that the fight with Kevin in McNally's had been just another part of the night-mare. But then I realized no, it had happened.

I had to go to work. Like an atomic cloud, a massive hangover was waiting for me as I sat up in bed. I knew I'd have to puke to purge what was left in my stomach. In the bathroom, I knelt in front of the toilet like I was praying and in between bouts of violent heaving, I really did pray. Please God, make this better. *Maybe I don't deserve it, but please make it better.*

21

Mom and Dad

After I told Jane about the breakup, I called Gail. Now she was squeezing the last bit of metaphysical meaning out of me and Kevin breaking up. "This is what I think. The two of you were drawn together because you had left over business from a past life. So in a way it's progress that it's over." She softened a little, trying not to sound like some cosmic cheerleader, rallying around the breakup. "I know you were really into this guy, but maybe it's a sign you should leave Springfield. I mean, your sister's doing okay, right? Nobody's making you stay there."

I held the phone as close to my ear as possible, since Tabitha was screaming, royally pissed off about something. I was still hung over and my head hurt. Was there ever any peace for anyone, even in babyland? Life seemed too impossibly complicated to figure anything out, ever again.

"Look," Gail said. "If someone moves out of the house here in Leverett, I'll let you know. Maybe you could move in for awhile."

"Yeah," I said, unenthusiastically. Everything Gail said seemed stupid to me today. "Maybe I will." But at the Athena the next day, I found myself telling Ari I might be leaving in a month or two.

"You going back to school?" he asked, way too excited.

"No, but I'm thinking of leaving town. I don't know if I'm ever going to go back to school, Ari."

"You do what you have to do, my girl," he said, shuffling his order forms around on his clipboard so he didn't have to look up at me.

In the weeks that followed, I would catch Ari watching me from his spot behind the cash register, over the rim of his bifocals. With his head slightly bowed, he looked like an inquisitive old octopus. I'm sure he noticed that Kevin wasn't coming by the coffee shop anymore. But Ari, usually so chatty and inquisitive about my life, would not ask me about him.

With my mother, it was a different story. In fact, she offered to take me out to Friendly's for lunch after I told her, which had been our special thing to do when I was a kid, even in the dark years after Jane's attack. We went on a Tuesday when I didn't have to work. Under the merciless florescent lighting, my mother's face looked different. Time, almost like a small animal, had burrowed itself in between her eyes. It had pouched out the skin around her mouth, creating small sacks of extra flesh to live in. I was sad suddenly that my mother was getting old and that there was nothing I could do about it.

A waitress with shiny golden hair came by to take our order. I moved my eyes away from my mother's face and stared at this girl's nametag, which said her name was Jenifer. This generation's Jennifers spelled it with only one n. Time was passing. Hardly a new thought, but now I had evidence that it was making my mother old and pushing another generation right up behind me.

"Ma'am?" Jenifer was saying, waiting for me to order. I realized I had totally spaced out. Besides, when had I become a ma'am not a miss in these service situations?

"A hamburger special, French fries and a coke," I said quickly, ordering the same thing I'd always ordered as a kid. As Jenifer walked away, my adult self felt odd, like I'd been dreaming it up this whole time. At any moment I'd awaken, relieved to find myself back in childhood and my mother young again

"Laura," my mother said, breaking through my time warp. "I was thinking. Why don't you transfer to Springfield Community College in the fall? It'd get your mind off things. They have a great nursing program, you know." It just might have been the single worst suggestion she had ever made to me. My mother had this way of getting very practical at exactly the wrong moments in my life. Nursing had been what I'd wanted to do when I was a kid, before I knew any better. Why would anyone want to be a nurse these days and play step-and-fetch-it to some chauvinistic male doctor? How could my mother even think of such a thing?

"Mom, you've got to be kidding. You know I was thinking of law school eventually or journalism, something that *means* something. *Nursing*?" I was talking too loud and Jenifer, who had been flirting with the dishwasher, turned around and looked at us.

"Laura, you had a real hard time at UMass. Maybe you need to think about something closer to home, something a little easier…"

"Something easier? When did I suddenly become stupid? Why are you bringing this up now?"

"I think you need to get a direction, that's all, and now's a good time to stop and think. I mean, what are you going to do, spend the rest of your life working for that old Greek in his coffee shop?"

"What's wrong with working for Ari?" I was very angry. "I like Ari. Beside I'd rather work for him than go to some community college around here and run into every idiot I went to high school with."

"Will you keep your voice down?" I watched my mother's saggy face as she decided not to escalate the argument. She would try to reason with me instead. I pitied her a little for that. "Look, honey, I'm worried about you. In another month, it will be a year since you came home. You need to think about what you want to do next and SCC is right here in town and it's not a lot of money. This is the time in your life when you should be making some progress…"

"That would be progress? Becoming a nurse?"

"It would be a start."

"A start at what, exactly?"

"Your future." She took a sip of coffee, waiting just a moment before plunging into the subject. "Honey, maybe it's just as well that it ended with Kevin. What kind of life were you going to have with him? Not that it's all his fault, with his family. But at this point, you should be moving on with your life..."

"What you really mean is that I should be moving on *up*, right? With someone better off." This argument was rapidly becoming a retread. When I was in high school, she had tried to get me to date boys from "better" families. Now here we were again and it totally enraged me. "Screw that, Mom," I said.

Just then, Jenifer approached with our plates. Clearly, she had heard what I'd said. *Screw that.* She looked at me with a kind of detached curiosity. To her I was just another older person who belonged in some separate universe, one that she and her friends would never want to join. My mother waited for Jenifer to turn away, her lips tight.

"Laura, you don't need to swear."

"Then stop saying these things. It was a bunch of bull back in high school and it still is now. Kevin's a good guy, he was good to me..." It made no sense, but I felt like defending Kevin, defending our relationship even though it was over.

"If you had married him..."

"I would never have married him."

"Well then, lived together, whatever people want to call it these days, but it would have been the same thing." She had her right hand on the counter, with its painfully small diamond and matching wedding band. "Laura, you're so smart and pretty. I just want you to meet someone better. Somebody who can give you a better life."

"I want something better for me, Mom, but it's not about becoming some nurse or marrying some guy. It's not about that."

"Then what is it about? How come you can never tell me what it is you want?" She raised her voice, the exasperation she felt with me making her not care who heard us.

"I want to do something that matters with my life." Inside I wanted to cry, it was so frustrating. How could I explain anything to my mother, who had never sat in a political science class or read a book on psychology, who'd never been anywhere or done anything but take care of her family and work? "I want to be with people who live different, who think about things, who care about what's happening in the world, who aren't obsessed with making the next buck."

"Well, you have to think about making the next buck. Why do you think I went into real estate? How do you think you going to get this better life you're talking about? You have to make money so you can get ahead in life. Why can't you see that?"

I decided to just shut up. We finished our hamburgers in silence. Then as Jenifer nonchalantly bussed our dirty dishes away, it hit me. My mother's hopes for me were pinned on two things – getting a decent job, and marrying somebody better off. All she was trying to do was share the same map she had followed. She would never understand, I realized. Because where I wanted to go was off her map entirely.

As we got up to leave, a sudden fit of what could only be love overtook me. My heart actually ached – for her, for me, and for time passing and changing everything.

When we got into the Pontiac, I looked over at her. "Mom. Sorry I swore before. I know you love me and that you're trying to help me." She stared straight ahead as she started the car but I could see the unshed tears that had collected in the corner of her eye.

"I love you too, honey" she said suddenly, even though I hadn't been able to make myself say that I loved her.

I had a much shorter conversation about Kevin with my father. His cousin Lou Rinaldi had gotten him a job running the produce section at the Stop'n Shop. Most nights now, he'd return home with bags of overly ripe fruit and vegetables he'd rescued from their next stop, the store's garbage bins. "It's the beauty part of the job," he'd announce. "All of this, free for the taking. Can you believe it? During the Depression, my mother could have fed us for a week on what that store throws out."

One night, about a week after I'd broken up with Kevin, he was enthusiastically loading up the refrigerator with heads of wilted lettuce and vast quantities of bruised tomatoes. I knew for a fact that my mother would be throwing out those rotten tomatoes in a few days, but this rescue of food, giving it one last opportunity to be useful, made him very happy. It didn't take a shrink to see that he saw himself in those fruits and vegetables.

When I told my father I wasn't seeing Kevin anymore, he welcomed the news, thinking it meant I was finally changing my ways, "wising up" as he put it.

"I'll tell ya, you don't need that guy in your life. You ever meet his father, Andrew? Wait twenty years. That's what you'll be married to. You're better off, believe me."

It was strange. Sometimes my father said things to me that my mother never could. As he delivered this judgment in the cold air of our open refrigerator, I didn't say anything. Because it was, in a weird way, exactly what I'd been afraid of.

22

No Big Deal

Summer descended upon New England overnight. The old air conditioner in my room upstairs was in the process of breaking down – some days it worked, some days it didn't. So when it was too hot to hang out up there, I sat out on the porch steps after supper, where I could watch the neighborhood's lights blink on, one by one, and smoke a couple of cigarettes. I heard a kid's voice from a backyard a few houses over saying "No, I don't wanna," the voice of a mother, tired at this hour, insisting, "You have to," and the sounds of a husband and wife arguing further down the street. The neighborhood's normal evening soundtrack had kicked in.

Kevin and I had been broken up for a month. The resolution I'd made, to use the break up to quit smoking, had gone by the wayside. In fact, I was smoking more cigarettes now because they reminded me of him. But the more I smoked, the more I missed him. The night's humidity didn't help. It made me think of things. Like sex. I made myself feel the wanton throb in my pussy, take a breath and let it pass, Zen-like. As I tried to transcend, I noticed that I was grinding my left fist, the one that wasn't holding the cigarette, into my gut, making it hard to breathe. That's it, I thought. I crushed the cigarette into the cement's hard unforgiving surface and went back inside.

My mother was gone, already scooped up by Peg Benner, leaving my father to his usual amusements. Looking past the kitchen, into the living room, I could just see the top of his head over the edge of his chair. The TV was turned up loud. After coming home and filling up the refrigerator with fruit, mostly blackening bananas and some banged up nectarines, he was happily dozing. A day's worth of dishes were piled up in the sink. The little pastel-colored plates and bowls my sister used for Tabitha sat on the top of this mess.

"Jane?" I yelled over the canned drone of the TV. Usually Jane and Tabitha would be hanging out downstairs at this hour, either in the living room or the kitchen. My eyes darted around both rooms, looking for signs of them. Then I saw the baby.

Like some wayward explorer, Tabitha had crawled underneath a forest of pine legs, which was actually our dining room table and chairs. With a hand small enough to be a doll's, she was reaching up, grabbing a fistful of tablecloth. Before I could get to her, a tall green glass, part of a set my father got from a local gas station, slid off the table and shattered on the hard wood floor. The glass didn't hit Tabitha, but you wouldn't have known it by the way she screamed.

I snatched her up and sat down with her on the floor, avoiding the pieces of the broken glass around us. I held her tight, kissing the thin cap of dark hair that covered her little head, desperate to calm her down.

"What the hell was that?" The commotion had woken my father up. Since his chair faced the other way, he couldn't see what had happened,

"Nothing," I said. "A glass fell and it scared Tabitha. I'll clean it up in a minute."

"Why isn't someone watching her, for chrissake?" He burrowed back into his chair, putting his hand back where it was, cradling his head.

Tabitha's crying had wound down a little and she gasped for breaths between sobs. As I sat on the floor, those other smashed glasses the awful night in McNally's came back to me. I got real shaky. My god, I thought, what was I becoming, some deranged Vietnam vet, having flashbacks? But before I could get too into that particular analysis, I heard my sister coming down the steps. She must have heard Tabitha. Looking sweaty and reeking of pot, she joined us on the floor.

"What happened?" Jane and I talked in the low murmur we used when a parent was around, although I suspected my father had already nodded off again.

"She pulled on the tablecloth and the glass almost hit her. She's okay, but it totally freaked her out. Where were you?"

"I was upstairs, just grabbing a smoke."

"Jane, you can't leave her down here alone. She's crawling now."

"It was just for five minutes. Dad was here and you were out on the porch. I figured she was okay."

"You know how he falls asleep in his chair. You can't leave a kid her age alone, ever."

Jane gave me a stoned, vaguely pissed off look. "Will you fucking relax? She didn't even get hurt. One of dad's cheap glasses got broken. It's no big deal, Laura." She took Tabitha from my arms and got up. "Where did you put her bottle? She needs to go to sleep anyway."

Jane was right. It was hardly a big deal. Just one of the million things that happened to kids, when they started to crawl. They were always bumping their heads, hurting themselves. All part of them becoming toddlers. But this incident marked something and it wasn't Tabitha's newfound strength and mobility.

After six months or so of loving her kid and reveling in her new role as a mother, Jane was slipping. At first, I didn't want to see it but there were these small but real changes I couldn't ignore. She wasn't dressing Tabitha in the cute little outfits people had given her anymore, saying it was too hot to bother. In this heat, I could see her point, but that meant Tabitha often hung out for days in the same stained little tee shirt. She had begun to seem a little oblivious to Tabitha's comfort. She let her sit in a dirty diaper a little too long and sometimes skipped her bath for a day, sometimes two. And it seemed like I was always running out to Merinski's to buy Tabitha cereal and baby food, because Jane would forget to keep enough in the house. The food mill that I'd bought her, so she could make her own baby food, sat in the cupboard still in its box. It had gone the way of her vow not to give

Tabitha formula, just breast milk.

The truth was, Jane had never liked routine. Even as a kid, she'd gotten bored playing the same old games and the newness of having a baby was wearing off. I wasn't unsympathetic. The tedium of looking after a kid was major and it didn't make me want to go out and become a mother any time soon. But something in the way that my sister slung Tabitha over on her hip like some bag of groceries while she chatted away on the phone, something in the lack of attention to that smiling eager little face, broke my heart.

The other thing was, she was going out to the bars with Kimmy again. What had started as an occasional night out was rapidly becoming three or four a week. It wasn't that I minded so much when she'd hit me up to babysit. Since I'd broken up with Kevin, I was around most nights anyways. But when I'd hear her crawl in around two, drunk as a skunk, I'd be furious, knowing it meant she'd let Tabitha cry in the morning until me or my mother got up to feed her.

One morning, while Jane slept it off, my mother got up. Since I had to be at the coffee shop early, I got up too. At this point, Jane was still breastfeeding in the morning and sometimes at night. After changing her diaper, she wrapped Tabitha in a yellow blanket and pounded up the stairs to Jane's room. My mother's shoulders looked as square and tight as a military guy's. I followed, in case things got ugly.

When my mother marched into the room, Jane tried to ignore her by putting both pillows over her head. My mother handed me the baby, now screaming her head off, and wrestled the pillows away from Jane. Then she tore the covers off the bed and pulled the blinds up so hard they made a huge bang when they hit the top of the sash. Chunks of sunlight hit the messy room.

"Get up. Your baby's hungry. Your daughter needs you." My mother kept repeating those three sentences in a kind of monotone like some maniac, until Jane finally sat up and put Tabitha on her breast.

"Does she realize what the hell she's doing?" My mother asked me later that night.

"I don't think she does. She just wants to have some fun and go out. You know, get her old life back."

"But she's got a child now. She can't just forget about Tabitha when it suits her purposes. Your sister really had no business becoming a mother."

"Yeah, I know." I thought back to the conversation I'd had with Jane on the phone when I was still at UMass, which seemed like a lifetime ago.

What I knew for sure was that my mother had her own flashback thing going. My Grandma Kate, who'd believed she would become a fabulous singer, had often wandered off to sing in the taverns at night, leaving my mother, the oldest of eight, to take care of her younger siblings. An old sadness clung to her these days, impenetrable and powerful.

"Your sister's never been right. Not after what happened. She can't handle that baby on her own. And she never will." The lines that time had burrowed between her eyes, the ones that I'd noticed at Friendly's, seemed even deeper.

"Mom, I'm always going to help her, you know that."

When I heard myself saying this, another part of me started screaming "No No No" somewhere else in my brain. Protecting my sister had always been something I knew I'd have to do. But the original debt had tripled, like a bet unpaid with a bookie. There was my sister, there was Tabitha, and now there was my mother. She was counting on me, not just for now, but for the long haul.

I tried to talk to Jane again, on the porch, on another unbearable hot night. We lit cigarettes and I tried to pull on the old currency between us, the stuff where we were a team united against our parents.

"I know Ma gets crazy, like the other day when she dragged Tabitha up to your room, but you need to slow it down. You've got a kid now. You're going out all the time and it's starting to fuck things up"

As she lit what I realized was a joint, the sudden flash of her lighter gave a hard opaque animal sheen to her eyes that scared me a little.

"Just stop, okay? I'm not going to be some perfect mother. It's not in the cards, Laura. Can't you see that? Tabitha's just going have to cope with how I am."

"Don't you want things to be better for her?"

"Sure, and they will be. You're getting too serious about this stuff. Sometimes you're as bad as Ma."

She handed me the joint. "Let's just smoke this doobie, Laura. Tabitha will be fine, I'm telling you. It's no big deal."

23

The Great Divide

Gail had been incommunicado for several weeks so I was glad to finally hear from her.

"What's up?" I said into the phone, perkier than I really felt.

"A lot," she said. There was a long pause on the other end. "We're getting thrown out of the Leverett house." Even though Gail had quit UMass, she'd stayed on in Leverett, "building a community," as she put it.

"You're kidding." I grabbed the phone and sat on the floor with it. "How did that happen?"

"You remember Leon? That cool black dude from Chicago who was into the Rasta stuff? He ran off with all our rent money."

"What the fuck was he doing with all the rent money?"

"Well, about six months ago, he got hepped up on managing the house's money, you know, paying the gas bill, making sure the rent got paid, all that stuff. Because nobody was really into it. Dealing with money is so boring." I twisted the phone cord tightly around my index finger. Of course, Gail would think that. People who had money could afford to be bored by it. I would have pointed this out to her, but she sounded too awful.

"Some people in the house were against it, but Leon got all bent out of shape and said we were being racists, that we didn't trust him because he was black. I was the one who said maybe he was right, you know, that the culture's racism was unconsciously poisoning us and we weren't copping to it. So I talked everyone into letting him be the house manager. We found out today that he took all the money, but it wasn't just for this month. Nobody knew, but he was screwing the landlady and had jived her into letting him pay every four months. So he actually took off with a lot more. This woman's husband found out about everything and was so pissed you couldn't believe it. Now they're getting a divorce and he's throwing us out, since the rent hasn't been paid since April."

"That really sucks." I was sad and mad at the same time. Now the Leverett house was gone, a total disaster.

"Laura, I feel so ripped off and it's not just the money – who cares about the fucking money – but he just played us. Me in particular. We hung together. We trusted him. He was even teaching us about Rastafarianism and using pot as a sacrament. I don't understand how he could do what he did. How this could happen…"

I had the decency to shut up and just let her cry. I remembered Leon from years back, when he'd breeze into the dorm some evenings. With a gold front tooth, a wide grin that rarely left his face, and dreadlocks (the first I'd ever seen). He was a sometime musician who liked "the ladies" and liked his smoke. He'd been friendly but there had been this aggressiveness about him. When he chatted you up, he always made you feel like, white girl, you *better* be friendly back.

Leon never talked about where he came from, but you knew it had been from some urban horror show. It wasn't hard for me to imagine the stealing from his perspective. He'd seen a bunch of entitled white kids and figured, "Why not? So what if they had to go back and live in their parents' nice big houses?" He probably hadn't considered it anything more than a little equitable redistribution of wealth.

If I'd been living there, I would never have trusted him with the money and I wouldn't have let him con Gail with that unconscious racism shit. Gail was vulnerable to this sort of thing. For starters, she was an Aquarius and she had a schoolteacher mother who had raised her to feel sorry for the downtrodden. What she'd learned at home, whipped together with the hippie stuff, had created this kind of soufflé of sucker-ness she had about people sometimes.

"What are you going to do?" I asked.

"I'm going to move home for awhile, I guess."

Even though my memories from the equinox party were bad ones, the Leverett house had meant something to me. As long as Gail was there, some part of who we'd been at school, with our hippie dreams about changing everything, was still alive. The house's collapse also meant there were fewer places for me to go if I decided to leave Springfield.

"I feel so bad, escaping back to Newton and my bourgeois parents," she said, "like I'm sleeping with the enemy or something."

"I know how you feel," I said. "Do you think it's a lesser crime for me, since I sleep with the rank proletariat?" At least I got a small laugh out of her with that.

I had to work that night. As I put on my apron, I told Ari that I didn't think I'd be leaving town, at least not anytime soon. He accepted this information the same way he had the last time I'd talked about my plans. He peered over the top of his bifocals, giving me the old octopus once over.

"You do what you have to do, my girl. You are a good girl. You know what I think. But you always have job here, as long as you want."

The next day was Saturday. By nine o'clock, when I woke up, it was already getting hot. When we were kids, Jane and I wouldn't even bother getting dressed on a day like this. We'd have just put on our bathing suits and headed down to the pool. As I lay in bed, I got that feeling again, like I had in Friendly's weeks before, that my entire adult life was some sort of dream. The feeling started freaking me out a little, so I got up and pulled on a pair of cutoffs and a tank top and went downstairs.

My father was drinking a cup of coffee at the kitchen table. "Bout time you got up."

"Where is everybody?" I asked.

"Gone to Bradley's. Some big sale on kid stuff," he said. I was glad I had slept late and missed that particular junket. On a Saturday morning, the aisles would be teeming with babies strapped into shopping carts, screaming like caged monkeys pushed around by their wild-eyed zookeeper mothers. It should be required attendance for any girl thinking about getting knocked up. I was sure many would bail on the idea immediately.

It's going to be a scorcher out there," he announced. "You wanna cup of coffee?"

"No, it's too hot for coffee," I said. It was actually never too hot for me to drink coffee, but I wasn't in the mood to sit down and talk to my father. The ghost of the unreal feeling I'd woken up with was still there, making me feel fuzzy and weird. "I'm going out for a walk."

"In this heat? You're crazy." My father looked up at me over his newspaper. "Suit yourself. I got bananas in the refrigerator. Better eat'em up before they go bad."

"Okay."

I opened the refrigerator and stuffed one almost-black banana into the back pocket of my cutoffs. These days, I was discovering that it was just easier to cave about certain things my family asked of me.

I walked outside, into the heat. In the summertime, taking a solitary walk in the neighborhood wasn't easy to do. There were older neighbors on their porches who always wanted to talk to you and bunches of hyped up kids on their bikes, racing around and screaming at each other. It was high summer and the neighborhood was enjoying it. I wanted to be outside, but alone.

I started walking up Chestnut Street and headed for St. Thomas cemetery. Even from a distance, its green grass made the place look like an oasis. As I crossed King's Highway, I reminded myself that the grass got that way by feeding on the remains of the humans underneath it. Morbid, yes, but I didn't care. The sun was starting to climb in the sky. I could see the last of the workmen, who'd probably been there since dawn, getting ready to leave, their day's mowing finished. The cemetery would suit my purposes this morning; it would be quiet and deserted.

The oldest graves, with headstones dating back into the eighteenth century, greeted me. The names and dates on these graves were beginning to fade away entirely. Soon, certainly in the next few years, the headstones would be wiped clean by the elements and the names would pass from the world's knowledge. I moved on and so did time. There were graves from the nineteenth century, the Yankee names giving way to Irish ones as the century progressed.

As I reached the cemetery's midpoint, what must have felt like an invasion of the dearly departed began. Graves from the twentieth century appeared, closer together and many with longer Italian names crowded on to the headstones Things got a little hectic-looking here, with all the Sacred Heart of Jesus carvings and Mary Mother of God statuettes – along with all the (god forbid) plastic floral arrangements hanging around. I could imagine whispers from the more austere Yankee graves: "Very tacky. But they're Italians, what would you expect?" I smiled. Yes, these were my people. They had all rushed over here to the New World with their dreams and their exuberant Guinea emotions. Even grief got decorated. As much as I wanted out of Springfield, these people had seen opportunity here and desperately wanted to come. For them, it had been a place to dream a better dream.

I looked over and saw a fence in the distance, with iron bars and granite posts that marked a separation, a formal boundary between St. Thomas' cemetery and the Jewish cemetery next door. I hadn't known any Jews growing up in Springfield. But as a little kid, the nuns had explained to us about them. Besides the fact that they forsook Our Lord, the nuns told us that the graves in their cemeteries stood suspiciously close to one another because Jews buried their people the wrong way, standing up.

At UMass, the Jews there had found that story horrifically amusing. When I went away to school, I deliberately sought out Jewish friends, since my father had warned me away from them. What I discovered was a dueling affinity. They looked like long lost cousins – dark, usually curly-haired and just as dramatic. But there was a difference. Somehow, they were always more confident than I was, even the ones who hadn't grown up with money. Maybe it was something in the religion. For a while, it had made me wish I were Jewish.

Right before the newest section of the cemetery, where my mother's mother had been buried only a few years ago, I turned left and wandered back up towards King's Highway. I hadn't realized where I was heading until I got there. The bench grave of little Lisa Higgins, the one that Kevin and I had had sex underneath, was suddenly in front of me.

I sat down on the bench and lit a cigarette, remembering the romp Kevin and I had that day. But in the silent intense heat, it felt like it had happened a long time ago, instead of a few months back. Strange how it hadn't bothered me that day, that the woods behind this cemetery had been the place of my sister's rape. Or maybe not so strange. Lust was a drug. Now, sober and alone, I felt like a stranger to that self that had merrily fucked Kevin with my leotard on. I took the blackening banana out of my back pocket and put it on the ground so it could fulfill its destiny and rot in peace. I had been flirting with the idea of a life with him that day. Now I was flirting with nothing and nobody.

Sitting on that bench, with the headstones surrounding me, the sun felt too hot on my shoulders. The great divide was here, among the living and the dead, and I was the only one around on this side of life. As if to remind me, the blood flowed faster through my limbs, my heart, my brain.

I thought about Gail and the collapse of the Leverett house. No big surprise there, but it made me sad. We had all believed, not so long ago, that if we just lived together, not like our parents, in the cramped stupidity of nuclear families, but really lived together and shared everything – lovers, politics, natural foods – that things would work out. I stared at the graves of lives that had gone by. Maybe the cemetery was the place the hippie dream really belonged, I didn't know.

I put my cigarette out and looked down at my arm, the skin glistening a little in the sun. In high school, I'd spent a summer working as a nurse's aide. A patient with bad arthritis had grabbed me with her twisted claw-like hand. "What I wouldn't give for an arm like that!" she'd said. The flesh on my arms still looked firm and perfectly smooth, like it had that day. Still young. Somehow, after all this, I was still young. I still had time.

Once I thought I'd seen what time could actually look like. In junior high, my class had taken a trip to a textile mill and I'd seen vast rolls of uncut fabric, which had looked luxuriously inexhaustible, if you were to try and unroll all the fabric they held. Of course they weren't. As full as they looked, those rolls would run out, like rolls of cheap toilet paper did. So would my life someday. I felt it then – in that way you know something finally, irrevocably. By the fall, I would have to get my life going again. I would have to do something different, no matter what. The heat was suddenly more than I could stand. I got up from the bench grave and walked home.

As I approached the house, so did my mother, Jane and Tabitha, getting back from their trip to Bradlee's. They had taken my father's old station wagon. It was moving too fast, churning up the gravel in the driveway like a tank in a war movie. Something was going on in the car and it wasn't good.

I stopped at the foot of the driveway. Jane got out of the car, with Tabitha's small arms wrapped around her neck. Ten seconds later, my mother got out of the driver's side, slamming the door shut.

"You don't like what I do, you can go to hell," Jane said.

"Don't you dare talk to me like that! I'm still your mother."

"Well, I'm a mother too now. So I get to make my own rules."

"Why would you want to let that man in our car? Everybody knows he's strange. For chrissake Jane, he's been in and out of the state hospital."

"He needed a ride. Besides, he's not so bad. People never give him a chance. Don't see why you have to get so high and mighty and decide who we can give a ride to."

"But Tabitha was with us. What if he's in one of his moods and says strange things? Why would you ever want to take a chance and let Gordon Valeaux be in the same car with her?"

My sister didn't answer this question. The look on her face would have been impossible for most people to read, but not for me. She was making herself keep quiet about something, which was torture for Jane who liked to say whatever was on her mind. She turned and took the porch steps too fast, disappearing into the house with Tabitha who was wailing now, and clinging to her neck.

Jane's car door was still hanging open, looking like it would break off if it were opened one inch more. My mother walked around the car and gloomily slammed it shut. She acted like I'd been there all along.

"Laura, can you help me get the things out of the trunk? Apparently your sister isn't going to help."

Before I did, I stood there for a moment, looking into the dark of the screened porch where Jane had just been. I knew even though I didn't want to know, even though I could never prove it. Gordon the weirdo who Jane stuck up for when nobody else did. It would figure. Gordon was Tabitha's father.

24

Night Out

In the morning, the coffee shop always smelled the same – coffee left on the Bunn warmer too long and the gross but kind of comfy smell of grease coming off the grill. I put on my striped polyester smock, tied on my white work shoes and got to work setting up for breakfast.

Could this world, my known world, get any duller? I thought about Santa Fe and wondered whether Sonya Bernstein was there and how her new life in the desert was going. Then I thought about Kathmandu, because Gail always talked about going there. I realized I had absolutely no idea whether it was in Nepal or Tibet, which let me know how hopelessly unsophisticated I was. Maybe I should resign myself to a life in Springfield right now and get it over with.

I tried to make myself stop thinking about all this stuff as I got ready to open up. I even chanted "om" while I stacked plates under the counter, which I only did when I was totally desperate, but it didn't change anything. It was one going to be one of those days. Malvina was already grumbling to herself as she put out the ketchup and mustard squeeze bottles – never a good sign, especially early in the morning.

Ari was nowhere to be seen. True to his Mediterranean soul, he was a man who liked to take his time. Sometimes I appreciated this about him, that even on the busiest days, he'd chat with people who came into the coffee shop, no matter how feeble or crazy they were. He was probably engrossed in a conversation with somebody out back – with one of the delivery guys, or maybe Juan the cook who'd been having marital problems, who knew? Wherever Ari was, it was time to open up and I was totally annoyed.

I unlocked the front door and the Fairley's, an old couple who used to raise horses and still wore cowboy hats came in and sat down at the counter. I made myself be nice to them. As I poured them coffee, Ari appeared, all smiles, and got them laughing about something or other. The man could be Mr. Personality when he wanted to be. But it was not one of those days when I was in the mood to appreciate Ari, or anything else about the coffee shop.

So later, when Jane and Kimmy stopped in and wanted me to go out that night, I said yes when I usually said no. A night out with Kimmy and Jane didn't usually appeal to me, but the day had been so bleak, I figured anything would be some kind of improvement. Besides, I hadn't hung out with my sister and Kimmy for a long time. I'd been mad at Jane a lot the past few months and a truce might be in order. Whatever I was going to have to face with Jane in the future – about how she was behaving and my growing suspicions about who Tabitha's father was – I knew it wasn't going to help if we were at war with each other.

At the end of my shift, I went to the Ladies Room, took off my smock and white shoes and gazed at myself in the mirror. I looked like hell. I probably needed to get out and have a good time.

We went to hear a band at the Paramount, an old movie theater we used to go to when we were kids. When it went bankrupt a few years ago, some ex-radicals turned hippie entrepreneurs had bought it for next to nothing. After ripping out all the seats and the rest of the fixtures, they had started getting bands to play there.

Jamie and the Lame Boys, some band I'd never heard of, was playing as we walked in. It was a pretty good guess that the lead singer was Jamie – he of the long dark tresses, glitter leotard top, and skinny hips. Lately I'd noticed that male lead singers were getting far too pretty, even for my taste. We sat all the way up front, because Jane and Kimmy never felt like they got their money's worth unless they were sitting directly in front of the band.

Jane rummaged through the diapers in her backpack, got out a bottle of Southern Comfort and passed it to me. With Jamie and the Lame Boys playing, it was way too loud to even think about talking. I settled myself on the floor and took a very sturdy slug from the bottle. I handed the bottle back to my sister, wondering if she was remembering what I was remembering. We'd seen *Mary Poppins* here.

It had been an Easter Sunday. We were still small, because we were wearing white gloves and Easter hats, the kind with the rubber band strings that held the hats on our heads but left red marks under our chins. After the attack, we stopped dressing up for Easter. We even stopped going to church for a couple of years. Then when my mother had made us start going again – all that trudging off to St. Thomas' for Mass and celebrating the holidays stuff – it had seemed pathetic to me, a bad try at copying what had gone on before.

I lay all the way back on the carpeted floor of the Paramount, which was probably filthy but I didn't care. Just behind Jamie, I could still see the old movie screen, its Art Deco frame intact. I guessed nobody had figured out a way to get that down and sell it yet.

We'd been happy that day, me with a huge package of Raisinettes, Jane with her Junior Mints, as we watched Julie Andrews and Dick Van Dyke, who we'd seen on TV, romp around on that bigger screen. All dressed up in our Easter clothes we felt safe and sure of the world we inhabited, with that thing that the nuns droned on about in Catechism class – evil – no more than a distant buzz in our ears, from some bee out there who might, if you let him get too close, sting you. We had no way of knowing what was coming.

I could smell the pot smoke starting to circulate. Even though people weren't supposed to light up, everybody did once the night got going. Jane and Kimmy were passing a joint between them and they offered it to me, but I decided to stick to the Southern Comfort. When the old sadness found me, getting stoned was dicey.

Jamie and the Lame-os (a better name for these guys, I decided) were in the middle of their set when I saw him. Or should I say them. There were a lot of people there, but of course, I would spot Kevin with some girl, whose mane of straight black hair reached all the way down her back and brushed her ass. They were leaning up against a wall on the other side of the theater. Kevin's face was turned but I could see him in profile, talking to the girl with the hair. He looked jokey and happy. He even had his Happy Face tee shirt on, the one I'd never let him wear anywhere because it looked so totally stupid.

Since there were only so many places to go out in Springfield, I had known I would see him like this, eventually. But the inevitability of the event didn't make it any easier, now that it was happening.

Deciding not to say anything to Kimmy and Jane, I reached for the bottle again. If there ever was an occasion for me to drown my sorrows, this was it. After another few songs from the Lame-o boys, some very tall guy kneeled down beside me. He wasn't un-attractive; his long blond hair and beard reminded me vaguely of Gregg Allman or some other Southern rocker-type.

"Hey darlin' how 'bout sharing that?"

"Sure," I said. He sat down and I passed him the bottle. As Jamie and the Boys played on, we kept repeating this same exchange. He would say, "How about…" and I would have absolutely no idea what he said, but I'd shout back "Sure." Meanwhile, I watched Kevin and Pocahontas, or whatever her name was, talking and laughing. Visions of John with the chick from the dorm, all over again. But this time I had no one to blame for the situation but myself. Jamie and the boys finished up and were replaced by an all-girl folk rock trio called "Fancy This," who'd had some hit on the radio awhile back.

The guy who looked like Gregg Allman was actually named Gary. I got that much from him in the break between the bands. He was involved with promoting Jamie and the Lame Boys in some complicated way that I never quite followed and he had to go to Alba-ny with them the next day. Overall, he thought they sucked. We finished off the Southern Comfort, making the inevitable toasts to Jamie and the Boys' total lameness and our hopes for their demise as a musical entity.

When the music stopped, he said "Hey sweet thing, how bout hangin' out at the Sher-aton with me?" And I said what I'd been saying all night, "Sure." He took my arm and helped me off the carpet into a standing position. Where were Jane and Kimmy, I asked him, as if he'd been keeping track of things for me. He dramatically shrugged his shoul-ders and I laughed, amused at this gesture. The fact was, I was too drunk to care about my sister's whereabouts or anything else. Nonetheless, Jane appeared to pick up her stuff as people started leaving. She and Kimmy were moving on to McNally's. Did I want to come? No, I said.

Jane gave Gary/Gregg Allman guy the quick once over, noticing how I was staying upright by holding onto his arm. "You okay?" she asked.

"Yeah." Talking to Jane was giving me a strange flashbacky feeling, back to the night I'd met Kevin. "We're going to the Sheraton. I'll call you in the morning, okay?"

"Attagirl. Have a good time. See ya tomorrow, back at the ranch."

As we headed through the lobby and made our way outside, I actually saw Kevin standing alone on the street, like he was waiting for something. He looked over at the Gregg Allman guy then looked back at me. He didn't say anything and I didn't either. Be-ing drunk helped. There was this fuzziness around everything that made me think of those Impressionist pictures that were made with tiny dots, or maybe a TV set with no reception. Things formed and then they went back to being just dots. Kevin's eyes came to life for a moment and registered the weirdness we found ourselves in. Then the dots returned and the Pocahontas girl appeared and they went off. I stood there for a moment, not sure of what I wanted to do.

"Say darlin' what's going on? Whatcha doing?" Gary was ahead of me, walking towards his van, which was parked down the street. I turned away and caught up with him.

At the Sheraton, Gary turned on the TV and the dots appeared again, this time on the screen where they belonged. Since it was so late, most of the channels were off the air but I made him keep looking through the UHF channels until we found an old movie that was still on, *Intermezzo*, with Ingrid Bergman, my mother's favorite actress. She was passionately playing the piano as some older guy lasciviously looked over at her and played the violin. I was still pretty drunk. When I had trouble getting out of my jeans, Gary laid me back onto the bed and helped me get them off, one leg at a time. Then he got inside me, but it was sort of a non-event, sex-wise.

I was very tired and for a large man, he had an awfully small penis, which felt like an annoyance more than anything else. Ingrid seemed to be having a better time than I was; she passionately played on through the whole thing. While Gary was on top of me, I kept my eyes on Ingrid's surreally beautiful face and just waited for things to be over with.

I woke up very early the next morning and had that awful eye-opening moment, remembering exactly where I was and what I'd done. It felt much worse than the time I'd slept with Tommy Boy. The guilt from cheating I'd had then had acted like a buoy in the water. At least I was somewhere, holding onto something. Now I was adrift in some open sea of my own making. Why had I done this? I sat up in bed. Gary looked up at me and squinted warily.

"It's like 6 in the morning. What's goin' on, babe? Go back to sleep."

"No, I have to go."

"*Now?*"

"Yeah, I'm sorry. I have to call my sister and get home." Gary sighed, turned over heavily and pulled the blankets over legs so hairy and long they reminded me of a praying mantis.

"Hey, whatever you gotta do, Lorraine."

"It's Laura"

"Sorry. Laura. Just stay, darlin'. Relax. I don't have to get the Lame-o guys going until ten and I can drop you off, wherever you want."

"No, I have to go now. There's stuff I need to do at home."

"Okay, darlin.' You're the boss."

After I called Jane, Gary got out of bed long enough to write down his phone number in Boston on a piece of Sheraton stationery. He gave me a slobbery kiss at the door, which I endured because it seemed only polite, given the fact that I'd had sex with him the night before. On the way to the lobby, I threw the piece of paper into a cleaning lady's cart.

Jane had driven the old Ford station wagon to pick me up. I could see her elbow poking out of the driver's side window and Tabitha standing up in the back seat.

"Hey" Jane said, too brightly, when I got in.

"Hey yourself," I said. Jane looked over at me and lowered the Doobie Brothers tape she had going in the car's tape deck.

"Looks like somebody had too good a time last night."

"Yeah. Well. Thanks for coming but I don't want to talk about it yet, okay?"

"Sure," she said. We drove down Riverdale Road, passing our old high school. The Doobies played softly on and Tabitha made happy little kid sounds in the back seat.

I watched my sister's face as she drove. In the morning light, I could see the family resemblance. Her eyes were set into her head at exactly the same angle as mine and our mother's upturned Irish nose had made its way onto both of our faces. Because she was fat and I wasn't, it wasn't so obvious that we were sisters. But we were.

Sitting there in the car, with what Gary had left in me slowly leaking out and wetting my panties, it occurred to me that morning how easily my life could become like Jane's. I'd gone off the pill after Kevin and I had broken up. Nature could have its way with me like it had with Jane. The difference was, I could and would stop some freakish pregnancy if that's what happened. But I wouldn't be able to stop what too many more nights like the one I'd just had with Gary would do to me. What was left of the other person, the one Gail knew, who'd gone Sufi dancing and read Rimbaud in the original French (okay, one poem) would wash away completely.

Jane didn't say anything until we hit the driveway. Then the sister mind-reading thing we'd always had kicked in.

"All right. I know you're freaked out. Look, what did you expect, screwing that Duane Allman guy, true love?"

"*Gregg* Allman. Duane's dead."

"Whatever." Jane stopped the car and we both just sat there. This was not a conversation we were going to have in the house. "Ever since you and Kevin broke up, you're either totally pissed off about what I'm doing, or you're walking around like you're half dead. Then you finally go out and get laid, and you use it to start mind fucking yourself. If you love Kevin, go back to him. If you don't, get over it."

"It's not so easy, Jane." I was shouting and hearing myself was startling. "I don't know what I want. Don't you get that? Even someone like *you* should be able to get that…" I trailed off.

Jane looked at me intently. "You mean someone as *stupid* as me, don't you?"

"I didn't say that."

"Look, I know what you think about me, about everyone back here. Well, even a loser like me knows you shouldn't go picking up some guy when you know ahead of time it's not gonna be what you want."

Tabitha's patience for being in the back seat was running out. Or maybe our arguing had upset her. She started wailing so we got out of the car.

Jane silently gathered her up and went inside. I sat out on the porch for a long time and realized my sister was right. How she could be so right about what I did and live the life she lived was beyond me. Maybe, I thought, that's what being sisters came down to. I went inside to change my underwear and apologize.

25

The Other Half

On Sunday afternoons when I was eight years old, long before she became a real estate agent, my mother began to take Jane and me for drives through Longmeadow, Springfield's nicest suburb, so we could see "how the other half lived," as she put it.

In my family, that phrase, "the other half," might mean a variety of people who had more money than us. Sometimes my father said it meaning millionaires or Hollywood types, but for my mother it had come to mean the people who lived in Longmeadow, her Gold Standard of achievable affluence.

It was November, just before Thanksgiving. We'd been at it for hours, cruising street after street of the suburb as the afternoon slowly went dark. Jane was so bored she had spread out on the back seat and gone to sleep, but I was as excited as my mother. Like Peeping Toms, we began to catch glimpses of life through the windows of various Colonials, Expanded Ranches, and Tudors as the lights inside were being turned on.

We saw a living room with lemon yellow walls, white carpeting, and a man in a suit playing a grand piano. In another house, two children sat in front of a blazing fire in a flagstone fireplace in what must have been their family room, my mother said. Then, through the long vertical slice of a sliding glass door, we saw a woman who looked a little like Jackie Kennedy working in a marvelously modern kitchen. Its blue appliances, walnut cabinets and expanses of yellow ceramic countertops made me think of that magazine *House Beautiful*, which I got to look at whenever I went to the dentist's. My mother actually stopped the car in front of this house so we could get a better look. Now her face lit up as she took in this real-life dream kitchen. "Look at that, Laura. Isn't it *gorgeous*?"

I frowned, thinking of our own kitchen. Our stove and refrigerator were white and old-looking and there were no counter tops to do stuff on, just the swirled gray surface of our kitchen table. "Mommy, why can't we have a kitchen like that?"

"Because it costs too much money," she said, pulling her eyes away from the house. My mother moved the gearshift and we drove on, coming to the end of the street, which was called Windy Way.

Different strands of knowledge seemed to gather together in my head. "Mom, the people who live in that house. Are they millionaires?"

"No, honey. It's not like that." She explained that the people who lived in these houses might be rich, but there was no way of knowing if they were really millionaires.

I had another question. "So Mom, are we poor?"

My mother raised her chin. "No. We are *not* poor. Never let anybody tell you that." She was carefully maneuvering the car now, merging with traffic to get on Route 91, the fastest way back to Springfield. "What we are is *middle-class*," saying the term with an enthusiasm only someone who'd grown up destitute herself could muster.

It wasn't until I went off to UMass that I realized my mother's estimation of our social class was a bit off. By anybody's standards, we were actually "working class," or in the more Marxian terms I would get familiar with in college, we were the "proletariat" – uneducated workers, tethered by ignorance to a system that would exploit us.

I thought back to those Longmeadow houses, as I sat down to dinner at Gail's parents' house in Newton. Their house, a large three-storied Tudor, was actually grander than most of the homes my family would drive by and gawk at years before. Gail had been bugging me to visit but I'd never been there before.

But after the Gregg Allman-guy fiasco, it had seemed like a good idea to get away and come out for a weekend. I'd met Gail's parents, Robert and Betsey Caldwell, a few times before at our old dorm. Now, under a chandelier just big enough to be taken seriously, Betsey was serving dinner, placing a shiny wok of something that looked like a stew in the center of the table, which was set with simple but elegant white china. Underneath my slightly sweaty fingers, the ruby red damask tablecloth felt thick and luxurious.

Besides being drop-dead gorgeous, Betsey had that kind of charm-school poise that I was sure had come with her DNA. According to Gail, her mother was from old New England stock that had been rolling in money for a while. ("My mother's great *grand*parents were loaded," was how she usually put it, with just the right amount of contempt in her voice.)

"I wasn't sure if you ate meat, so I made a seafood paella. I hope you like it," Betsey said, carefully ladling whatever it was she had just said into our soup bowls. She had jeans and a peasant blouse on and her hair, long and blond like Gail's, was pulled back in a leather barrette-thing.

"We're all in for a treat. Betsey's seafood paella is legendary." Gail's father Robert had just arrived home a few minutes earlier. He took off his suit coat and sat down at the table and smiled at me.

"Yes, it really looks delicious." I gave him a somewhat fakey smile back, deciding not to sound like a hick and ask what paella was. I didn't think I could even say the word right.

"Come on, Dad. Mom made it, but it's Rosa's recipe." Gail rolled her eyes and filled me in. "Rosa's our cook. She's Portuguese. Tonight's her night off."

"No one's trying to take anything away from Rosa, Gail. Let's just declare it a joint creative effort of hers and your mother's."

Robert was a public interest lawyer with eyes the color of cool water and longish chestnut hair. Sitting there, with the sleeves of his white Oxford shirt jocularly rolled up, he had all the charisma of a Kennedy running for office. (Years later he would, in fact, get elected to the state legislature.)

"Indeed. I owe most of my cooking inspiration to Rosa." The ever-gracious Betsey laughed congenially and raised her glass. We followed her lead and did the same. "A toast to Rosa, please!"

I felt uncomfortable, suddenly, sitting at their table. After the toast, I put my napkin (red damask, like the tablecloth) in my lap. I knew it was damask because of my father's sister, my Aunt Doreen, who was into these things. I waited for everybody else to start eating and I made sure I didn't grasp my soupspoon too close to its business end, remembering how John used to complain about the way I held flatware.

Betsey and Robert were nice people so they made polite conversation, slow-pitching me their guest questions about Nixon, who'd finally resigned a few months before.

Did I think Nixon should be pardoned? (No, I said, knowing that they felt the same way.)

Was it fair, what had happened to John Dean? (He had to pay a price, I said, but I hoped that he didn't have to stay in prison too long.) Again, they made soft sounds of encouragement, urging me to expand on what felt like my rather puny opinions on the subject.

Finally, Gail got bored with her parents' niceties. "So they finally catch that bastard Nixon and drum him out of office and we're supposed to rejoice in how the system works in the end? Just shows you how the system is rotten to the core…"

Gail was off and running, intent on convincing us that the Socialist Workers Party (her latest infatuation) could save the world. It was a relief, in a way. At least I could stop pretending to be so intelligent and finally eat more of the fabulous paella and drink the expensive red wine her parents kept pouring.

After the second refill, as Gail and her father got into a lively debate about the future of communism, I slipped back into my own thoughts. I realized that this house didn't just make me think of those houses we used to drive by, in Longmeadow, it made me think of a medieval castle.

Certainly, this had something to do with its size and Tudor styling. But it was more than that. Ensconced within its domestic horn of plenty, you could begin to feel sure of things. By the time Betsey served the flan, I felt myself teeter then fall under its exhilarating influence. *Yes*, I belonged in this hip Norman Rockwell scene – where culture and conversation came as naturally as breathing, where status and success in the world would surely follow…. *This* was more like it.

Later on, Gail and I went into Cambridge, to a dive she knew about near Central Square. Some reggae band was playing. In the packed bar, we danced in each other's arms, aping the hetero couples around us. We liked to do stuff like this sometimes, making people wonder if we were lesbians. Lost in that hypnotic sexy music, I felt safe and outrageous at the same time, like the world might actually be my oyster. When we finally sat down at the bar for a break, Gail kept her arm around me.

"Have you ever wondered why we've never slept together, just to say we did it?" she asked. We were drinking rum now, getting silly and stupid.

"Why, do you wanna?" I yelled over the bar's din.

"NO! Do you?"

"My god, no. Things get fucked up enough just doing it with men, like with that promoter guy last weekend. It was so awful. I don't think I told you – he had small penis syndrome, and you know I'm a size queen…"

"Girl, you were so gypped!" Gail laughed, shaking her blond mane and looking so beautiful that for a second, I could imagine sleeping with her. Then I saw a gleam come into her eye and I knew what that meant. She was about to share her latest greatest profound insight.

"Laura, remember how we used to think you should be able to sleep with anybody, anytime, and get off on it? This Native American healer I heard talk last week said that when you have sex with a guy, the stuff in his aura clings to you for months afterwards, sort of like the lint you find, in a dryer filter. Sleeping around can really fuck you up."

"Are you serious?"

"Well, he sees this stuff in peoples' auras. He should know!"

I looked at her through the bar's smoke screen. If I ever did really want to go lesbo with Gail, I knew this trait of hers, of madly embracing whatever the last philosophical approach to life she heard, would drive me crazy. Even as her best friend, it was hard to take. Now she was retreating from one of the tenets of the sexual revolution we had vowed eternal allegiance to. But I let it go. We were having a good time and I didn't want to get into some big debate.

"Your parents are still pretty into each other," I said, changing the subject.

"Yeah, they are."

"I liked hanging out with them tonight," I said, feeling a little shy admitting to the feeling.

"For parents, they have their shit together. You know, they donate a lot of money to good causes and they're pretty radical in some ways. My father is part of this big class action suit that's going to integrate South Boston. You wouldn't believe how racist the Irish are over there."

"Yeah I would. What do you think my neighborhood is like? It's full of racists; they're just not all Irish."

"Yeah, but *you're* not. You're a changeling. You forget that sometimes. You should come and stay at the house more. Being back here is turning out better than I thought. Really. We're not fighting so much and my parents like having my friends around. They see it as part of nurturing the future of the planet and all that."

Not too much later, we called it a night. In an upstairs room down the hall from Gail's, I crawled under sheets that felt ironed and smelled slightly of lavender. I fell into a deep sleep, not needing to dream of anything on this side of the castle's tender walls.

The next day, I had to get back early so I could work at the coffee shop that afternoon. Ever the perfect hosts, Betsey and Robert got up to have coffee and croissants with Gail and me.

What would it be like, I thought, as we sat in the sunlight of their perfectly decorated eat-in kitchen, to have a house, never mind a family, like this one? Then like somebody was sticking pins in a voodoo doll of me back in Springfield, I felt treacherously disloyal. The memory of my mother in the car that day in Longmeadow, her chin pathetically raised up. *We're not poor. Don't ever let anybody ever tell you that.*

We finished our coffee and I said my goodbyes. When I got back into the Pontiac, I was aware of how crummy it looked in the Caldwell's circular driveway. I drove back through town to get to the Mass. Pike, watching Newton's beautiful homes grow smaller in my rearview mirror.

Traitor or not, it was time for me to return to the other half, the half that sat on the bottom, where, no matter what happened, I would always come from.

26

On Monday

"Hi," he said. "I thought you still worked here." It was the day after I got back from Gail's and Kevin was standing right in front of me, in the coffee shop. My brain froze. Then the coldness from the glasses I had in my hands seemed to give me back my powers of speech. "Yeah. So how's it going?" I finally said. Then I started blabbing, talking about any kind of bullshit that came into my mind, because I didn't know what else to do.

"Laura," he said, finally interrupting me. "You know, it's okay. I just stopped by. You look kind of busy and I..."

"No," I almost shouted it. No way did I want him to leave, now that he had appeared like this, out of nothing. "I'm not. I'm not busy at all. I just have to bring these to a table in the back. Don't go, okay?" I rushed away to deliver the Cokes, my heart thumbing a mile a minute, just as Ari reappeared. In the few hours he'd been away from the Athena, he'd gotten himself a haircut and had put on a new loose white shirt, the kind older Latin men wore so they could look neat without tucking in a shirt. It made me suspect that Ari, widowed for years, was dating somebody.

"Hello young man," he said to Kevin, taking his place behind the cash register. Ari was bad with names, but I was sure he knew that this was the guy who'd been my boyfriend.

"Hello, sir," Kevin said.

"Well, you come to my coffee shop you must sit down, my friend."

Looking like an actor who'd been waiting for a cue, Kevin finally took a seat at the counter. Feeling awkward and really stupid, I walked past him and took my place behind the counter. That was my role in this play today, I told myself. I talked myself down. *Okay, you're a waitress, so ask him what he wants.*

"So you want coffee, a piece of pie or something?" I said.

"Yeah."

"Which?"

"Both," he said, looking at me like he was making the biggest decision of his life.

Slowly and carefully, I wrote "cof" and "p" down on the order pad. As he watched me, he lit a cigarette. The slightly grimy fingers I knew so well flexed to hold the lucky cigarette. I saw him again the way I had that first time in McNally's, the way any woman would see him, at least all the ones I knew. He was beautiful. Who wouldn't give it up to have that face smiling in her direction, to keep that body on the other side of the mattress? But none of this meant that I wasn't still afraid of him becoming the tricky slippery prelude to a life in Springfield I didn't want.

What would happen, I asked myself again, when the body and the beauty bloated and came apart some year not so far away from this one? Would he end up being just another pot-bellied guy in a dead end job who drank and watched too much TV? And where would I be? Going crazy in some lousy two-family with a bunch of kids? The questions whipped around in my brain like they always did. But suddenly they stopped.

"What a bunch of crap," I thought instead, as I stood there in my stained apron looking at him. In the now of that moment, I only knew that he was beautifully irrevocably uniquely himself and that I missed him.

I didn't ask him what kind of pie he wanted. Instead, I opened the case and pulled out the cherry pie because I knew that was the kind of pie he liked best. I heated it up in the new microwave oven Ari had just bought and put a lot of whipped cream on top, because I knew that this too was what he liked. I brought it over to him along with the cup of coffee I poured from the freshest pot. I placed the coffee and the piece of pie in that precise sweet spot of the counter that was in front of him.

"Thanks," he said.

"You're welcome," I said, really meaning it.

"I saw you that night at the Jamie and the Lame Boys show."

"Yeah, I saw you too." I hesitated and then decided just to go for it. "I'm sorry, you know, about everything that happened."

"Me too." His face was still unfathomable. Then his lips parted again, just enough to let these words pass through them. "I want to see you again, Laura."

I had to tell myself to breathe. "Tonight, after I get out of here, let's get together. We'll talk, okay? Kevin, I…"

"Look, I can't tonight. I'm on my way to see my mom. She's up the street, at Mercy Hospital."

"What happened?" I asked. There was always something happening with Kevin's family, it seemed.

"Some female thing. She had to have a hysterectomy and my dad's gone, like usual. I have to go back to the house and take care of the little kids. You working tomorrow?"

"Yeah, the morning shift."

"When are you done?"

"Around three."

"I'll come by after work and pick you up, okay?"

"Okay," I said, wondering how I was going to make it through the rest of the shift, never mind the rest of my life, without him.

He wolfed down the rest of his pie and got up to leave. Then he looked at me one more time, over his shoulder, as he left the coffee shop.

"See ya at three," he said, taking his beautiful blue-jeaned ass out of the coffee shop.

27

Push Comes to Shove

"So these Ricans got thrown out of McNally's last night." Kimmy was talking loud enough so that everybody in the Athena could hear her. It was the Tuesday after my weekend in Newton and the day after Kevin had showed up. He was supposed to pick me up at the end of my shift and, as far as I was concerned, this day couldn't go fast enough. I hadn't really been in the mood to see Kimmy and my sister, but they'd just strolled in with Tabitha.

Kimmy plunked herself down in one of the booths near the windows. "This one guy is way smashed and he and his chick start dancing around, like the Ricans always like to do. Well, the thing is, this chick's got no underwear on. You can see everything she owns, every time she twirls around. Some dude from Chicopee, he asks the Rican guy if his chick's pussy is so hot she has to take her panties off. So they get into it. Finally Mick just throws them all out."

The coffee shop was mostly empty but I could hear the story as clear as day across the room as I waited on old Mr. Walters, who was ordering a hot turkey sandwich, like usual. Luckily, in his case, the tale was falling on mostly deaf ears.

"The dude should of kept his mouth shut." Jane said, as she strapped Tabitha into a booster seat. You could always count on my sister to weigh in on these sorts of things. "If you ask me, Mick wrecked a good time. If that Rican chick wants to come over here and let all the guys in Springfield see her pussy, that's her business."

"You don't get it," Kimmy said, somewhat miffed. "These Ricans are always coming over here and doing weird shit. They should just stay over in the South End where they belong."

I looked across the room at them and thought of Robert and Betsey, just for contrast. The Caldwells would never understand how different people turned out, if they never went to college. Sure, Jane and Kimmy looked like hippie chicks, but they had prejudices that ranked right up there with my parents' generation. I made my way over to their booth. "Hey, can you guys keep it down? Everybody in the world doesn't need to hear that story."

"God, Laura. Sometimes you are way too uptight. We're just talking," Jane said.

The booth, I noticed, stank slightly of some kind of booze. They'd already had a few, for sure. "Yeah well, just lower the volume a little, okay? You guys want burgers and fries? I'll bring some milk for Tabitha."

I went back behind the counter to get their drinks. If Betsey and Robert had been flies on the coffee shop wall, they would have shipped Kimmy and my sister off to some consciousness-raising program. In fact, they could have shipped off most of the people I knew in Springfield for the same reason. I was lost in these thoughts, pondering the cultural divide among the white people in my own state that nobody ever wanted to think about, when I heard a loud crash out front, near the entrance.

At first I thought that one of the heavy poles that Ari used to rope off the foyer when we were closed had just fallen over, which happened sometimes. Then I saw one of the Gang of Three guys, the one that always wore the red bandana, just standing there. Right next to him was Timmy Morton. By the look on his face, I knew it was Timmy who had pushed the pole over.

Ari looked up, the old grey eyes rising evenly over the bifocals, noting the sudden squall on his calm home sea, otherwise known as the Athena. I don't know if he'd seen Timmy do it, or if he just knew he had. "Young man…" Ari started to say.

Bandana Man and Timmy registered Ari's attention with identical sneers. "Ah, sorry about the pole," Timmy said, interrupting him. With a voice malevolent under a thin veneer of fakey politeness, he sounded like a psycho Eddie Haskell. "We thought you were closed or something. You know, you shouldn't leave that pole out there. Somebody might get hurt."

Then they sauntered in, stepping over the pole like it was a body in a battle they'd already won. There were only a handful of people in the coffee shop, but they all turned to watch Timmy and Bandana man, sensing an ominous change in the air. I looked across the room and saw my sister's face, red with a kind of ferocity, and Kimmy's, which had gone a dead white. Tabitha was happily playing with a saltshaker, sprinkling salt all over the table.

"You two, you are not allowed in my shop. You, the boy with the red kerchief, you and your friends steal from me. You are not human beings, the way you act." Ari was pointing at them, his short stubby fingers making chops in the air, like miniature karate moves.

"Shut up, you stupid old Greek," Bandana Man answered, turning around as he and Timmy walked into the center of the coffee shop. "We go where we want. Anyways, this ain't your country."

Sometimes when I go back to that day and play things back in my mind, they come into the shop like they did, acting like assholes. They knock down the pole and say the stupid things they say. Ari yells at them. Almost nostalgically, I see them like the more ordinary delinquents they might have been. They make some noise; they get everybody riled up. Then they get bored. They leave. But that's not what happened.

Timmy spotted my sister sitting over in the booth. He and Bandana Man started moving over towards her, as if drawn by some irresistible force. The smirk on Timmy's face totally disappeared as he approached the booth. In that first look he gave my sister, there was no antagonism, no violence. She could have been a long lost friend or a relative he hadn't seen in a while.

"Say, good to see ya. Been awhile," he said to Jane, in some weird halftone between who he actually was and some friendly neighbor he might have been in a different life.

I didn't want to understand but I did. There was naked need that passed through the void of blue in his eyes, like someone falling out of a plane. The thing itself was recognizable, even ordinary. He wanted to be noticed and loved, like everybody else. But he knew he never would be. Without hope, the need gained momentum and lost control. In free fall, it let him do whatever he wanted to do.

"Yeah." Jane's eyes were strangely alive, gleaming like the holes of a lit up jack o'lantern. "We used to know each other. But that was before you switched from girls to boys, like that little spic you're with. Whadya do? Go to P-town and get all homo? Man, you are the *loneliest* fuck I ever met."

Years later I would wonder whether it was courage or recklessness that made her say this. But violence is a very intimate interaction, a sickness trying to fix itself. As his victim, Jane knew things about Timmy. She'd paid a terrible price for it but she knew.

Timmy seemed stunned for a moment. She had struck back at him, called him a homo. But almost worst, she'd called him a lonely fuck.

It was actually Bandana Man who lunged towards her, screaming. "Fuck you, you fat bitch! We're not fags, you dumb twat!"

Even in that moment, I knew what my sister said wasn't true, that Timmy and Bandana Man weren't what we called "homo" back then. It didn't matter, really. Since the attack against my sister, Timmy had been labeled as a pervert, an outsider, a creep. Now my sister, an outsider herself, was taunting him with it.

Ari had already moved out from behind the cash register. Now he came rushing over to the booth, the ends of his white Latin shirt flapping.

"You both go out now, or I call the police. Out now! Out!" Recovering from the little funk Jane's words had put him in, Timmy turned and moved back towards the center of the shop, where he intercepted Ari and hit him hard enough to knock him over.

My terror began to take on this trippy quality, making things slow down and seem less solid, less real, like they did when I was really high. Two ancient Jehovah's Witnesses dressed in baggy suits who'd been sitting near Jane and Kimmy stumbled out of their booth and were approaching Ari, who lay sprawled in the middle of the floor.

"Call the police right now!" I screamed at one of them. As one of the Jehovah guys kneeled next to Ari, he looked over at me like I was speaking in a foreign language. Did the Jehovahs have something against the police? Or was it just doctors, I thought frantically. No, that was the Christian Scientists. "Never mind, you fucking assholes," I screamed, suddenly more angry than terrified. "I'll do it myself!"

I raced around, desperate to escape the confinement of the counter and get to the phone behind the cash register to call for help, but I never took my eyes off Timmy. The police would ask me later if he had actually touched my sister, or Kimmy or Tabitha. In fact, they would ask me what happened over and over again. What I remember is this.

After Timmy hit Ari, Bandana Man took off and ran out of the coffee shop, probably assuming more trouble than he bargained for was coming. But Timmy got strangely calm. He left the center of the floor, once again moving towards Jane and Kimmy's booth. Then he stood in front of it, giving them his Eddie Haskell smile, seemingly oblivious to everything else.

"Say, this must be your daughter, huh? She's a real cutie, isn't she?" My sister stared as he bent down into the booth to be closer to Tabitha, lightly touched the very top of her head. "Don't worry," he said to her. "I still like little girls."

The jack o' lantern smile never left Jane's face. She leaned back against the red leatherette booth as her arm reached deep into the diaper bag. When it emerged out of the diapers and baby wipes, there was a knife in it.

Why? People would ask me that a lot, afterwards. *Why in God's name was she carrying a knife in the diaper bag?* I would shake my head to let them know I didn't know why my sister did certain things. But this is what I do know. Jane never forgot. Nobody had ever let her forget how she had been changed. The world could and would do anything to you. It was what my sister knew in every cell of her being. And in some cellular sisterly way, I knew it too.

"Jane," I screamed at the last moment, whether it was to stop her or to tell her to be careful, I'm not sure. Kimmy was screaming, too. She'd covered Tabitha's small face with her hands so she wouldn't see what was coming. Because Kimmy knew what I knew. That Jane wouldn't stop, that she would indeed do it.

When he saw the knife, Timmy stepped back, but it wasn't fast enough to stop my sister.

"Yeah, good to see you too. *Been way too long*," Jane said, as she buried the knife in Timmy's chest.

28

Fade Away

The blackness came next. One second I was standing up, trying to get to the front of the coffee shop and call the police, the next second I was going down. I hadn't fainted since I was a kid, on that day when Mrs. Merinski told me Jane had gotten hurt. Now Jane had hurt somebody, maybe even killed him and I was making the same trip into the dark.

My senses began to peter out, like the sonar in a sinking submarine. I remembered how things had been the other time. The linoleum of our old kitchen floor, rising up like a big green sea, ready to swallow me. Mrs. Merinski sucked to the end of an expanding black tunnel, mouthing words I couldn't hear. This time the sandy-colored tiles of the coffee shop floor ran together, becoming the million grains of sand it takes to make up a beach. All the noise in the Athena became one thunderous tide crashing. Then that shore seemed to glow, all lit up, right before it went dark and I hit the floor.

In this dark, everything was calm. It let things be just what they were going to be. Jane's words echoed in my brain. Been way too long, she'd said. Maybe it had been too long for a lot of things. Maybe it was time to let them all go, I thought idly, before everything dissolved into nothing.

When I woke up, somebody who looked like Paulie Garabini, a kid I'd gone to elementary school with, was standing over me. When we'd played games back then, like Motor Boat or Ring Around the Rosy, I never wanted to hold his hand, because he had this habit of picking his nose and eating it. What was he doing, all grown up and dressed like a Springfield cop?

The scratchy chatter coming out of the radio on his belt, right next to his gun, brought me back to the present. A cop. Paulie Garabini actually was a Springfield cop and I was lying on the coffee shop floor because Jane had just stabbed Timmy Morton. The information leapt through my body, like that first jolt people must feel from the electric chair. I totally freaked. I tried to sit up, but things began to go black again. Then Paulie was kneeling next to me, talking to me like he'd seen me at recess the day before. "Hey Laura, take it easy."

I lay back on the floor. "Paulie Garabini," I said, looking up at his face.

"It's Paul these days," he said. "You got a big bump on your head. You need to relax and slow down, girl."

"How long have I been out?"

"Not so long. A few minutes."

"Where's my sister? What are they doing to my sister?"

"She's over there, talking to the officers," he said.

I looked across the coffee shop. A man without a uniform on, who must have been a detective, was asking Jane questions and Jane, with Tabitha on her lap, was grudgingly answering them. It made me think of how she'd been when she'd gotten out of the hospital all those years ago. There had been the same blank expression, the same emptiness in her eyes.

"I'm gonna throw up," I said to Paulie. And I did a little.

Paulie got me water from behind the counter. "Drink this," he said.

I had to hold the glass of water he gave me with both hands, because I was shaking all over. Even in that state, I couldn't help wondering if he still had that nasty habit of his.

"Your sister and her friend and the little girl are okay, you know. Even that asshole over there will be okay," he said, pointing to where Timmy Morton lay on the floor. Then his radio crackled again. I couldn't understand what the scratchy disembodied voice said, but Paulie translated. A patrol car had just picked up Miguel Santiago, who I knew as Bandana Man, over in Holyoke.

I noticed Ari then, who was up and about now, talking to the EMT guys and the cops, reclaiming his domain. The front of his white shirt had a large crescent-shaped smear of dirt on it and he held a towel to his forehead. Beyond that, he didn't look too bad, which was mildly reassuring to see. But as I watched the EMT guys getting ready to move Timmy Morton onto a stretcher, I started to panic. There were blood streaks on the floor next to him and he looked very pale and wasn't moving. Maybe Paul Garabini was lying. Maybe he was dead. And that would mean my sister had committed murder and would be locked up forever. She would be lost to the dark side. It was the thing I was never supposed to let happen, not ever again.

I closed my eyes, still hoping what I'd just seen was a nightmare, but knowing it wasn't. Then suddenly Kevin was there. I actually felt his presence before I opened my eyes. Yes, he was supposed to come and pick me up today. We were going to talk about getting back together. Now he was standing over me, talking to Paulie. "Is she hurt? What the hell happened? I saw the ambulance outside…"

I noticed he had his Happy Face tee shirt on, the one that I thought was so stupid. "I'm okay," I said. "But Jane just killed Timmy Morton."

Kevin didn't try to reason with me; he knew I was beyond that. "Babe, I'm so sorry this is happening." He sat down next to me on the floor and took me in his arms.

I started crying and then, as if from a great distance, I saw myself hitting him, my fists no more effective than a baby's as they beat against his chest. "Why weren't you here? You should have stopped him!" It made no sense but I was blaming him. He held me tight and didn't try to stop me or shut me up. "Where the fuck *were* you?" I kept yelling and I couldn't stop.

29

Losing It

It was touch and go for a while, but the scumbag Timmy survived the stabbing. As it turned out, my sister had missed his heart by half an inch. Mostly because of Paulie Garabini who knew what had happened to Jane, the cops let my sister go as long as she agreed not to leave town.

Kevin didn't leave my side when I had to go to the hospital. They said I had a slight concussion but, because I was so hysterical, the doctors let him take me home that evening. It was Tabitha's face, pressed against the screen door, and her small voice saying "Auntie Laura!" that finally made me stop crying and freaking out when I got home. I didn't want to scare her. I figured her small psyche had been through enough.

Ari opened up the Athena the very next day with a small white bandage planted on his forehead, taking his post by the cash register as if nothing had happened. When I stopped in to pick up a few things I'd left behind in the craziness of the previous afternoon, I asked him why he didn't just take time off and close the shop. He shrugged off my suggestion.

"What use? This shop, these customers, they my life. Do no good to close. I sit home, think too much." He paused, as if giving the matter his deepest concentration. "Besides, I lose money."

Kevin called me the day after, acting like my boyfriend again. It was what I'd wanted, what had seemed like a dream about to come true, the day before in the coffee shop. But when he talked about coming over, a massive knot formed in my stomach. *It's not safe,* some part of me whispered. I didn't know why I was being so weird but the idea of seeing him freaked me out.

"Let's wait a few days," I said to him over the phone. "It's kind of crazy around here."

"Sure," he said, sounding a little hurt.

I went back to work five days after the attack. It was time, I told myself. Since it was Sunday, the Polish ladies came in for pie and coffee after church. They quickly got busy making up for whatever seriousness they'd had to endure at St. Stanislaw's by cracking bawdy jokes in Polish. (I didn't understand a word, but you could get the gist by the way they gestured to various body parts and laughed.)

Usually the old ladies made me laugh too. There had always been something reassuring about their appearance at the Athena. But again, something in me whispered, clenched my stomach up into a knot. Now all I could think of was how they were old and they'd die soon. In fact, the same clothes that they wore now, their Sunday best, would probably be the clothes they'd be buried in. The more I tried not to think about this, the more I did.

It wasn't just the Polish ladies. Everything around me began to seem unbearably fragile. The cups, the counter, Juan as he cooked behind the grill. And my own tiny smear of self, as substantial as a fingerprint on a piece of glass.

I poured their coffees and tried to smile. They were nice old ladies and I knew I was being totally creepy. *Okay*, I told myself. *You have weird shit in your head. It's natural after what happened.* As I often did when I was working at the Athena, I thought of an imaginary hamster wheel and willed myself to stay moving on it.

Since the ladies all wanted Boston cream pie, I got a new pie out of the cooler. As I pushed the knife through the pie's layers – spongy cake, thick yellow custard and the heavy ledge of chocolate frosting – I started shaking. I kept seeing Jane putting the knife into Timmy, the way it hadn't gone in neatly, like stabbings happened in the movies. Instead, it'd had to make its way through Timmy's real flesh and tissue – the human meat of him. He'd been screaming. In my head, I saw and heard it again, that sound and the look on my sister's face as she forced the knife into him.

It felt like a bad acid flashback. I ran into the Ladies Room out front. There was a stool small enough for a twelve year old under the sink. I sat down on it and sobbed. When I looked up, I saw Malvina. I hadn't realized it, but she'd followed me in.

"I think I'm losing it," I said to her, without turning around.

"Well, you'll get it back again, white girl," she said, using her most affectionate nickname for me. Malvina went over to the nearest stall and came back with a wad of toilet paper and handed it to me.

"The Polish ladies. I was getting the pie and I left it on the counter…"

"Don't worry 'bout that. They all got their pie." Malvina pulled up a broken kitchen step stool from the far corner of the room. The cracked red vinyl squeaked rudely as she sat down next to me.

"Can't say as I blame ya, being upset. Shoulda been me working that day. Those motherfuckers, they done a job on you. Gonna need some time to settle."

They done a job on you. Her words made me cry more.

"Girl, you not the Lone Ranger, you know. Everybody lose it sometime. You still young, you gotta learn how to come back."

She looked at me fiercely then, like she was making some kind of appraisal. Then she did something very un-Malvina like. She reached over and gripped my arm, strong and hard, with her right hand, the one she used to clobber women with in the ring. Malvina had never touched me before and her hand felt rough and tender at the same time.

Like a transfusion, something came into me, ignoring the barriers of our separate selves. I didn't know a lot about Malvina besides the basics, that she was a black lesbian who lived alone and that she'd been a lady wrestler. I had wondered, sometimes, how she had managed to survive a world that always saw her as some kind of freak show. We just sat there for a minute or two. Neither one of us said anything or acknowledged her hand on my arm. I stopped crying.

"I'll tell ya what," she said, finally. "You go home now, girl. I be here 'til Anita comes in. I don't mind." What she had given to me started ebbing away as she released my arm. Even then, I understood and I wouldn't forget. *I would have to find my own strength.*

I went home.

After Jane stabbed Timmy, this picture kept coming to me. I didn't know where it came from. A child who could have been Tabitha comes along and blows on a dandelion, not a yellow one in full bloom, but one that's already gone to seed. The dandelion explodes. Just a fluffy shell of what it had been, its seeds fly away. For better or for worse, the seeds have to find their own crazy way now. The little girl drops the stem and moves on.

It was what I thought was happening to my family. After the attack, we began moving away from each other again. My father started going out at night, something he hadn't done in years. After his shifts at the grocery store, he liked to hang out with a bunch of crazed Vietnam vets who practically lived at the VFW. He still brought an endless supply of damaged fruit into the house but he didn't seem to care, one way or the other, if anyone ate it.

My mother was once again all business, all the time. She and Peg Brenner opened up a new office together in the center of town. They went to the trouble of getting it professionally decorated and having a slick new sign made to hang out front. Brenner and DiStefano Realty, it announced in bold black letters, with pink slanty lettering underneath that said, "A Woman's Place Is In the Home."

Strangely, my sister didn't show much emotion about what had happened that day in the coffee shop. Even though she faced an assault with a deadly weapon charge, she seemed indifferent about having to go to court or the event itself.

"Too bad I missed," was all she would say, whenever the subject of the stabbing came up.

When I tried to get her to talk more about it, drawing her out over a joint in our sanctuary, the upstairs bedroom, she looked at me blankly and said, "Don't go there, Laura. I don't want to talk about it"

"Well, what if *I* want to talk about it?"

"Well, then that's your fuckin' problem." She took another long draw on the joint.

"What about the charges? You could go to jail…"

"It'll never happen. I'll plead out. Gordon told me what to tell 'em. I'll end with probation and have to talk to some shrink. Nothing I can't handle." As she sucked hard again on the joint, her eyes became black knobs to a drawer that no longer opened to me.

Gordon Valeaux, ex-mental patient and Tabitha's father, probably. Now he was the one she talked to.

In the weeks after the attack, Jane started going out with Kimmy every night. I became Tabitha's permanent babysitter. But I didn't mind. I knew I was hiding behind a toddler, but I didn't want to see anybody, especially Kevin.

I used to picture the everyday me like the insides of an old-fashioned watch, all springs and levers and little wheeled cogs. A little hammer hit some thingamajig, which tripped off some other contraption and kept me moving. Now something had gone terribly wrong.

The truth was, I was turning into some kind of psycho, and I didn't want anybody to know. There were bouts of shaking and a kind of paralyzing fear that seemed to be waiting for me, even when I tried to do simple things, like go to Merinski's or just walk down

Chestnut Street. I didn't even try to explain this to Ari when I had to call him and tell him I couldn't work. Instead, I chalked it up to family stuff.

"That okay, my girl." As usual, Ari was the perfect gentleman. "It is I who is sorry for terrible thing that happen in my shop. This country full of crazy people. Not like Paros. Not ever. You take care of your sister and the baby. I kiss you on both cheeks. You come back anytime."

"I will, Ari," My eyes filled with tears. "As soon as things are a little better, I'll come back." I hung up the phone.

But I never would go back to work at the Athena. I was down for the count now, afflicted. Being home was no longer a choice. While everyone else in my family was scattering, I was becoming a prisoner, under house arrest, held fast by the strange shiftings of my nerves.

Gail was the only person in the world I wanted to talk to about any of this. I finally reached her on the day she was leaving for India for a three-month yoga retreat. When I told her I was completely losing it, she made a quickie diagnosis.

"I think you're blaming yourself for what happened," Gail said. "You're afraid somebody's going to punish you. Some Freudian patriarchal hang-up, probably. Well, it's not your fault, you know." I could hear a taxi honking its horn, ready to take her to Logan. "Gotta go, babe. Call you from India, okay?" And then she was gone, onto another continent entirely.

I think I'm losing it, I'd said it to Malvina, that day in the coffee shop and I'd said it to Gail. What did I think I was losing, exactly? After I put Tabitha to bed that night, I sat with my father in the living room. It was dark except for the gloomy blue light of the television. My father was back from the VFW and the whiskey on his breath was strong. I could smell it from across the room as he nodded off.

Gail's voice came back to me. "It's not your fault," she'd said. But the memory of her tinny voice coming out of the receiver and into my ear was easily drowned out. Because it seemed like it was all my fault. *If I'd been there for my sister more, it wouldn't have happened. If I'd been stronger, smarter, better somehow, I could have made things different, for Jane, for myself.*

The black tide washed over me and I felt myself slipping under it. I knew why my father drank. At some point, you got tired of all the might-have-beens and the regrets. You wanted peace. You wanted the demons of your fears and mistakes to just shut the fuck up.

And that night, I was going to have a little of my father's poisoned peace. I went into the kitchen, reached into the cabinet over the refrigerator where he kept his booze. I filled a plastic tumbler most of the way full with Seagram's and sat back down in the dark of the living room.

Whatever it was that had let me think I could make a new life for myself, that had let me think I was something special – yeah, I was losing all that.

30

Going Mental

When Jane and I were still kids, there was a song that would come on the radio about going crazy. It was called, "They're Coming to Take Me Away, Ha Haaa!"

As the singer's voice got increasingly loopy, so would we, shouting out the lyrics and "going mental" ourselves. We'd keep singing long after the song on the radio had ended, until an adult finally told us to shut up.

"Going mental," had been our funny kid's way of expressing two things we heard adults discuss: going crazy (with the high antics and drama the song promised) and mental illness (something to be terrified of, like cancer). But even words themselves could become dangerous, I would find out.

My father's sister Doreen had been a buyer for Steiger's, the biggest department store in town. A busty brunette who dressed better than anybody else in the family, she and my Uncle Tony lived in a split-level house in Ludlow (the town was sort of a poor man's Longmeadow). They didn't have any kids. Instead, Doreen doted on her two toy poodles and filled the house with antiques, cut glass, and fancy dishes. She had her job, her Tupperware parties, played Mah Jong, and seemed happy enough. But when I was seven, Tony left her for a Portuguese girl he'd gotten pregnant, who worked at their dry cleaner's.

Doreen became a classic Italian hysteric, smashing wine glasses and crying to the Mario Lanza records she played incessantly at all hours of the day and night. After what everyone called "the breakdown," she got what I later suspected were botched shock treatments. Almost overnight, my Aunt Doreen became a fat woman who took to wearing the no-color housedresses of women who'd given up on life. Once when we were visiting, I heard her mumbling swear words to herself in the kitchen when she thought no one was listening. I found this so upsetting that I asked my father if Auntie Doreen had gone mental when we got home. I got a swift slap across my face as the answer.

"Nobody in our family has mental problems, you understand?" It was winter and even though it was only five o'clock, it was dark out. Passing under the glare of the porch light, my father looked confused and afraid. "People who are crazy get locked up in the state hospital. Your aunt's not crazy. She's got problems with her nerves, that's all."

The sting of my father's slap had been scary enough, but the look on his face scared me even more. He pushed open the storm door with more force than was necessary. "Now, you get in the house. Your mother's got supper ready and I don't wanna hear another thing about this."

I took my father's lesson to heart. Apparently, going mental was like committing crimes or being guilty of mortal sins: it involved some shameful exile outside the bounds of respectable behavior. And in those years, my family believed in respectability more than they believed in Jesus.

All of that changed after Jane was attacked. A terrible thing had happened, something that should never have happened. It was as if the rules had abandoned us, along with any assurance of safety and predictability, of knowing what would happen next in life and what we should do about it.

I started having dreams about bridges collapsing and rickety stairs that led to the nothingness of an open sky. In the neighborhood, even after the trial, people avoided us, acting as if we smelled bad. I think they were afraid, worried that what had happened to Jane was contagious. I would watch them, as they walked by the house and gave it (and us) their scared little looks. Just like in the comic books, I started imagining their thoughts written in balloons over their heads.

Well maybe things go on in that house nobody knows about.
Like attracts like, you know.
There must have been something wrong with that girl, for that to happen.

My mother knew something was wrong with me when I quit the Athena and stopped leaving the house that summer. But I was afraid of the same kind of cartoon thoughts appearing over her head, if I told her what was going on with me. It had been my mother, after all, who'd freaked out the most when the neighbors had shunned us. And in the hallway of my fearful mirrors, where the past became the present that became the future, I knew what those cartoon balloons would say. *My god, she's having a breakdown, like Doreen.* And the caption after that one was even worse. *Now this one's ruined too, just like Jane.*

31

Wasteland

The way I got through these days was by watching television. And not just a little television. I watched TV all the time now, for as many of my waking moments as possible.

Actually, this wasn't the first time I'd been saved by TV. Television had been both Jane's and my chilly savior in the bad years after the attack, when both my mother and father were sort of missing in action and the big Motorola in the living room never got turned off at all.

I could still track the passage of those years by the shows Jane and I used to watch. Our favorites were *Bewitched* (A housewife who was really a witch magically saves the day for her family. The series Tabitha's name came from), *Please Don't Eat the Daisies* (a widow and widower with tons of kids marry and everybody lives happily ever after), and *Family Affair* (orphaned traumatized kids get adopted by a generous and understanding uncle). If there was nothing my parents could give us anymore, the television in the living room still provided. We chewed on each of these shows like it was the last strip of gum in a pack, hungry for whatever flavor we could suck out of it. And most of the time, it worked. We got something. Maybe not the best thing, but something.

Then, in some strange symbiosis, TV seemed to change along with me as I entered puberty. Or maybe it was just the stuff we were watching by then. When Jane and I saw the Rolling Stones on *The Ed Sullivan Show*, I zeroed in on Mick Jagger's skinny hips and realized that my new restlessness had something to do with boys and, well, sex. Later that year, after I bought my first box of Tampax, the images from the TV started to materialize in my real world. At school, boys were growing their hair long and girls were bucking the dress code by rolling up the waistbands of their skirts to create instant (and reversible) miniskirts. Slightly older kids trying to be like the hippies they saw on TV in San Francisco began to turn up in Forest Park, playing music and selling pot.

In the neighborhood, all the adults started talking about "what was happening out there." The drugs. The sex. Never mind the anti-war radicals and the restless Negroes. In a way, it was freeing. What had happened to Jane, to my family, became a tiny storm in what was coming now, a virtual cyclone of change and confusion that would leave nothing as it had been before.

And that was what happened, to me, to the neighborhood, to everybody. I stopped watching TV (except on Monday nights when *The Mod Squad* came on), because I didn't need it any more. The old order was in the process of being overthrown and I knew that I was going to be part of the new one. As proof of my conversion, I let my hair frizz out and (sort of) lost my virginity to the first willing guy I met at a rock concert in Forest Park. (No actual intercourse, but everything else.) I smoked dope for the first time by the window of my upstairs bedroom, doing it alone before I tried it with other people around. Jane smelled the smoke, came in, and offered instructions.

"Give me that. You're never going to get high that way." She took the joint from me, and showed me how to inhale and hold the smoke down long enough for it to do some good. It wasn't surprising that at thirteen Jane was better at this sort of thing than I was. She had already crossed over to the other side, even more eager than I was to get out of the dead zone that was our parents' orbit.

By the time I left for UMass, I was secure in the swell of hippiedom, safe and set apart, having left the beliefs I'd gotten from my family, the neighborhood, and the Church like the trash people left out by the side of Chestnut Street. I was done with all that, ready to forge on into a new place, into an entirely new state of being.

Or so I thought. But now I'd lost my way and woken up in some wilderness I no longer recognized. Whatever path I'd been on, if it had ever really existed at all, had disappeared entirely. I'd been such a brave little hippie and now I was afraid of everything. Afraid of walking down Chestnut Street. Afraid of going to the store, afraid of people, afraid of feeling afraid. Afraid of what it actually meant that I was this afraid.

Reruns of *Leave it to Beaver* and *The Donna Reed Show* were my favorites now. In the state I was in, there wasn't as much comfort in anything that smacked of the changes that had happened since these shows were made. I'd watch the reruns every morning after I'd gotten Tabitha up, angling her high chair so I could watch the TV from the kitchen as I fed her cereal and made coffee for my parents, now always in a hurry to leave the house. The game shows and soap operas that came on next were not nearly as good as the old reruns, but I'd leave the TV on anyway, nervous for its tranquilizing effect. After I dressed Tabitha and put her in her playpen, I'd contemplate whether I should attempt to leave the house that day. And each day, the same answers would float up through the black waters of my psyche, like the Magic Eight Ball answers Jane and I would get when we were kids: No, Not Now, Try Again Later.

The panic would be around me by then, just starting to percolate. By eleven o'clock, Jane would get up, hung over and grouchy, finally ready to take Tabitha off my hands. But it wasn't like I had any place to go and anything to do. She would put Tabitha in the stroller and go off somewhere – with Kimmy, I liked to assume, but maybe it was Gordon Valeaux. I never asked because I really didn't want to know.

In another hour, usually around noon, there would be a call from my mother. That summer she called me every weekday, the want ads spread out in front of her, as she ate lunch at her desk. Her tone would be cheerful and never too pushy. She was calling, she'd say, "just to check on me, see how I was doing." But the conversation would always progress to the same subject. At some point, she'd let me know she was looking at the want ads, and that she saw "some opportunities out there." I could be a nurse's aide, a dietician's assistant, a cashier at Bradlee's. One week, there was a typing job at Mercy Hospital she got very excited about. A week later, she was especially keen on a job behind the counter at Grinder Village.

"It wouldn't be too hard, Laura. You could do it. It's close to the house, right down on Westfield Street. And it would get you back to work."

My mother would never refer to my problem about leaving the house directly. She knew I wouldn't talk about it. But she still clung to the belief that if I could get myself back to work, I'd magically bend back into shape, like some Gumby claymation figure.

In some ways, I must have been clinging to it too. All summer, I answered that phone when it rang, like clockwork, each weekday, knowing that it would be her and that we'd go through the same ritual with the want ads. Even though I never once followed up on any of those jobs. Even though I had succeeded in smashing every expectation she'd had for me and that I'd had for myself. Even though I was bordering on becoming some hippie version of my Aunt Doreen.

After my mother's call, I'd make myself a tuna sandwich and spend the rest of the day watching the afternoon soaps until they ended at four o'clock. It would hit me then, as *General Hospital* faded from the screen, that I'd let another day go by and not left the house. The panic would ratchet up at that point in the bizarre bell curve of my day. *What if I can never leave the house?* I would think. *What is going to happen to me? Did some Never-Never Land of a life led solely within the confines of my parents' house await me? Maybe I was as crazy as my Aunt Doreen and had never realized it until now.*

Like clockwork, the nightmare thoughts would overtake me then. By evening, they would drive me out of the living room and into my bed where I would hide and shake underneath the covers. I'd turn on the small black and white set on the bureau in the upstairs bedroom because it was better than having nothing at all and its crappy sound helped a little. I would hear Jane return with Tabitha and my parents coming home from wherever they'd been. But I didn't want to see them and I knew they didn't want to see me like this.

Lying there, fear twisting up all the muscles of my body, my heart beating too fast, all I could count on was the passage of the hours, of time itself, to fix things. Like clockwork, when the evening passed and turned into the solid dark of night, I would be released from the binding terror that the thoughts created. I didn't know why this crazy cycle repeated itself, why the fears would strike at certain hours then leave again at other hours, but they did.

Around nine o'clock, the cycle for that day finished, I'd wander out into the living room again, relatively fear-free. Jane would usually be gone, out at the bars. Tabitha would be in bed. I'd eat something, maybe drink something, and have short nothing kinds of conversations with my parents if one of them happened to be around.

I could relax in front of the TV again, its quiet roar as comforting as some mountain stream. The later it got, the more I felt like myself, the self that was a grownup, living in the Seventies, that could perhaps still function in the world. I'd stay up past midnight, well into the small hours of the morning, watching Johnny Carson, Dick Cavett, old movies, anything that was on now, enjoying my reprieve. In the true-blue light of late night television, I could think again, hope again. Maybe tomorrow, maybe things would be different for me then.

32

With Kevin

"Let me come over," he said. It was almost eleven o'clock on a Thursday night. Ever since he'd taken me to the hospital, two weeks ago, Kevin had been calling pretty regularly, very set on seeing me. What happened that day in the coffee shop may have freaked me out, but it seemed to have made him surer about our future.

"No, we better not," I said. It was exactly what I'd said before when he called a week earlier. But Kevin was cagey. He knew something was going on with me. How he knew this, I didn't know. But he believed he could save me from it, given half a chance.

"Why not? I bet everybody's asleep over there. And your sister's out, right?"

"Yeah, you know Jane."

"So let me come over. I'll leave when Jane shows up. Anything you want. Really. We can just talk, if that's all what you want to do."

"Kevin, we have never *just talked*." The *we can just talk* part amused me, given our torrid sexual history. Talking had always followed sex with us; it was never something we just did.

"So let me come over," he said again, this time with the emphasis on the word "come."

I couldn't help it but I laughed. It was the first time I'd laughed since that day in the coffee shop and it felt strange, like putting on a pair of shoes I hadn't worn in a while. Kevin was very persistent, once he decided he wanted something. He turned up at the back door ten minutes later, knocking softly. I opened the door.

"Hey," he said.

"Hey yourself," I said. "I didn't say you could come over."

"So you want me to leave now? I'll do whatever you want."

I didn't say anything. Instead, I stepped out on to the porch and into his arms. Maybe he would always be irresistible to me. I buried my face in his shiny copper hair, smelling cigarettes, sweat, and the pizza he'd had for supper. His hands stroked my face, then my breasts, rough with impatience and need. We moved together towards the old sofa my father had recently put out on the back porch, against my mother's specific wishes. He lay back, pulling me on top of him, reaching under the long tie-dyed tee shirt dress I had on, intent on being inside me.

"We can't. My sister might come home…"

"No she won't."

There was authority in his voice and it made me wetter. Besides, I knew it was true. Jane wouldn't be home for hours.

Afterwards, we lay curled up next to each other, the blanket that usually covered up the rips in the sofa cushions thrown over us. The sex had been mind-blowingly great. Maybe it was because of the crazed state of my nervous system, I didn't know, but I'd come hard and fast with him inside me, not my usual way. And fucking him had temporarily run off my fears. What I really wanted was for us to lie still for a while in this small pool of peace we had created, without thinking, without talking, enjoying it for as long as possible. But Kevin had other ideas.

"So tell me. You still wanna screw other guys?" The way his eyes opened, as wide as a child's when he looked at me, made me think of the first time we'd been together.

"After that, what do you think?" Hoping to delay any further conversation, I began to lick the sweat off his beautiful hairless chest. I was making my way down his torso, hoping to suck him into hardness again, when he reached for my shoulders, pulling my face close to his.

"I'm serious, you know. I feel like some chick saying this, but I need to know where you're at. I didn't come over here just to get laid. You know that."

The fear began to churn in my gut again. I pulled my head out of his hands and put it on his chest, where I could hear the strong thumbing of his heart.

"Kevin, it's amazing being with you like this again. And no, I don't want to be with anybody else. It's just…"

"Just what?" He reached across me, retrieving a pack of Marlboros from the floor. He lit one for himself and then one for me.

There was no way around it; I was going to have to talk. I sat up, thankful at least for the cigarette. It made the reentry into my normal conflicted state of being slightly less horrible. "You know that I'm really fucked up right now, right? How can I be with anybody? Ever since the thing at the Athena, I've been a fucking wreck. I can't do anything. I can't even work." I took a long drag, thinking about telling him the rest of it, the part about not being able to leave the house, but I didn't want to risk what his reaction to that level of weirdness might be.

"You know what I think?" he said.

I just shut up, knowing what Kevin would do now. I had presented a problem, so like every other man I knew in Springfield, he would attempt to solve it for me. "Laura, you're always getting into your head too much. You're way too uptight. What *you* need to do is to learn how to relax," he said. The six-pack he'd come over with was still sitting by the steps abandoned in our lust. Never the least bit modest, he got up from the couch buck-naked and brought the beer over. He took a can out of the plastic loops and opened it for me. "You need to drink more. Seriously."

I put the cigarette down and took the can from him. "C'mon. That's bullshit. What did drinking ever really do for anybody? Just take a look at your father or mine. Having a beer or three isn't going to take care of anything. And neither will sex by the way."

"Look, don't get all heavy with me. I'm just saying, it's one way to mellow out." He looked at my breasts, which had worked their way out of my tee shirt. "And excuse me, but it seemed like sex was making you feel better a few minutes ago."

"Yeah. Well. Can't deny that one." A little bit of the warm peace I'd felt before returned as he reached over to touch one of my breasts. For sex to have been that good, while so much of the rest of me was falling apart, was astounding. I kissed him lightly on the side of his face then took a long slug of the beer as a sort of conciliatory gesture.

After he'd copped a quick feel of the other breast, he continued on. "Look, here's my point. You're freaking out because of stuff in your head. It's not like somebody's actually trying to kill you or your family or take you to a concentration camp. You know, I'm reading this book about Auschwitz. Now those people were really fucked…"

He was off into some long rap about the German extermination of the Jews in Europe. In the months we'd been apart, I hadn't missed this trait of his, to get totally obsessed about a subject and talk it to death. I wouldn't have been surprised if he was reading his tenth book on the Nazis. In the light of the almost-full moon, I watched his face closely as he talked, noticing the lines that had begun to appear around his eyes, which hadn't been there a year and a half ago when we were first together. The churning in my gut got more intense.

"You're not listening to me," he said, finally.

"Well, how can I, when you get going about the concentration camps?"

"I got talking about it, trying to make you see that you don't have real shit to worry about."

"I've got all kinds of things to worry about. There's my sister and Tabitha for starters, and not being able to work, even as a fucking waitress in a coffee shop. Never mind not knowing what to do with my life."

"Look, I get it. When Jane stabbed Timmy, it brought back all that crap, from what happened when she was a kid. But what you're missing is that, in her own way, Jane took care of things. Timmy's not a total moron. He knows your sister might really kill him if he tries something again. And a motherfucker like that, he's going to move on. Jane's too much trouble. Now you need to move on. Nobody got killed. Just let that shit go."

I didn't really disagree with his reasoning. But I already felt hollow and lonely inside listening to him and he wasn't even finished yet.

"And the part about what to do with your life. Here's what I think. We tried breaking up and it didn't work out. I love you and you love me. At least, when you let yourself, you do. I want us to get married, have kids, get our own place. Then you wouldn't be freaking out…"

"So you think I'd be fine, if we just got married and settled down."

"As fine as anybody else is."

"What if it's not what I want?" Was it really how I felt, or was it just some hold over from my women's lib period, way back when? Somewhere, the person who had believed all that was still around, but just as quickly as she'd spoken up, she was gone again.

"Why the fuck not? What else do you think there is in life anyway?" Kevin said.

I knew the man loved me so he deserved my most honest answer. "I don't know what else there is," I said. I could have given him a million reasons why I didn't want to stay in town and marry him, but the truth about all this stuff was like a shell game. It always seemed to turn up under a different shell then the one I'd just picked. I was so tired of trying to figure it out. Saying I didn't know was a relief, but it made me feel utterly exhausted.

We were both quiet. I could hear a train going by, as it made its way past the paper mill down near the river.

"You cold? You're fucking shaking." Kevin rubbed his hands up and down my arms and took the cigarette out of my hand.

"I just can't do this."

"Do what?"

"Argue like this, about getting married. About any of that stuff. I just can't."

"Okay." he said. The look on his face told me he'd buttoned it up again, that part of himself he probably shared with no one but me and maybe his mother.

"Kevin, can you hold me again? I don't want to fight anymore."

"Okay."

We had sex again, this time more tenderly. I think we both knew there was a goodbye in it, but neither one of us could have admitted it.

33

Day Break

I knew something was going to happen; I could feel it growing inside me. But on the night it finally happened, I didn't see it coming at all.

It was way too late to get woken up by anybody, least of all my drunk sister. Only half-trying to be quiet, I heard Jane fumbling with the back door, making her way into the kitchen. I'd never been a good sleeper and my insomnia had only gotten worse that summer, like everything else. I was pissed off and decided to let her know about it, so I went downstairs.

"You could have been quieter, you know," I hissed. "You're lucky you didn't wake the whole house up." I had on the same long tie-dyed tee shirt I'd worn when Kevin came over weeks before. These days, I often wore it all day long and slept in it at night. I sat down on one of the kitchen chairs. Jane sat across the table from me. Even from where I sat, I could smell what she'd been drinking – the sharp edge of the whiskey up against the sodden wall of the beer.

"Hey, I was trying to be quiet. Why'd you get up?" She was looking over at me, her eyes glassy and bright from the booze.

"You woke me up. I didn't really have much choice."

Jane burped loudly. "Oops. Sorry about that, Sis."

"Which, that totally gross burp or waking me up?"

"Whatever you want, Sis." Jane laughed and slung her feet up on another kitchen chair.

I waited for some of my anger to pass before I said anything. I hated it when she called me Sis, which she only did when she was completely in the bag.

"It's 4:30 in the morning, Jane," I said. "You could have woken Tabitha up. Or Dad. Why don't you just go to bed?"

"Hey, I'm on my way, but I got to wind down first. Mick had to practically throw me and Kimmy out of McNally's tonight. We were doing shots with some Navy dudes from New London and nobody wanted to call it quits." She rummaged around in her bag, retrieving a battered but empty pack of Salems. "You got some smokes? I'm out."

"Yeah, sure." There was no way I was going back to sleep now, I realized. I went into the living room and picked up my pack of Marlboros and a sweater I'd left next to the couch where my father slept. "Let's go out on the porch so we don't wake anybody else up."

Like we used to do when we were kids, we sat down on the cement steps. The sky over the Pacettis' roof next door showed signs of lightening up, but Jane was wide awake and chatty.

"So what's going on with you anyway, Sis? What's up? We don't talk so much anymore," she said.

That was true. I didn't talk to Jane much these days. But telling my drunk sister at 4:30 in the morning about the breakdown I was having wasn't exactly what I had in mind. Nonetheless, it came out anyway, much like my sister's burp had.

I took a deep breath. "You know, I'm going through this thing where I can't *leave the house*," I said, feeling real shaky about actually releasing this information out into the open air.

"What do you mean? I don't get it."

"I have to stay in the house or I get too nervous and start freaking out."

"You're kidding. That's why you quit your job and you're always hanging out here?"

"Yes. I think I'm having some kind of a nervous breakdown."

My sister blew smoke a little too fast in my direction. "So, like, what does that mean? You're ready for the funny farm?"

The line from that song came back to me. I watched the red burning tip of Jane's cigarette so I didn't start to cry, remembering who we were when we used to sing that song. "Look, I'm trying to explain this to you and it's hard enough for me to talk about it. So don't give me any shit, okay? I freak out if I try to leave the house. That's why I don't go anywhere." Because I was trembling all over, I pulled the sweater around me tighter.

Now Jane's eyes were on me, taking everything that I'd said in. "All right, that's pretty fucking weird. You know how much I hate shrink talk, but you've got to have some idea what that's all about…"

I stared at the battered wooden fence that marked the edge of our backyard and, these days, the edge of my fucked up little world. "It started after the thing happened with Timmy in the coffee shop."

"So let me get this straight. You'd be all right if I hadn't taken care of that motherfucker that day?"

"That's not what I said, Jane." I was trying real hard to remember she was drunk so I wouldn't get totally furious with her.

"But that's what you meant. Well. Now it all makes sense," she said, sarcastically. "Your freak out is all my fault. I told you before, you should forget about what happened. It had nothing to do with you. It was between him and me. Now you're fucking going crazy about it and you won't even leave the house?"

She was making me think of my father, the way she ratcheted up everything I said and then aimed it back at me. I lost it and started yelling. "I tell you I am living in this hell, that I can't function like a normal human being, and you tell me I should just forget about it. Thanks a lot! What if I can't, goddamn it? I can't!"

It felt good to say it, so I said it again, louder. "I can't Jane. I can't. I can't! I started to cry. Jane's face was a piece of stone. Her lips stayed closed over her clenched teeth, moving only enough to make these words.

"Sure you can. You can do anything you want. You're the smart one, remember? But you'd rather mope around here and do nothing but watch TV and be Tabitha's fucking babysitter."

Next door, the Pacettis' screen door slammed. Mr. Pacetti was a bus driver for the city who went to work early. He was one of those weird old guys who never talked much. Some part of my brain saw him looking over at us as he walked to his car, his head turning just enough to take the scene in: those DiStefano girls, one half dressed, smoking on the porch and screaming at each other. Then he turned away like he hadn't noticed a thing but I knew Mrs. Pacetti and the rest of the neighborhood would get an earful when he got home.

Rage was freeing me up. I took a deep breath and spewed, "I take care of your kid, because you sure as hell don't want to, and you're putting me *down* for that?" I was shouting now and I didn't care.

"Fuck that, Laura. Anybody can sit around and watch soap operas all day and take care of a kid."

"I don't see you doing that. You drag her around all day, god knows where, and at night, you can't wait to ditch her so you can hit the bars. Has anyone told you you're a fucking lousy mother?"

There was a beat of absolute silence.

"You know you're right. I *am* a lousy mother. Well, let me tell you something, Sis. You're a lousy psycho. Who do you think you are, Aunt Doreen? You're not fucked up because of me, you're fucked up because you thought those rich kids were your friends and that all of that hippie commune stuff really meant something. Well I'll tell you something, I always knew it was a bunch of bullshit."

Jane laughed and crushed the butt of her cigarette under one of the toes of her clunky work boots. "If you were so in love with all that shit in Amherst, you should have just *stayed* there."

Suddenly I thought about the conversation we'd had, in the upstairs bedroom, when I'd first moved home. I had wanted to protect my fat sister, in her Salvation Army clothes, with her barely concealed tragically stupid pregnancy. I had been afraid for her, because of what Timmy Morton had done to her, and what the world would continue to do to her. But now everything had turned into its opposite. My damaged, fucked up sister might be both, but I was the one who felt so fucked up I couldn't even walk out onto Chestnut Street.

Jane lit another cigarette.

"You don't like what I do, you don't like what's going on around here, then get the hell out. You're not doing us any favors by sticking around, believe me."

I don't know what, if anything, I would have said then, but Tabitha started screaming. My sister kept smoking her cigarette. When I got up and went into the house, she probably assumed I was going in there to take care of Tabitha, because that's what I usually did: Spell Jane when cracks appeared in her mothering. And that's what I thought I was going to do.

But when I went inside, it felt like somebody or something else took possession of my body. Tabitha's cries had wound down to a quiet whimpering but I walked past her and Jane's room. If I entered that room, I knew I would never leave. *I'm sorry I'm sorry I'm sorry but I can't be your mommy, Tabitha. I will die if I stay here for you.*

Inside my own room, I pulled my jeans on under my tee shirt, then quickly located the knapsack I'd been using for a purse, which was under the bed. I opened the bottom drawer of my bureau and found a small baggie of Quaaludes Gail had given me when I went to see her in Newton and $196 in cash that I'd stowed away while working at the Athena. There was an old notepad from school in the drawer and a couple of pens. On one of the notebook's faded lined pages, I scrawled two lines:

I'm going to New Mexico. Don't worry about me.

I tore the sheet off the pad and left the note on top of my bureau. Then I stashed the Quaaludes and the money in my knapsack

I went downstairs, moving past the door to my parents' bedroom, through the living room where my father lay passed out on the couch. The TV was still on, its canned voices softly murmuring. I clicked the thing off because it seemed like the right thing to do.

Very quietly, I opened the front door and looked out at Chestnut Street. The sun was coming up. I could hear the birds chirping in the trees and the far away sounds of cars on King's Highway. I thought of my mother, the way she had called me every day from her office that summer, trying to help me. I had to believe she would understand. I thought of Kevin and knew he wouldn't.

I looked back once, into the darkness of that house. My legs were shaking, but I put one foot in front of the other. I closed the door and left.

34

Bus Ride

After I had the fight with Jane, I hitchhiked to the bus station and bought a ticket to Santa Fe from the pimply-faced guy behind the Greyhound ticket counter. By seven o'clock that morning, I was on a bus going west.

I really didn't know how someone who'd been terrified of leaving her parents' house for two months could actually get on a bus and let it take her away from everything she knew, but that's what I did. For two days, I sat in that big metal tube, so shocked by my own decision that I did nothing but take one breath and then the next as the bus barreled on, leaving towns, highways, entire states behind us.

On the third day, we got to Kansas, Dorothy's home in *The Wizard of Oz*. Through the blurry bus window little white farmhouses and vast expanses of cornfields passed by, along with normal-looking people who looked like they knew who and what they were doing in this life. No surprise, the actual place didn't connect up with the intensity of the movie at all.

It was hot in the bus since the air conditioning only worked occasionally. I started noticing how the powerful smell of my own BO was permeating the space around my seat every time I lifted my arms up. It figured, since I was wearing the same tee shirt I'd left the house in. This was beyond gross, I thought. Maybe I could wash the tee shirt in a restroom at our next long stop. The bus was half-empty now. Maybe I could dry it overnight on the seat next to me. I would be all right in just my sweater. I would be all right, yes. All right. I was saying this to myself a lot.

I *was* all right. Because I had figured out how to dose myself with enough of the Quaaludes to manage things, so I could keep being all right for the entire trip. I took one and a half tablets every nine hours, with the other half of the tablet saved for the occasional, unpredictable bout of terror.

The other thing I was getting good at was scavenging what people left behind on the bus. Acquiring these things made me feel taken care of and happy. The important finds were a big linty blanket, a smart red travel pillow, three oranges and a banana, and a number of magazines, which I read from cover to cover, even the *Seventeen* magazine with its article on "How to Know He's Serious About You." I also found a Gideon Bible, which I didn't read but kept close in the space between my seat and the side of the bus.

Especially when it came to eating, I was learning that life on the road revolved around the power of breakfast foods. Each time we stopped at a Mom and Pop diner, I made myself eat enormous quantities of the stuff (eggs, hotcakes, potatoes or grits, sausage or bacon, slices of buttered toast) whether I was hungry or not. Food was fuel, same as gas was for the bus, and once I tanked up, I was good for the day.

What I didn't do, was talk to people. If someone showed signs of being chatty, I pretended I was sleeping and covered myself up with the big linty blanket. If someone really kept at it, I'd answer so stupidly they would think I was retarded. In most cases, this shut people up.

Our last stop in Kansas was a place called Burgettstown whose Texaco station doubled as a bus station. There was a group of kids hanging out there, smoking cigarettes, with nowhere to go and nothing to do. Their restlessness, and the way they kept punching each other's arms reminded me of kids I'd known so long ago, in Springfield.

A guy my own age, tall and thin and with hair the color and texture of corn silk spilling out of his cowboy hat, got on the bus and took a seat across the aisle from me. He was beautiful in a sort of a hippie Marlboro man way, with eyes the color of a sky I'd never seen, only dreamt about. I was sure the world he saw with those eyes was better than the one I saw out of my own tired brown ones. I started sneaking glances at him, out from under my blanket.

The yearning came upon me then. *Maybe this is the man who will save me, who can solve all my problems*, I thought. Faces of the men I'd actually loved (John and Kevin) and dozens of others I'd slept with flickered through my brain, like an old black and white movie someone had sped up. Even with all the pain, all the mistakes, I still yearned, I still hoped, looking into the face of this stranger. I thought of the sex we might have, he and I. *How those strange blue eyes would look as he moved inside of me, how in that moment I would change and so would he and we'd be together always.*

The power of this wanting cut through my Quaaluded feelings. I felt warm, alive, the actual flow of my blood getting faster and stronger, moving past even the panic I knew was hanging out there, underneath.

Oblivious, the guy across the aisle kept reading, totally engrossed in his magazine, which looked like it was about horses and other livestock. He got off the bus in another small town before I figured out what, if anything, I should do. As he walked up the aisle away from me, I decided that it was just as well nothing had happened. For one, I stank too much to possibly get it on with anyone, even a fellow hippie-type.

And then there was this fact: Men were dangerous, and I knew I couldn't afford getting messed up with one now. I had just enough money and Quaaludes to make it to New Mexico, which was twenty-four hours away. I had to keep going, no matter what, and that was that.

Under the faucet that night, at the rest stop, I rubbed an old piece of bar soap into the tee shirt, trying to make enough suds to wash it out. I was hoping it would dry so I would have something clean to wear the next day, when we were supposed to arrive in Santa Fe.

When I left the house, it had seemed important to take very little and to go very quickly. It was as if even an extra ounce of baggage, even an extra second of time might hold me back, might sink me forever.

I'm leaving for New Mexico, the note I'd left had said. *Don't worry about me.* Two sentences, that was all I could handle. Left on top of my bureau, where I knew Jane would find it.

I tried to wring as much water as possible out of the tee shirt, but it was still pretty wet. It was ridiculous, really. I should have taken another tee shirt and a change of underwear. I should have done a lot of things, like call Sonya Bernstein during one of the rest stops to tell her I was coming, but I hadn't.

I got back on the bus and spread the tee shirt out on the empty seat next to me so it could dry as much as possible.

Then I freaked out. Fear came, a downpour in my brain that I was sure I would die of. *This bus ride was just some movie I'd been watching. It was unreal. Where was I? What was happening to me? I should have never left home, not that first time for college, not ever. Was I dying? Or was I finally truly going crazy?*

I started shaking. The dark corridor of the bus seemed to extend into some terrible infinity. The silhouette of the bus driver's head with its sinister-looking cap on it, moved like a bat in the dark. A patch of the strange road outside eerily lit up as the headlights hit it. *I have to get out of here*, I thought. Saliva stuck solid against the insides of my mouth and my heart pounded against my ribs, like it was hatching its own escape plan. But I knew there really was no way out. If I started screaming and really lost it, the driver would pull over and call the cops. They'd carry me off the bus as the other passengers watched and whispered. I'd be hauled off to some hospital in the middle of nowhere. And that would be it. I'd lose control over what happened to me.

Into the dark, I prayed in two syllables, *Please God, Please God*, over and over again, as I searched for the baggie of Quaaludes in my knapsack. I gulped two whole pills down with what was left of a can of Coke I'd saved from the last rest stop. There was nothing then. Just me in the dark, my breath coming and going in fits and starts, as the bus drove on and on across that never-ending prairie.

But what I'd started to think about before I fell off the cliff of panic was still there and eventually I had to look. There was my sister, the last time I saw her, smoking a cigarette on the back porch, her profile looking like our father's, especially the set of her jaw. Then, from somewhere, her words came back to me, the last thing she'd said that morning: "Get the hell out."

She'd been very pissed off at me when she'd said it. But she had meant it. And she had meant Springfield, not this bus. *She wanted me to be free. She knew Springfield was not for me, that I had to find a different life.* Like a key turning a lock, her words released me now. She had told me. I was free to go.

I sat there for a while. With a ticker tape end-of-World-War-Two kind of peace breaking out inside me, I watched the lights of some town I'd never visit pass by. The Quaaludes began to kick in then, bringing with them a wave of slightly buzzy numbness, but I knew I was already okay.

What I really had to do now most urgently was pee. I got out of my seat to go to the toilet in the back of the bus. The closer I got, the more it stank back there, but I didn't care. On the way, I looked at my fellow passengers, who were mostly middle-aged working people. They looked tired and kind of knocked around by life. I realized, after four days of being on a bus with some of them, even though we never talked, there was something familiar and comforting about their presence. In a way, the bus was my home for right now.

I thought again about the cowboy guy with the shiny corn silk hair and smiled, imagining what it would be like, giving him a blowjob in the back of this bus right now, stink or no stink.

I slept soundly then, the bus rocking me like a cradle

35

Santa Fe

That night, I slept more than I had on the entire trip. When I woke, it was morning and we were crossing into New Mexico. Outside my window, there were strange mountains in the distance that were higher than any I'd ever seen. Someone on the bus said that we were going through the Raton Pass, part of the Old Santa Fe Trail, a place I remembered from my schoolbooks. People had been coming west this way for more than a century. Now so was I.

As we made our way south on I-25, the light coming through the tinted bus window seemed to wash out everything, fraying it around the edges, the way it does in an overexposed photo. It was the way I felt, actually. The light was so strong it seemed like it was dissolving where I usually ended and the rest of the world began. There was something good about the feeling but also something scary, too. Just for protection, I took my last Lude.

By noon we were driving into the center of Santa Fe, a densely built up Spanish-looking town clustered around a central plaza. In some ways, the town seemed like a mirage. Most of the buildings were made of adobe, making it seem to me as if they'd somehow grown out of the earth rather than having been built.

Everybody on the bus got chatty all of the sudden as we approached the bus station. An older Mexican-looking guy with a baseball cap on and eyes that looked too wet, turned around to talk to me. I asked him where he was from.

"Acoma," he said. "You like Indians?" I was surprised that's what he called himself. The guy looked Mexican to me. Besides, I thought Indians called themselves Native Americans. When he asked me where I was from, I thought about saying Springfield, Massachusetts but realizing he would have absolutely no idea where that was, I just said, "Back east."

He wanted to buy me a drink, but I said no. "You sure?" he said, looking me up and down.

"Yeah," I said. I knew I looked like hell and smelled bad. Once again, I was amazed at the tenacity of the male sex drive.

"Hey babe, I gotta bottle of tequila right here. You're in the wild west now. Have a shot." He opened his jeans jacket and revealed a flask peeking out of a crushed and dirty paper bag.

"No, thanks. That's all right." The idea of placing my mouth on that bottle totally grossed me out. Indian or not, this guy was creepy. Undaunted, he turned back around and started talking to some other woman.

We came to a complete stop. As we got off the bus and collected our stuff, everybody seemed a little confused, like parakeets suddenly let out of their cage. Putting my feet down on Santa Fe's soil for the first time, after all those miles and all that fear, I took a moment to stand apart from the others and if not to exactly pray, at least give thanks.

The noon sky above me was as blue as the hippie cowboy's eyes. But in this light, with its supernatural intensity, there would be nowhere to run, nowhere to hide. The time I'd spent hidden away inside my parents' house flashed through me, making me shudder. For better or for worse, I was here now, out in the open. And I would have to survive somehow, even though I was almost out of money, totally out of Quaaludes and a long long way from Springfield.

I found a payphone and pulled my wallet out of the knapsack. Tucked behind my Massachusetts driver's license there was the scrap of a napkin from that day in Northampton at Beardsley's with Sonya's name and her number at the Women's Center on it. It had been a cold wet day in the northeast when she had scrawled it down in the café so many months ago. The fact that it existed at all seemed like a miracle. Now I prayed to whatever forces ran this crazy universe, as I dialed the number, hoping for another miracle: that Sonya still would be working there.

"Hello, Santa Fe Women's Center." It was Sonya, with her professional voice on.

"Could I please speak to Sonya Bernstein?" Even though I knew it was Sonya, I felt too shy to say so, right away.

"This is she. Can I help you?" Sonya's professional voice intoned.

"It's Laura. Laura DiStefano, Gail's friend from UMass," I said. My own voice sounded squeaky and weird. "I hope you remember me. I'm here. In Santa Fe, actually," I said, still trying to convince myself that it was true. "I just got here. I'm at the bus station. I took a bus from Springfield and…"

"Oh my god, you took a bus here all the way from Springfield?" she interrupted, with genuine excitement. "Of course I remember you. We met at that café in Northampton. And you're here! You made it. You came all this way. You made it."

"I did." Then I started to cry, a silent geyser of tears erupting, getting the grimy receiver of the pay phone wet. "Yes," I said. "I'm here. I made it."

36

Being There

Sonya came to the bus station and we walked to the old bungalow where she and her girlfriend Rachel lived. I didn't say much as we walked, still bowled over by the simple fact of being in Santa Fe. I kept stealing glances at her. Sure, she was a friend of Gail's, and we'd made a real strong connection because of her and my sister's rape, but who was this woman, who I'd only met once?

I sat down in her small square living room, grateful for a seat that wasn't moving. After asking me if I wanted something to eat (I didn't), Sonya went into the kitchen and brought us each back an enormous glass of iced herbal tea.

"That's one long trip to make on a bus," she said, sitting across from me on the couch.

"Yeah, it took four days."

"So, you're welcome to stay here. You know that, right? Rachel and I have an extra bedroom. We get a lot of people coming through here."

"That'd be great, Sonya. You know I really appreciate it. I should have called before I got here, but I didn't want to call you collect. Besides, it's not like I really planned this."

"Yeah. So what happened that made you leave?"

It was natural for her to ask, but her question made me nervous. She noticed the look on my face and shrugged her shoulders. "I don't really care, you know. We don't have to talk about it. But it sounds like something major went down."

"Well, I'm not running from the cops or anything like that." There was Jane inside my head, doing it again, the knife entering his body. Then the screaming (my own? hers? I didn't know). I met Sonya's hazel wolfish eyes. "My sister almost killed somebody. She stabbed the guy who raped her when she was a kid, the guy I told you about. It happened in the coffee shop where I was working," I said, suddenly very talkative. Now that I had started, I couldn't shut the talk faucet off.

"He survived, but my sister Jane had to go to court on a malicious wounding charge. I just sort of freaked after that. I kept seeing it happen and I couldn't leave my parents' house without feeling like I was going to die. It made no sense, but I felt like it was somehow my fault. Then my sister and I had this fight – about everything, really. What happened, how she was fucking up being a mother, how I had fucked up at school, and how I was losing it in general. I knew I had to leave. That if I didn't, I never would."

The lids of Sonya's eyes lowered as she listened to me. They were almost translucent, I noticed, like seashells held up to the light. I finally stopped talking. Sonya seemed to go away for a few seconds, to touch bottom somewhere inside of herself, before returning to the surface of our conversation. When I looked at her again, she had become, if possible, even more the Sonya I knew from memory. Her gaze was stronger, almost feral; the hairs on her face suddenly more obvious. She was a warrior, an Amazon woman who did not fear or need men and I was grateful to be near her.

"It sounds like you did what you had to do," she said.

"Yeah, I think so." I blinked back tears, willing myself not to cry. I didn't want to fall apart, not here, not now.

"It's all okay, you know," she said, acknowledging my supreme efforts at self-control. "Sorry if I made you get into all this heavy shit. There's lots of time to talk. You just got off the bus, for god's sake." Her face changed with an actor's adeptness. A kind of mischievousness broke out around the corners of her mouth and her eyes. "Rachel would tell you, sometimes I get too into other peoples' dramas. Helps me cope with my own bizarro life, you know?"

Her self-deprecating insight did the trick. I laughed and the air in the small room felt lighter. "Anyways, I have to get back to the center. My group of teen incest survivors meets this afternoon. You must be exhausted."

"Yeah, I'll probably take a nap. Do you mind if I take a bath?"

"Not at all. There's extra towels and everything in the bathroom. Rachel and I will be home around 5:30. Maybe we'll walk down to the Plaza, have dinner, drink some margaritas. How's that sound?" Sonya picked up her house keys and gathered an armful of files.

I worried again about being an imposition on her and Rachel. "That sounds great. And Sonya, sorry, I hope crashing here won't be a problem. I've already fucked up your day."

"No you didn't. And nobody gets to fuck up my day but me. I'm glad you're here."

I fell into a deep sleep on the couch and woke up a few hours later, totally disoriented, thinking I was still on the bus. *No, I'm in Santa Fe now.* I made myself look around Sonya and Rachel's tiny living room. Light flooded in through the two windows directly opposite me. Neatly tacked up on opposing white walls, I saw a *Take Back the Night* poster, with a group of smiling women holding candles above the words, and a poster for the Santa Fe Opera, performing *La Traviata*.

Underneath the Opera poster, there was a bookcase made from planks of wood and bricks. I knew it would be full of books on women's issues and even from here, I could see *Our Bodies, Our Selves* sticking out at the end. There was no TV. The place was clean, verging on immaculate. I thought back to the disorder of the Leverett house. This house was their home, not just a hippie group house.

I sat up, not sure of what to do with myself, surrounded by what was so clearly two other peoples' space. Rummaging in my knapsack, I found a cigarette I'd bummed from somebody on the bus. I went outside and sat down at a table out on the patio, letting the sun wash over me. I thought about calling Springfield, but decided not to. I told myself it was because I hadn't asked Sonya if I could make a long distance call.

After awhile, I got too hot and went inside. In the kitchen, there was a door that I suspected led to a basement, where there just might be a washing machine. I was desperate to wash my clothes but shy about wandering around their house. As a kid, my mother had put the fear of God into me about poking around other peoples' houses.

Still, I cracked open that door. I could see a washer and dryer at the bottom of the stairs. Feeling like a thief, I crept down the steps, irrationally afraid that Sonya or worse, Rachel, who I hadn't met yet, would come through the door and bust me for going down there.

Suddenly, at the bottom of the steps, I laughed at the absurdity of it. This was Sonya and Rachel's house, two radical lesbians who lived in New Mexico, for god's sake. What would they care? I stripped off everything I had on. Standing there naked, I put all my clothes into the washing machine, poured some detergent in, and turned the knob. The machine started up, clunking noisily to life in the semi-dark. As it did, it occurred to me that my life, too, could start up again. I opened the lid and watched the clothes and the soapy water, now turning gray with dirt, churn around. After awhile, I bounded up the stairs and joyously drew a bath.

For five days I ate, slept and explored Santa Fe. With Sonya and Rachel at work all day, I did this on my own. Walking around town and being out in the open was hard at first. As therapy, I made myself sit on a bench in the Plaza each day as people wandered by. I gradually increased the time I sat there. Baked by that Santa Fe sun, the fear began to peel off me like a layer of old wallpaper.

Still, what I couldn't seem to do was call Springfield. The note I'd left had told my family where I was going and not to worry. But I knew too much time had gone by and they would, in fact, be crazed with worry by now. Each day I thought about making the call, but couldn't quite make myself do it.

On Sunday, Sonya and Rachel were having people over for a big dinner at the house. When I walked into the kitchen that afternoon to help out, Rachel was hard at work, flipping rectangles of tofu in a pan. Chatty and blond, she reminded me a little of Gail, although she was older than any of us, possibly even forty. Sonya had told me she had a PhD, which probably explained the feeling I got, that she thought of me as part of some kind of social experiment. But so what? I was hardly complaining. After all, she was letting me, a total stranger, stay at the house. From the window, I could see people already arriving, putting covered dishes on the glass table in the patio.

"Can I help with anything?" I asked her.

"Nope, but a glass of wine while I cook would sure be nice. Pour yourself one too, hon." I poured red wine into two hefty glasses, delivered one to Rachel, then wandered outside with my glass.

The group was mostly women, with a handful of kids under five running around and a few token men. Even though Sonya and Rachel were vegetarians, some of the Hispanic women from town had brought a pot of posole and several pans of chicken enchiladas. I was sitting on a bench next to an adobe wall, finishing off my second glass of wine and enjoying my enchiladas when a skinny woman with the long brown braids and two identical little girls in tow approached.

"Do you mind if we sit with you?" she asked. The twins, who looked to be around three years old, had long messy mops of blond hair. They wore blue gingham dresses that made me think of that book, *Little House on the Prairie.*

"Not at all. I'm Laura, a friend of Sonya's from Massachusetts," I said, practically oozing fakey friendliness.

"I'm Heidi Wildflower. And this is Spring and Summer," she said, with a Southern hick-type of accent, as the girls crawled up on the bench. "How long are you visiting for?"

"Well, for a while. I might try living here." I said, working hard to keep a straight face. *Heidi Wildflower? With twins named Spring and Summer? She had to be kidding.*

Heidi put two plates down between the girls and tried to tuck paper towels under their chins as they squirmed around.

"Welcome to the land of enchantment! You're going to love it out here, I just know it. The spirit guides are very active here, you know…"

This woman is a total flake. I could hear Kevin's voice in my head, but I was in the mode to be nice so I let her ramble on about spiritual vortexes and crystals for a while then asked, "Where are you and the girls from?"

"We're from Tennessee. I got divorced and just knew this was the place for us, so we came out here eight months ago. I live right next door, with my friend Serenity and her little boy. I work at La Terraza."

"What's that?"

"It's a restaurant. La Terraza is Spanish for balcony, I think. It's right down on the Plaza. I waitress there three nights a week."

"Do they need any help?" The words were out of my mouth before I knew it. I was my mother's daughter after all.

"Well, they might. You should come by and ask for Suzie. Somebody's always leaving or changing their hours."

"Thanks, Heidi. Maybe I will do that."

Even then, I knew I'd be going down to La Terazza first thing in the morning, asking Suzie for a job. Because I knew for sure I would be staying in New Mexico; I just hadn't totally owned up to it yet. Then either Spring or Summer – it was impossible to know which – fell off the bench and started screaming bloody murder. It was nothing serious, just a scraped knee, but when we were in the bathroom and I was helping Heidi bandage the child's tiny knee, I thought of Tabitha and my guilty heart skipped a couple of beats.

When we got back on the patio, everyone was carrying dirty dinner plates into the kitchen, getting ready to walk up the road behind the house to watch the sunset.

"We always end our dinners like this," Sonya said to me, as we headed up the road. "It's sort of a tradition. You'll see. Not a bad way to end the day in Santa Fe, believe me."

After fifteen minutes of walking, made longer by the need to carry some of the little kids, we reached a small dirt plateau by the side of the road. Below us, the patchwork of the city stretched out, only partially filling the vast bowl of space in front of us. Heidi spread out a quilt for the kids. The rest of us either crouched or stood on the hard packed dirt. A few joints got lit and were passed around, but I abstained. Since I'd stopped taking the Ludes, smoking pot was chemically still too unpredictable.

The red ball of the sun was sinking fast, bathing the mountains in the distance with pink and lavender light. Such a wide horizon was a little overwhelming but the light was strangely familiar. I remembered how I'd driven home from Northampton the day I met Sonya, imagining that the sunsets in Santa Fe would be something like the light behind Holyoke's paper mills. And now here I was. My heart beat faster, with all that was both behind me and in front of me.

Like she was reading my thoughts or maybe I looked scared standing there, watching my first western sunset, Sonya came over and stood next to me. "It could be okay for you out here, you know. This is a good place," she said. Then we stood there, silent as the sun disappeared behind the Jemez Mountains.

When I got back to the house, I called my sister and my parents and told them I was okay. With most of the continent between us, it was safe now.

37

Love and Fear

"Hello, Laura?" Kevin's phone voice didn't sound right. It was almost eleven o'clock my time and I'd been studying for a final I had in the morning.

"What's going on?" I asked quickly.

"It's my father. Andrew's dead."

I held the receiver close to my ear and listened as the usual boundary between the life I'd left behind in Springfield and the one I had now seemed to collapse.

Three years had gone by since I'd moved to New Mexico. In that time, I'd left Santa Fe and gone back to school in Albuquerque. By carrying a huge class load, I was finishing up my bachelor's degree fast so I could start law school in the fall.

After everything I'd been through – all the weird shit in Amherst and the descent into hell in my parents' house, I felt much older than my fellow students. These days, I lived like a monk in a cheap efficiency off campus and was actually looking forward to the demands of law school. I welcomed being challenged. For me, it was an improvement on the old craziness.

It had been Gail, the perpetual hippie, who had made me realize I wanted to become a lawyer. Six months after I arrived, Gail had shown up in Santa Fe. She'd come west to help start some yoga ashram that would be attached to the one she had visited in India and was staying with Sonya and Rachel just like I had. On Sundays, we had this ritual of walking down to the Plaza for croissants and coffee. One of those times, I told her about a dream I had.

I'm in the courtroom of mother's favorite show, Perry Mason. *In flat gray TV tones I see my family and lots of other people from Springfield – some like Ari who I'll always remember and love, others like Timmy Morton who I wish I could forget. Perry himself is approaching as I sit on the witness stand. I'm scared to death. Why am I there? Am I on trial, or is somebody else? Perry Mason begins to ask me a question, but all I can hear is the tinny sound of a television turned down too low, like I was back in my parents' living room. I know that what he's asking is important; somebody's life, maybe my own, depends on my answer. I try to speak, to ask him to repeat the question, but the terror that took me down in real life returns and takes my words away. Then suddenly a gavel I can't see bangs down – and I understand that the time is up. Whatever has happened, whatever I was going to say or do, it's too late.*

"Well, I think it's pretty clear what the dream means," Gail said when I had finished.

"You do? Well tell me, because I don't."

"Laura, the dream is practically screaming at you. Instead of being afraid of Perry Mason, you need to *become* him. It's your dharma in this life to turn the whole thing around. Your sister was fucked over by a guy and then by the system. You need to take the power into your own hands and stop being crushed by the patriarchal establishment."

Gail had never really gotten out of using the language of the Sixties. "Dharma" was definitely hippie-dippy and "the system," never mind "the establishment" sounded so Chicago Seven to me I wanted to laugh. But I didn't. Gail's face had taken on the Madonna-esque expression she got when she thought she was being a channel for divine inspiration. So I drained my teeny cup of espresso before I said anything. If nothing else, it was a generous thought.

"You really think I should become a lawyer? And how would I go about doing that?" From where I was sitting that morning, I could see La Terraza across the Plaza. Practicing law was a long way from my present occupation, waitressing. Still, I felt a strange rush of excitement, either from caffeine or the idea, I wasn't sure.

"You could go to law school like everybody else does. Look, if some of the idiots I went to school with back in Newton can do it, you can. It would settle some of that weird shit you still have about your sister. And you could do good things in the world."

Once Gail had said it, the idea somehow began to take root in me. Soon enough, I was thinking about it all the time as I served up enchilada platters and bussed tables. I hadn't come to Santa Fe to be a waitress, that much I knew for sure. Years ago, I had yearned for Perry Mason's intervention after what happened to Jane and now my dreams wouldn't leave me alone about it.

After another year, when I qualified for in-state tuition, I went back to school. Then, without telling anyone but Gail, I applied and got into the law school at the University of New Mexico. It wasn't some illustrious Ivy League law school, but it would get me to where I needed to go.

When I'd told my father about law school on one of my infrequent calls back home there had been silence on the other end of the line. When Sal finally spoke, he sounded older and softer. "Now that's really something. Hell, nobody in our family's even gone to college before." Even though he had quickly handed the phone back to my mother, I knew I'd made my father proud. Like the astronauts landing on the moon, which we'd watched on TV so long ago, I was about to do something he'd thought was impossible.

But I knew I'd already done the impossible by getting on the bus that morning in Springfield, shaking with fear and going after my own life. Even making it through law school would be easier than that. And while my becoming a lawyer probably had something to do with what had happened to Jane, I couldn't bullshit myself and say that I was doing it because of my sister.

What I wanted was an identity, a role in this world. For the first time in my life, I felt like I had the right to have one. And it wasn't just me. The hippie culture, a whole generation of us who had said we'd never sell out, was now buying in, one way or the other. Because the gavel was indeed coming down. We were all going to have to figure what to do with our lives, before it was too late.

I had known Kevin was hurt and pissed off when I left and we didn't talk for a long time. But a year before, after he started taking drafting classes at Holyoke Community College, I began hearing from him again. Maybe he'd been wrong about college, he'd said. He didn't want to build fences his entire life. He was thinking about becoming a landscaper, or maybe even an architect.

Sometimes I let the calls get sexy. Given our past that was probably unavoidable. (I couldn't put on a leotard without thinking of him.) Still, when I talked to him there was a space I kept in my head between the person he'd known who'd broken into a million pieces after flunking out of UMass and the person I was now. That would be different tonight. The phone lines that connected us were humming with more than electricity.

"Tell me what happened," I said finally, knowing it would be terrible.

"He fell. He was drunk and he was walking on the tracks, on that overpass in the South End that goes over Route 20. There was no train coming or anything. He must have just lost his balance and he fell twenty feet onto the side of the highway. It was two in the morning. Some trucker saw it."

"God, that's awful."

"I know."

"How's your mom doing?"

"Like you'd think. Sad, but you know, relieved in some ways, like I am. He was such a pain in the ass and he was drinking himself to death anyway."

"But still, he was your father."

"Yeah, well, we buried him today, Laura. And all I could think of, when we were putting him in the ground, was what a fucking waste his life was. All that whoring around and drinking and the stupid shit he did…" His voice was breaking. "I loved him, you know. But I'll tell you one thing – I can't end up being that much of an asshole. No matter what, I can't end up like him."

I thought of Jane then. Mostly my sister and I had short, forgettable conversations at Christmas time and on birthdays, when my mother would hand the phone to her. Every once in a while, she'd call me up drunk and try to make me feel guilty about leaving town. First there would be the soft "Tabitha-misses-her-auntie" routine, followed by a descent into a sulky "how-could you-have-moved-west-and-fucking-forgotten-about-us" rant. Hearing her on the phone, no one would have believed that it had been my sister, after all, who had set me free that morning.

It wasn't that I'd stopped loving Jane. But after she got pregnant for the second time (a Puerto Rican guy, now serving time for armed robbery), I realized that my sister really did have her own life, even though she would only occasionally take responsibility for it. Whatever the past had done to her, I knew I couldn't save her from things she herself didn't see as problems.

"Laura, are you still there?" I'd gotten distracted thinking about my sister as Kevin monologued on, and he'd heard the distraction in my silence.

"Yeah, I'm listening. I was just thinking about my sister a little."

"Look, I'm sorry to call and lay all this on you, okay?"

"It's okay. I mean, your father just died."

"I know I'm kind of drunk, but I need to ask you something."

"What is it?" I knew where we were going but I proceeded anyway.

"How would you feel if I came out there? Just for a while. I could try to go to school even. I know what I'm asking, okay? It's not just because of Andrew or because I'm wasted tonight. It's because of you. I want to be with you. I always have."

I told him I'd have to think about it and, pleading a need to finish studying, got off the phone. Then I stared at the phone's face of numbers and letters for a long time, wondering how I had let the conversation get to that point. Now he had asked me and I would have to give him an answer. Kevin wasn't the type who would ask something like that and forget about it, even if he'd been half in the bag.

As I tried to study, a list kept forming in my head of every single reason why I shouldn't let him come, why trying to live with Kevin in New Mexico would end in disaster.

Later that night, after I had given up first on studying, then on sleeping, I got out of bed and sat at my kitchen table. I thought about a lot of things. Actual things. Like the endless miles of highway that stretched from New Mexico to Massachusetts and the millions of houses between here and there, full of families with their own secrets and sadness, watching television in the gloom of their living rooms. I thought about all the noisy bars you could find if you went from the East Coast to the West Coast, into all those nothing working towns that filled up all the spaces in between. There were millions of them, too, and they were full of hippies and construction workers, black, brown and all kinds of white people, who had family problems or drinking problems or both. Who were scared like Kevin, of becoming what they didn't want to be. Or who were like me, terrified of never becoming anything at all.

I could still feel some part of that terror, a fourteen-wheeler of fear, under the surface of my skin, in the highways and byways of my own vast nervous system. I shuddered underneath my bathrobe. *Even if you have a law degree. Even then. The world will do what it does.*

The ghost-like memory of my sister again, the way she had looked when she came home from the hospital, the funny pink skin over her eye, where the plastic surgeon had tried to fix her.

Then it came to me like truth does sometimes, whether you're ready for it or not, that my fear might not be any worse than anybody else's, that it just might be the price of being alive.

When the morning came, I called Kevin back, my fingers quickly dialing his number from memory. Whether it was love or the past that I was surrendering to, I didn't know.

"I want you to come," I said.